Smokescreen

Love in Flames 2

Elouise East

Contents

List of Characters

Al, barber, Harry's best friend
 Ave, George's wife, foster parent, friends with everyone
 Casey, paramedic
 Charlie, manager at Crush bar, Josh's boyfriend
 Clay, White Watch firefighter
 Clemency, model, Harry's best friend
 Dean, Red Watch firefighter (Out of the Frying Pan)
 Dillon, Jason's brother
 Esme, Harry's mother
 Ford, Jason's roommate
 George, Ave's husband, foster parent
Harry, photographer
Ian, Red Watch firefighter
Isabella, Matias's sister
Jasmine, wedding planner assistant, Jason's best friend
Jason, Red Watch firefighter
Joey, Detective
Josh, employee at Crush bar, Charlie's boyfriend
Kade, Detective

Layton, Green Watch firefighter
Leticia, works for Addams Advertising
Maddox, Green Watch firefighter
Matias, Blue Watch firefighter
Mitchell, gang leader, teenager Jason's past employer
Naomi, Harry's sister
Nash, Blue Watch firefighter
Niall, Red Watch firefighter
Oliver, Owner and Chef of Nourris Moi (Out of the Frying Pan)
Paul, Cam Fire & Rescue Station Commander, Quinn's husband
Quinn, manager at Shelter Kitchen, Paul's husband
Scott, Red Watch firefighter
Stefan, Green Watch firefighter
Tom, owner of Crush bar
Ulrich, Jason's roommate
Valerie, Red Watch firefighter
Zuri, Harry's studio assistant

Chapter 1

Jason

What did a man do when he was half-naked with another man in a compromising position with witnesses?

He made a joke.

"How many firefighters does it take to change a lightbulb?" Jason Townsend grinned. "Five. One to change the bulb, three to cut a hole in the roof and one to hold the ladder."

The occupants of the room groaned, several rubbing their hands over their faces. The one person who didn't glare at him stepped closer, raising the camera to his eye.

"Keep still. That's it. Stay there for a moment. Dean, can you turn a little to the left? That's it. Hold. Okay." The photographer stood upright, his hands dropping to his sides. "That should be it for these props." He glanced at his assistant. "Can you remove these and grab the other items ready for the next set of photos, please, Zuri?"

Jason smiled at the girl, who blushed a delicate shade of pink when she took the proffered bucket and sponge.

He didn't want to think about the photos they'd managed to get of Dean washing his abs. That was...weird. Not that Dean wasn't a nice guy, but he was his colleague and had a boyfriend. Jason wasn't interested in being the third wheel, even if Dean had been interested, which he wasn't.

"What is it with the need for half-naked photos?" Dean grumbled, crossing his arms over his chest as if to hide his body.

"Women love them, and I suppose gay men do, too. It helps to sell." Jason scratched his stomach while stretching and yawning. "God, I need more sleep for this."

"Why do we need watchers? It's creepy."

"Dean?" He waited until the guy looked at him. "Chill. Who cares who sees us? It's not like we're naked and rolling around on the floor, is it?"

Dean shuddered. "I suppose."

"It was your idea, anyway."

"It was not!"

Jason had known that would rile Dean up, which was why he'd said it. Dean Tyrell was a recent addition to Cam Fire and Rescue Service. From what Jason could gather, he'd received a lot of trouble from his previous station and requested a transfer to Cam. The lucky son-of-a-bitch snagged a local chef within weeks of arriving, and they were in love. Dean had wanted to help his boyfriend, Oliver, raise funds for a shelter he often cooked for and had come up with the idea of a calendar, thanks to their station commander, Paul. Though it wasn't Dean's idea, Jason loved annoying him.

"It might as well have been. You put the bee among the bonnets." Jason raised his eyebrows and stared at Dean until he fidgeted.

"It wasn't my fault you all agreed," Dean shot back.

Jason snickered. "Like we'd care about showing our bodies. Look at us! We're perfection!"

"And modest, too."

Harry, the photographer, rolled his eyes and dropped the props on the floor in front of them. He crouched, making him the height of Jason's crotch, and held out a hose like what they'd use at the station. Jason automatically grabbed it and frowned.

"What am I supposed to do with this?"

"Are you sure you're a firefighter?" Harry raised one eyebrow.

Jason narrowed his eyes. "I know what to do with it outside of this room, but where would you like me to put it in here?" *Except where the sun doesn't shine.* He didn't say the words aloud. Instead, he simpered sweetly.

Harry's left eye twitched, and he rubbed it. "Please rest it on the floor around your feet and let it drape over your shoulder, then hold the nozzle in front of you."

"Yes, sir."

Dean elbowed him, and Jason shrugged. Dean shook his head and took the hose from Jason's hands. "Stop winding him up."

"I'm not doing anything." Dean stared at him long enough that Jason sighed. "Fine. You're no fun."

They worked together to do what Harry asked, but the man wasn't happy. "No, we need another one. Zuri?"

The assistant raced to the pile of props and dragged another one out, carrying it over to them. She was only a small slip of a girl, and those hoses, however fake, were not light. Jason took them from her the instant he could reach, then glanced at Harry.

Harry twirled his finger. "Same but for Dean. You'll be the mirror image of each other. Can you take it over your right shoulder, please, Dean?"

Jason tucked his hose under his arm and helped Dean get his situated without tumbling over the damn things.

"I know hoses that are much easier to manage." He smirked.

"Jason!" Dean glared at him.

"Jason, rest your right forearm on Dean's left shoulder and hold the nozzle pointed towards your groin. Dean, same with the nozzle, please."

Jason grinned and did what Harry had asked. "Are you wanting to see comparisons? I think the trousers will get in the way."

"For god's sake, Jason, shut up." Paul Thompson, his station commander, stepped forward, finger pointed towards him. "If you don't behave, you'll be on paperwork duty for every minor maintenance job within the station for the next month."

Jason pouted, pressing a hand to his chest. "That hurts."

Harry positioned them, checking with his camera before repositioning them a few times until he was satisfied.

"Right, look at the camera and smile." Jason heard the camera click several times. "Dean, put your other hand on your hose, too. That's right."

"Got to keep hold of your hose, Dean," Jason murmured from the corner of his mouth while maintaining his smile.

"Fuck you."

Jason tried to lower his amusement level for the camera.

"Whatever you said, Dean, say it again," Harry said. "Those smiles were winners."

"Fuck you," Dean said louder with a smile.

Snorts of laughter rounded the room.

"That's about right." Harry moved closer. "I bet you say that to him a lot."

"More than you can imagine."

"Hey!" Jason's protests were without feeling because he knew he annoyed his crew, but he couldn't be anything less than he was. Being true to himself was all he had left, and he refused to hide it. It had been banked and beaten down inside him for too many years for him to allow it to happen again.

His troubled thoughts dimmed his mood, and Harry called his name.

"Yeah?"

"Joyful thoughts."

He met Harry's gaze and locked on him for several long seconds before Harry lifted the camera to his face again. Dean elbowed him, and Jason peered across at him, finding his humour once more.

"Isn't this where you're supposed to tell us to make love to the camera?"

"Jesus, Jason." Dean closed his eyes and rubbed at his nose, sighing.

"I could do that, but I think you'd take that too literally. My camera might break, and I don't think your insurance would replace it."

The room filled with laughter again, and Jason grinned. He loved someone he could banter with.

"I don't know. Would this be better?" He slid the hose between his legs and around his hips until the nozzle pointed at his groin once more, though now it hid behind the hose. Jason bit his lip and stared at Harry through the camera lens.

"I think that's a bit suggestive, Jason," Paul said. "We have to remember this is for charity and needs to be fairly clean."

Jason heaved a sigh. "Such a shame." If he wasn't mistaken, though, Harry's camera clicked to capture his pose. He unwound the hose and let it fall back where it had been before his move.

Dean exhaled. "Please behave. I want to get back into my clothes."

"Even though Oliver is watching?"

"Especially because Oliver is watching. There's an unbearable amount of inspiration there."

Jason snorted and rested his head on Dean's shoulder while he shook with laughter. When he'd regained his breathing, he said, "Don't go getting a hard-on, Dean. It wouldn't be clean enough."

Dean shoved him, and his feet tangled in the hose. He fell sideways to the floor with a crash, almost taking a light with him.

"Shit, sorry." Dean helped him back up again. It wasn't easy because Jason was laughing, but they managed. "I thought you had your balance."

Jason wiped his hands on his trousers and picked up his hose again. "Balance is overrated."

Dean snorted. "I knew you were going to make this photo session a nightmare."

"I don't know what you mean. I'm the epitome of innocent."

This time, Harry snorted. "If you're innocent, then I'm the Queen."

"I'd happily make you *my* queen," Jason quipped.

Harry hid his face behind the camera. "Let's try a few more pictures, then we're finished."

He moved them around into a few different poses, then ended the session, moving to the table at the back of the room. Jason watched his actions while he rolled the hose back up. There was something about the man that both irked Jason and had him wanting more. It wouldn't be ideal to start something with him. He'd be a notch on Harry's bedpost like he was on everyone else's who wanted to fuck a firefighter. And if Harry wanted more, what did Jason have to offer? Nothing.

Zuri took the hose, and Jason moved behind the curtain that had been placed in the corner of the room so he wasn't visible to everyone when he dressed. Dean had a separate curtained area. He pulled on his street clothes and dragged a jumper over his head before emerging from the changing area. Paul was talking to Harry by the table, and Jason felt a pull to go over and see what was happening. He ignored it.

Wandering over to Dean, he clapped him on the shoulder. "Bet our pictures will be the best."

Dean rolled his eyes and rested against Oliver. "Hmm, I'm not sure. I think your ego fills plenty of the photo. No one will see me." Dean tilted his head. "On second thought, that's brilliant. Ours will be the best."

Oliver chuckled. "You looked amazing. Stop worrying."

Dean beamed at his boyfriend. "You would say that. I hadn't planned on anyone else seeing what's under my clothes."

"How else will they know unless you show them?" Jason said.

"Um, because I don't want them to know." Dean blew out his cheeks. "You're hard work, Jason. Good job I like you."

Jason grabbed him in a headlock but found his gaze caught by shining emerald-green eyes, wide with panic. The familiar feeling of being berated for something he'd done came to the forefront of his mind, and his heart raced. He took in his surroundings and let go of Dean, making sure he had his balance before freeing him.

"Sorry." He held up his hands. "I'll go."

A small smile graced his lips, though he wanted nothing more than to curse and rally against himself. He gave a wave and left the room, ignoring the lift and thundering down the echoey staircase to the ground floor. It was only when the cool, fresh air brushed against his overheated skin that he breathed easier. Hadn't his brother told him enough times that he was a troublemaker, that he didn't take other people into consideration when he did things? He would've thought he'd learnt his lesson by now. Five years' worth of "training" wasn't enough, apparently.

The photography studio wasn't far from his apartment. He pulled his jacket closer around him, shoved his hands in his pockets and set off down the street, focusing on the light rain instead of his tumultuous thoughts. It was the kind of rain that drenched him despite the sprinkles he felt. He didn't care. It suited his mood.

After he reached what he called home, he had constant goosebumps and was soaked to the skin. He raced up the stairs to the third floor, his shoes squelching with every step. He struggled to unlock the door with his trembling hands but managed, then kicked off his shoes and headed to his room. Stripping off his clothes, except for his boxers, he threw them in the washing basket by the door—which reminded him he had laundry to do—grabbed a towel and stalked to the bathroom. The mirror and tiles were wet with condensation, meaning one of his roommates had not long had a shower, and he wiped the mirror, staring at his misshapen reflection.

He removed his underwear, switched on the shower and climbed in despite it being cool, to begin with. He braced his forearms against the tiles and inhaled when the water hit the top of his spine. While the water warmed, Jason moved forward and to the side to let the water pound his muscles. His eyes closed of their own volition, and he rested his head against his hands, recalling the scenes from that morning. It could've been an expensive photoshoot if he had broken anything from either falling or when he'd put Dean in a headlock.

He exhaled. He was nothing but a nuisance for most people. No wonder he was single with no conquests in sight.

He finished up and wrapped a towel around his waist, wiping at the mirror again to stare at his reflection. Some people called him a pretty boy. Some called him a troublemaker. It depended on what side of the law they were on. Shaking his head, he brushed his teeth and made his way back to his room afterwards. There were no plans on his agenda for the rest of the day, and he was at work tomorrow, so he laid on his bed, staring at the ceiling, and tried to decide what to do with his spare time.

A knock sounded before he got any further with the thought.

"Yo, Jase. We're heading out for an afternoon at the pub. You wanna come?"

Ulrich was one of two roommates who shared his apartment. The other was Ford. They were both factory workers at the same company and worked the same shifts, which rarely meshed with Jason's shifts. Despite having not seen them for more than a few minutes over the last couple of weeks, he couldn't bring himself to gather the energy to fake an afternoon and evening of fun.

"No, thanks. I have a few errands to run. Have fun!"

"All right. See you later."

A bump sounded, and Jason knew Ulrich had fist-bumped his door. Why he did it, Jason didn't know.

The air began to pebble his skin. He rolled to his side and heaved upright, moving to his drawers. He didn't want to dress in his jeans and T-shirt from earlier, and given that he wasn't going out, he chose joggers and a T-shirt instead. It was an old Cam Fire and Rescue shirt that had faded and stretched, but he kept it because it was nice and soft to lounge around in.

When he pulled on some socks—he hated having cold feet—the front door slammed, and he surmised Ulrich and Ford had left. He wandered down the hallway to the kitchen to grab a beer, the only one he'd drink that evening, and then into the living room, dropping onto the sofa to choose a movie. He could've gone to the cinema, but he didn't have the energy to be upbeat and pleasant right then. Mindless movies would be his companion for the next few hours, with takeaway and snacks in between.

When *Armageddon* finished, he switched over to *Equilibrium* and grabbed some lunch in the form of crackers, cheese, fruit and yoghurt. It would tide him over for a short time.

Early afternoon turned into late afternoon, which turned into early evening, and Jason stretched from his position. He had a kink in his neck and needed to move around. Picking up the leftovers he'd munched through the hours, he took them to the kitchen, putting them into boxes or bags and putting them in the cupboard or fridge, depending on what it was. The crumbs and packets he put in the bin. He wasn't a slob, though he wasn't always tidy either, yet when it came to the kitchen, for some reason, he needed to be tidy. He blamed his brother for that, too.

His phone chimed.

JASMINE: *Why didn't you come out with the reprobates tonight? I expected to see you.*

JASON: *Had a shitty day. Needed a breather. I'll catch up with you in the next couple of days.*

JASMINE: *Make sure you ring me tomorrow. I refuse to let you wallow for long.*

JASON: *I'm working tomorrow. I'll message, but I'll be fine.*

JASMINE: *Just because you put a smile on your face and others doesn't mean you're fine. I know you better than that.*

JASON: *I know. Just... I'm fine.*

JASMINE: *As I said, ring me tomorrow. No matter the time. I'll be up.*

JASON: *No, you won't. You'll grumble if I ring you before lunchtime.*

JASMINE: *Ring me after lunch. There're more hours in the day than before lunch, you know.*

Jason grinned and sent a kiss emoji back to her. She was right. She knew him well, and he would wallow until he found his footing again. Being at work would help bring him back to his usual self, but it would still take a bit of effort on his part. Jasmine had been his best friend since they were twelve, and she transferred into their school. They were like chalk and cheese in the early days, often arguing and debating different topics, until one of their teachers made them work together on a project. Ever since they had created their working ocean diorama, they'd been best friends, and despite the years that had passed, nothing had changed.

He settled back in front of the TV, needing another few hours of mindless entertainment before he slept. When *Battleship* began, he felt the tension melting away. Maybe tomorrow wouldn't be as painful as he expected it to be.

Chapter 2

Harry

Harry Jones had known he shouldn't take the job, but he'd needed the money it would bring in. He would've been fine if Jason "cocky shit" Townsend hadn't started with his comments. The second Jason said the first firefighter joke, Harry knew he'd struggle to keep himself from breaking down. How someone could be so nonchalant about fire, he couldn't understand.

But it terrified him. Although it could be the feelings he projected rather than Jason's.

While his assistant tidied away the props they'd used, making sure they were ready for a firefighter to come back and pick them up, Harry focused on transferring the data to his computer. While the images loaded, he closed his eyes, inhaling to breathe away his headache. The stress of dealing with firefighters might have been more than he could handle, after all. He'd thought he'd be fine because it wasn't like the sessions lasted long, but Jason's...exuberance had worn him down.

A clunk startled his eyes open, and Zuri placed a cup of tea beside him.

"Sorry," she apologised. "I thought you could do with a hot drink."

Harry smiled. "Thank you, and no worries. I was in my own little world." He used his middle fingers to make circles around his temples, hoping to dissuade the pain to no avail.

Zuri held out her hand, and Harry gratefully accepted the paracetamol. "You shouldn't have taken this on." She squeezed his shoulder. "It's too stressful for you."

"Then how could you get your firefighter fix?" He smirked.

Zuri's face lit up like a red traffic light. "I could've managed." She pursed her lips. "Okay, it's amazing seeing them so close, so real, so..." She waved her hand.

"Naked?" Harry raised an eyebrow.

She backhanded him on the shoulder. "No! Well, yes, but no. I was thinking larger than life."

Harry's left eye twitched, and he screwed his face up. "It's an apt description of them."

"You should've cancelled."

"I need the money, Zuri. You know I do. Keeping this place up and running takes almost everything I have."

"Surely, there's—"

"It's done. I won't go back on my word, especially not when I've already done half of the pictures."

"Give yourself a break from them, at least. Doing three sessions a day every day is not helping."

"Once they're done, I can go back to how I was before. The quicker that happens, the better."

Zuri crossed her arms, ready to argue.

"Look, you know my issues. Once the photos are done, I can push the memories down again."

Zuri slid her arms around his neck. The heat of her body against his back was a pleasant feeling, even if she was the wrong gender for him. She squeezed him, then let go, her steps letting him know she was leaving.

"I'll see you tomorrow, Harry," she said.

He spun on his chair and watched her leave. She put the phone to her ear, and he heard, "Joey? Yeah…"

Harry rolled his eyes. He loved Zuri. She was an amazing assistant, but she didn't know when to leave her nose out of things. That call would no doubt end up with his best friends at his door by the time he arrived home that afternoon. He didn't mind, but he wished she'd let him deal with this his way.

Spinning to face the screen again, he stared at the dozens upon dozens of photos he'd taken. His breathing increased, and his hands shook until all he could see were flames consuming his childhood home. He squeezed his eyes shut against the images, but they became more vivid, encompassing his mind. He could feel his mother's arm around him, holding him back, screaming in his ear while the fire devoured part of their lives. He watched the house collapse, taking his father and his brother with it.

Harry gasped and raced to the bathroom, flicking on the tap and splashing cold water over his face. His mouth was wide open, trying to get air in and not water. He repeated the action until his hands were numb from the cold, then braced himself on his forearms and gripped at his hair, resting his thumbs against his temples.

"One, two, three, four..." He continued counting the beats of his heart until the pounding receded.

With slow movements, he rose, avoiding his reflection in the mirror, and dried his face before drifting back to the studio area, unplugging all the electrical equipment he no longer needed that day. Grabbing a long pole, he tested the three smoke alarms, checked the fire escape door, double-checked the fire extinguishers and reminded himself of the routine should a fire break out.

He dropped into his chair by the computer with a sigh. There was nothing else he could do about his anxiety. He followed the advice he'd found online and let his mind settle with the knowledge that everything that could be in place was.

Harry inhaled and focused on the photos, ignoring what they depicted and concentrated on the intricate details of them instead. It was the only way he could get through them. When he reached the one he shouldn't have taken, he stared, feeling his body react, then set it aside. He shouldn't have taken it.

He hadn't even started his car at his usual finishing time when his phone rang. Harry glanced at the display, tempted to ignore Joey, but he couldn't, knowing Joey worried about him.

"Hey," he said after he'd exited the car park.

"Hey, man. How are you doing? Zuri called me earlier."

Joey Kirkland was a police detective, but he was also in the BDSM lifestyle that Harry had no interest in. How they had become friends, he didn't know, but they'd met in a bar called Crush one evening and had hit it off. They didn't see a tremendous amount of each other, but when they did, it was as if their friendship carried off from the last moment they'd seen each other. There were never any awkward moments like there could be when you'd not seen someone for a while.

Focusing on Joey's question, he said, "I've been better, but I'm okay."

That was his phrase for "I've had an episode, but I'm dealing with it" without saying the words aloud.

"Well, me, Al and Clemency decided to visit. We're currently on your sofa awaiting your presence."

Harry groaned. "Please don't tell me you let Al order the pizza?"

Joey hooted. "Sorry. You snooze, you lose."

"Joey! I'm going to have to pick off all the pineapple now!" Harry huffed. "I'll be there soon."

He focused on the road ahead of him. Despite the crap of his day, his mind had settled, and he relaxed a fraction. Although he wanted to have a bath and go to sleep, the instant he'd heard Zuri on the phone to Joey, he'd rearranged his plans in his head. His friends would take his mind off everything, and no doubt, annoy the shit out of him, but he couldn't complain—except about the pineapple. They knew he hated pineapple on his pizza, and Al always added it.

He parked in his designated spot and grabbed the equipment that he toted back and forth between his home and his studio. Feeling weighed down by more than his physical load, he held his fob to the sensor to give him access to his building. He had been lucky to find a small one-bedroom apartment when he left university and needed to get out of his mother's house. He had nothing against her or his sister, Naomi, but he'd needed his space. The building he lived in was well-maintained by the owner, and the manager was a lovely woman who loved to help if someone needed it. His apartment was on the fourth of five floors, and each floor held four apartments. What he loved most about it was the light he got in his living room. They had built each apartment into the corner of the building, and it had three windows bringing in light the moment the sun rose, facing east as it was. He'd lost count of the times he'd fallen asleep on the sofa and woke to a stream of light, enabling him to enjoy the sunrise. He had considered moving his bedroom there instead, but after hearing the noise from his neighbour one night, he'd changed his mind.

He exited the lift and strode to his door, bracing himself for the onslaught. Right after he opened the door, he received cheers from the occupants of the house, despite them not being able to see him. Shaking his head, he hustled down the hallway to his living room and put down his equipment in a corner out of Al's reach. He was a clumsy asshole, sometimes.

"Good evening, Monsieur Jones," Clemency said in a fake French accent.

"Your manager will be grateful you chose a modelling career instead of an acting career. Your accents suck," Al said, throwing what looked like popcorn at her from his seat on the only armchair in the room. *Harry's* armchair.

"They're not that bad." Clemency picked up the popcorn from the floor and threw it back, then settled herself back onto the beanbag.

Harry stared at them, then shook his head. "Evening, Joey." He ignored the "infants."

"Hey, man. Pizza will be here in about ten minutes."

"Thanks." He wandered around the room, checking the sockets and the electronics to ensure they weren't hot, then checked the rest of the apartment before he dropped onto the seat next to Joey, bouncing a bit before settling, and rested his head back with his eyes closed.

"Don't even think about it," he murmured several seconds later when the room went silent. He opened his eyes to see Clemency and Al poised with pens, halfway out of their seats. "Find some paper if you want to draw on something."

They both looked crestfallen, but Harry didn't care. He'd experienced several mornings where he'd found himself with pictures drawn on his face, fortunately with a biro, not a permanent marker, when he'd been too tired to stay awake. He wouldn't make that mistake again. Now, he kicked them out before he got to that point.

"We're watching *The Fast and the Furious* from the beginning," Al said.

"How else can we watch a film if not from the beginning?" Joey said, hiding a smile behind his hand.

Al threw some popcorn in his direction, too. "I mean from the first film, you imbecile."

The doorbell interrupted Joey's potential answer, and he rose from the sofa. "My treat tonight."

Harry went to the kitchen and grabbed some napkins and a glass of water for himself. The others could help themselves to whatever they wanted. By the time he returned, four pizza boxes were on the coffee table, three open, one not. He settled himself and opened the box, readying to pick off the awful pineapple but found none. He side-eyed Joey, who grinned back.

"I threatened Al with cutting off his popcorn supply."

Harry snorted. "I'll have to remember that." He nudged Joey's shoulder. "Thanks."

Joey returned his shoulder bump and focused on his food.

"How's work?" he asked Clemency when they'd eaten the first slice.

"Good." She turned towards him, the rustle of the beanbag audible when she moved. "I have to be in London tomorrow until Monday, then they're talking about flying me to Paris for a long weekend." She grinned, though she tried to contain it by biting her lip. "Think of the shopping I could do for Christmas!"

"It's October, Clem. Christmas is too far away to think about yet," Al said.

"It's two months. You always leave things to the last minute, then I end up helping you to find something for everyone. Think what life would be like if you organised yourself." She gasped and put a hand to her chest. Despite her lack of ability for accents, Harry could see her on stage acting. She wasn't as bad as Al claimed.

"I have to agree," Joey said. "Why buy things now when you have to figure out where to put them, and then you forget about them and end up buying new stuff?"

Harry tilted his head to the side several times in agreement. "I've done that before. This place is not big by any means, but I hid a present for my sister one year and didn't find it until two years after."

Clemency squinted at the three of them and shook her head. "Men."

"Joey, how's work?" he said to change the subject of how stupid men were. It was a topic Clemency could spend hours on if they let her.

"I should ask you that. How are the hot firefighters?" Joey waggled his eyebrows.

"Hot," he answered, then clapped a hand over his mouth. "I mean, annoying, busy, talk too much, joke too much." His cheeks were on fire.

His three so-called friends heckled him.

"Ah, you've met Jason, then," Joey said. A statement, not a question.

He nodded but ignored the elephant in the room. "The props are working out well. I'm glad they could bring something from the station to use instead of trying to source them myself."

"They're a good bunch." A dark cloud rolled across Joey's face, and his expression pinched. "Shame about the other guy. Goes to show you can trust no one."

His tone held more hurt than anything else, but Harry understood the sentiment. When Joey had first told him about the arson attack on his friend's restaurant, Harry's anxiety got the better of him, and he spent several hours locked in his home, trying to find a way out again. Joey had known how Harry would react and had waited until he was home before telling him in person and ensuring he would be okay. Over the years, they'd found it better to explain things to Harry as soon as possible. That way, it didn't blindside him on the news or radio, which had happened on more than one occasion.

For Joey, the concept of a firefighter setting alight a building was hard to understand. Firefighters were supposed to save people, not hurt them. Even with Harry's experience, he never believed it was the firefighters' fault his childhood home had collapsed.

"I think it's time for ice cream," Al said, rising from his seat and disappearing into the kitchen. Harry could hear him rummaging around in his fridge.

"Get the next film set up." He nudged Joey. "If we put on *Pitch Black*, he won't realise the change until it's too late. It still has Vin Diesel in it, after all."

Joey scrambled for the remote and flicked through the on-demand listing until it was ready and paused in a place Al wouldn't recognise. They didn't mind watching *The Fast and the Furious* franchise, but they'd watched some of them the previous weekend. There was no getting fed up with Vin Diesel, they all agreed, but there were plenty more films to choose from.

"Cookie dough, caramel or mint?" Al called to them.

"Cookie dough!" Clemency shouted.

"Caramel!" Joey said.

"Any!" Harry called.

Al knew their preferences, and Harry didn't understand why the man always asked. When he returned to the room, Al glanced at the screen. "Ah, already raring to go, that's what I like to see." He handed out the bowls and settled in his chair. "Play, maestro." He waved his hand.

Joey lifted the remote, but Harry caught his hand before he could throw it. "Down, kitty. I need that." He plucked it from Joey's hand and pressed play, then tucked his legs underneath him and cradled the bowl.

It took a good half an hour before Al shouted, "Hey, this should've been *Tokyo Drift!*"

They roared with laughter when Al grumbled, but he didn't complain any further. They watched through that film and most of *The Chronicles of Riddick* before Clemency declared herself out of the game. She kissed everyone on the cheek and left the apartment with Joey in tow to give her a lift and ensure she arrived home in one piece. Al stayed until the end of the film, then gathered the cups and rubbish he'd used.

Without words, they cleaned the living room, and Al put the cardboard into a bag to take outside to the bin when he left, knowing Harry wouldn't stand for it to be left in the kitchen until tomorrow. In the hallway, he stared at Harry.

"Do you need some relief tonight?"

Harry's mouth curled. "Thank you for the offer, but I'll be all right. Sleep is the best thing for me today."

Al nodded, though his expression showed he didn't believe it. "Ring me if you need me." He left the apartment with a wave.

Harry and Al had a mutually beneficial relationship. Neither wanted something permanent, but they were satisfied to scratch their itch with each other instead of trying to find someone else to fuck. It didn't happen often, but occasionally, Al helped Harry through his memories by pounding them out of him.

Harry locked the front door and wandered around the house, disconnecting the electrical items and switching off the oven at the mains before he could settle down. He considered sleeping on the sofa but could already hear the bass from the neighbour, which meant the guy either had company or *company*. Either way, Harry didn't want to listen to the result.

He wandered to his bedroom, closing the door behind him and switching on the light. The sea-green colour on the walls calmed him, and he felt the lingering effects of the photoshoot earlier that day wash away. Usually, he would've showered, but he needed sleep more than anything else.

During undressing, his phone chimed from where he'd lain it on the bedside table. Once he was down to his underwear, he climbed into bed and grabbed his phone.

MUM: *Are you coming for dinner on Sunday? Naomi would like to introduce her boyfriend. He's a singer. I promise to have a tube of cherry drops for you as payment. Love you x*

Harry groaned. Another new boyfriend. It hadn't taken his sister long to get rid of the asshole before, thankfully, but to replace him with a singer? Harry hated pop music, and knowing Naomi's taste in music, that was precisely what he'd be singing.

HARRY: *Are you providing the earplugs, or shall I bring my own? Of course, I'll be there. Love you x*

Chapter 3

Jason

"Car fire. Four Lamps Roundabout. Appears empty. Let's go."

Jason jumped into his boots and pulled the trousers up, then climbed into the engine. When the doors slammed shut, Scott gunned out of the station, siren wailing. Jason braced himself, shoved his arms through his jacket and put his helmet on.

"Control to 2524."

Jason grabbed his radio. "This is 2524. Go ahead, Control."

"2524, we have more information coming through. There are two cars involved, but no one knows if it's a car crash. Nobody heard anything to show it was a crash, but we can't rule it out. Paul will meet you there."

"Understood."

Jason exhaled, trying to lower his heart rate. The buzz from the alarm set him going, but he needed calm to do his job. Something must be troubling them to have Paul join them. In the role of station commander, he wasn't usually with them, but because Red Watch still didn't have a watch commander, Paul was doing both roles for the moment.

"Get out of the fucking way!" Scott growled while avoiding cars that moved aside, trying to help but not doing the best job of it. They meant well, and Jason would prefer them to try than not move at all.

No additional news came through before they arrived, so Jason assumed what they were attending was what Control had said. Until they stopped.

"Holy crap!" he muttered. "Dean, Niall, get the hoses on those cars straight away. Scott, move the onlookers away and start blocking the traffic. Valerie, without getting too close, see if you can see any occupants in the cars. There are four cars, not two!"

They scrambled out of the engine and raced to their jobs. Jason called through to Paul.

"2524 to 2596."

"This is 2596. Go ahead, 2524."

"There are four cars involved. All cars are on fire in the centre of a roundabout. We'll need help to divert the traffic." Jason's heart pounded while his brain considered all the implications of the fire. If they didn't get the fire under control, they could explode at any time. He had no idea when the fires had started.

"Understood. ETA is three minutes. I've called in police backup."

Knowing there were police on the way helped to calm Jason. He diverted his attention to helping Scott block the roads to keep traffic out of the firing line.

"No occupants in the cars that I can see," Valerie said.

"All right. Can you help block the other road? Typical that this happened on a fucking six road roundabout." He wrapped the tape around the pole and ran across the road to the other side to attach it. "Stay behind the tape, please."

"What have we got, Jason?" Paul's voice had him pivoting to meet him. There was a second guy with him, but he ignored him for now.

"Four cars were on fire when we arrived. No occupants that we can see. Dean and Niall are containing the fire now. I'm concerned about the possibility of the engines exploding, though."

"The fires seem to be lessening. I think we should be okay. Although the wind is an issue. I wish it would make up its mind which direction its blowing in. The smoke is going in every direction."

Jason saw Valerie running back to them. He waved to get her attention, then shouted, "Another hose on the trees!"

She diverted, and he refocused on the scene. He hated standing still and talking about a situation when he wanted to help put it out, but it was part of his crew commander's role to ensure that all members had the correct information. He caught Scott talking to a member of the public. Their body language was argumentative, and Jason excused himself and jogged over.

"What's the problem here?" he asked, standing beside Scott.

"This guy says one of these cars is his, and he wants it back." Scott's voice was deceptively calm, but Jason could see the irritation behind his eyes.

"I'm afraid, sir, you'll have to wait until the fire is out and the police have told you the car can be moved. Until then, it needs to stay where it is." Why would he want his car when it was lit up like a bonfire?

"I need that car for work, for fuck's sake."

"I would suggest making alternative arrangements for a while, sir. Your car won't be in any condition to drive yet."

"Jesus Christ! Can I speak to your boss or someone?" The guy waved his arms around as if he was on drugs or something and didn't know what to do with himself.

"Yes, wait here."

Jason pulled Scott with him towards Paul, who was now talking to a police officer.

"Sorry to interrupt, but we have an issue with a guy over—Fuck!" Jason dashed across the asphalt and took the man to the ground several feet from the newly extinguished cars.

"Get the fuck off me, asshole! I want my car!"

Jason kept his arms around the man until two police officers took the flailing man from him. Panting, Jason collapsed to the floor and stared at the sky. Why did he do this job again?

"You all right there?" Niall asked, holding out a hand to help him up.

Jason climbed to his feet and brushed himself off. "Yeah. I need a new life." Niall frowned at him. "My life flashed before my eyes. It's not pretty." Niall clapped him on the shoulder.

"No one's life is," the Irish man said.

They wandered back to Paul.

"Nice save. Are you okay?" This came from the stranger by Paul's side.

"Been better." Jason snorted.

"Jason, Niall, this is Ian, your new watch commander."

They shook hands. The man was stocky, held himself like a military man and had eyes that seemed as if they would catch everything.

"Ian will take over in a couple of weeks after some in-house training by me. He will attend the calls to see how you work together, too."

"Glad you could join us. Gives Paul a chance to catch a snooze in his office now," Jason quipped.

Paul shook his head. "I've already told him about your nasty joke habit. I have warned him."

"Who, me?" Paul loved to take the wind out of his sails. He could've played some wonderful jokes on the guy.

"The police will take over now if you want to get your engine sorted."

"Yes, sir." Jason nodded once and ushered Niall over to the engine, where Dean and Valerie were getting the last of the foam from the hoses before they rolled them up.

Now that his heart rate had returned to normal, anger coursed through him. That stupid asshole could've killed himself or Jason with his actions. He should've let the man burn, but then he mentally slapped himself for such a callous comment, even if it was inside his head. His first priority was saving lives, the second was extinguishing fires. It didn't stop his anger, but it cooled it. He refused to step over into troublemaker land like he did when he was younger.

Once they had tidied away, Scott drove them back to their second home. When they emerged, smoke clung to them as usual. He would've thought he would be immune to the smell now.

"I'm going to the cinema tonight. Does anyone want to join me?" he said.

Valerie yawned. "Sorry, I'm out. I need to sleep for at least twenty of the twenty-four hours I have off."

"Dean? Niall?" He glanced at them. "Jasmine's coming, too."

"That cute redhead you had with you at the pub last week?" Niall asked.

Jason winked. "The one and only."

"I'm in." Niall grinned and strode away.

"Dean?"

He could see the indecision wavering on Dean's face. "I'm not sure. Let me speak to Oliver. What time are you going, and what are you watching?"

"No idea and no idea." Jason laughed when Dean blinked at him. "When we go to the cinema, we choose when we get there. Whatever film is closest to our time."

"How...? Why...?" Dean huffed. "Never mind. I'll let you know."

"I don't suppose you'll be coming?" he asked Scott.

"Let me know what time, and if I'm there, I'm there." Scott wandered off, texting on his phone.

Jason watched him, wishing he could get the man to open up a little more. No one knew what he did when he wasn't working, and although Jason was nosey, he would never lower himself to intrude where he wasn't invited. He'd been working with the man for the last seven years, but Scott hardly ever socialised with them.

A car engine drew his attention, and he squinted at Paul and Ian climbing from it. "Everything okay?" he asked.

"Yes. The police have it sorted." Paul nodded at him. "Have you not changed yet?"

Jason looked down at himself. "Not yet. I was thinking this should be a new perfume. Smoke scented. What do you think? Will it catch on?"

"I doubt it. Find another side job."

Jason winked and wandered off to wash off as much of the soot and smoke as he could without showering.

"Dean's made homemade lasagne," Valerie called from the changing room. "It smells divine."

"Are you sure *Dean* made it?" Jason asked, drying his hands and arms.

"He said he did, and Oliver has been giving him lessons. Doesn't matter to me either way, providing I'm fed."

Jason exited the bathroom area. "You eat more than any of us combined, I think."

Valeria wiggled her body. "But I also burn it off a lot more, too." She winked and left the room, leaving Jason stunned by her observation. He was sure she bloody well did with that wife of hers. Other than Dean, no one else on the crew had partners, except maybe the odd one-nighters. It made Jason's earlier quip about getting a new life take on more weight. He needed to live more than he did.

He wandered through the hallways to the dining hall, contemplating what people thought of him. He was a "Jack the lad" or a "Heartbreaker" or worse. But no one realised how terrified he was of bringing a partner down to his level. He was too troublesome to put on anyone's shoulders, which was why he stayed away. Trying to figure out when was the last time he'd slept with anyone took him far too long.

"What's that face for?" Dean asked.

Jason frowned at him. "What face?"

Dean rubbed his nose. "Forlorn, maybe?"

"No idea. Been thinking about how to get you off your sofas and to the cinema tonight."

He sat next to Scott, who was still on his phone. Dean plated the food and placed it in front of everyone. Within seconds, the alarm blared, and everyone groaned but raced to the engine. Jason dived into the front seat and checked the computer.

"Car and garage fire. George Street off Chesterton Road. The garage doors are wooden and are going up quickly."

They arrived within five minutes. Ten seconds later, the crew swore and rolled out the hose jets. The garages—all three of them—were on fire, and it was creeping closer to the nearby houses.

"Valerie and Scott, get water on those fires. Dean, wet the ground around them and see if you can get to the back to stop it from spreading. Niall, evacuate the closest houses. Fast."

Jason pushed onlookers further away, explaining the need to keep them safe and ensure they didn't get hurt. Sometimes, it felt like no one cared about their well-being. Instead, they wanted to see whatever was happening with no regard to their safety.

It took well over an hour to extinguish the fire, and after several more call-outs, they were all exhausted. Jason considered cancelling the cinema visit but changed his mind.

"For those who are coming, we'll meet at eight o'clock. Whatever is on is what we'll watch."

He wasn't expecting many of them to join him and Jasmine, except for Niall, who had already confirmed, but regardless, it would be nice to relax. He drove home, jumping straight into the shower and cleaned as best he could, though he never got rid of the smoky scent. When he came out of the bathroom, he saw Ford.

"Hey, we're going to the cinema for eight if you're interested?"

"Sorry, man. I have a four o'clock start tomorrow; I'm off to bed."

Jason clapped him on the shoulder. "All right. Get some rest. I'll make sure to keep quiet when I come in."

His phone beeped.

JASMINE: Bumped into Matias. You know, firefighter Matias from the other crew. Anyway, I invited him and whoever he wanted to bring. Hope that's okay.

JASON: Doesn't matter if it's not because you've already invited them, but it's fine. He's a good guy.

JASMINE: Sweet. The more, the merrier.

Jason rubbed a hand over his cheek. Matias was on Blue Watch and often joined them on nights out when he wasn't working. From what Jason could figure out, he lived at home and had an on-and-off boyfriend. He yawned, second-guessing again his decision to go out, but he couldn't stay home now that he'd organised the whole thing.

JASON: See you in an hour.

The hour went by fast, which Jason was glad about because he'd been falling asleep on the sofa while he was eating his takeaway. He swung by Jasmine's house to pick her up.

"You will not believe the day *I've* had."

He let her talk. It was the best choice because she wouldn't settle to listen until she'd expanded on everything she'd experienced. He'd learnt that from experience.

Finally, she took a breath and said, "And how has your day been?"

"Busy." He could've gone into it, but they arrived at the cinema to quite a crowd outside. He parked the car and strode over to the group, shaking hands.

"I didn't realise you were bringing the entire brigade," Jason said.

Matias's face coloured. "I hope it's okay. I sent out a text to everyone. I honestly didn't think anyone would be free on such short notice."

"Nah. I'm only joking. I don't mind at all." He clapped his hands. "Okay, has anyone seen what's on yet?"

"I thought you'd already decided on the film?" Nash, another Blue Watch member, called.

"Nope. The whole idea is to turn up and see what film is on when we get here. No matter what it is—and now if we can all fit in—we'll watch it."

Several groans sounded, and Jason grinned. "You should've read the small print before deciding to come."

The twelve of them entered the complex, and Jason stared at the show listing, grinning.

"Aww, they have *The Boss Baby: Family Business*. I think that's a good idea."

"No way, man," Layton called. "If you're watching that, I'm out." Layton belonged to Green Watch, along with Stefan, Bryan and Maddox.

He knew that would be the reaction. "All right. How about *Dune*? The only other one is *No Time to Die*, but for that, we'll have to wait an hour." He glanced around the group, receiving some shrugs in return. "If you don't vote, I choose."

"You choose," Matias called.

Jason winked at Jasmine. "All right."

He wandered over to the checkout and bought twelve tickets, holding onto them while they headed for the snack counter. Once everyone was ready, he led the way to the entrance, handing over the tickets.

The usher raised his eyebrows, and Jason leaned closer. "They don't know yet. Let's not tell them."

"Thank you. Screen Four, which is down the corridor to the bottom and on your left." The usher tried to withhold his smile.

"Come on, you lot."

They entered the screen and settled in to wait. They had five minutes to spare, and once the trailers started, he received popcorn thrown at him from all directions.

"Hey! Everyone loves people who love animations. There's nothing wrong with it."

"I'm outta here," Layton said, rising.

"Sit your butt down," Maddox said. When Layton sat, Jason hid his smile. Maddox knew how to control his crew.

"I can't believe we're sitting here watching *The Boss Baby*." Nash dropped his head into his hands.

"Sit back and relax. You'll enjoy it."

Layton growled at him. "You are an ar—pain, aren't you?"

Jason glanced at him and saw him rubbing his ribs and glaring at Maddox. "I live to serve."

Jason settled down next to Jasmine on one side and Matias on the other. In his humble opinion, there was nothing wrong with animated films. They were awesome. And if he felt a little upset because he didn't have a partner to share this camaraderie with, then he pushed it way deep inside. Who needed a boyfriend when he had friends like these?

Chapter 4

Harry

"*Within the last forty-eight hours, there have been twenty-six car fires set off in various places around Cambridge, pushing the firefighter crews to their limit. Off-duty firefighters had to be called in alongside engines from further afield. There have been no arrests for these crimes yet.*"

Harry stared at the screen. Surprisingly, his first thought was not, "Oh, my god. This is bad." It was "I hope the firefighters were okay." That thought had him pausing for several seconds before the anxiety set in. His hands trembled, and he fumbled for the remote to turn the TV off. He sat with his head in his hands, his thumb caressing the scar on his cheek and breathing deeply while counting as he'd read about online.

When his phone rang, his hands didn't shake as he reached for it, but his voice was no more than a croak.

"Harry, it's Al. I wanted to check in with you."

Harry gave a self-deprecating laugh at his best friend's words. "I've been better, but how did you know?"

"I saw the news, and I know you watch the news first thing in the morning. I was worried."

His heart thumped painfully, but Al's voice took him down another step towards normality. Al didn't like it when he called it normal, but it was how he saw it. When Harry could manage without flashbacks or panic attacks, he was normal. It was his aim each day—to pass the entire day as if he was normal. He'd yet to manage a full day without some sort of anxiety crippling his time, but he was a lot better than before.

"I did the breathing and counting like I read about and switched off the TV straight after." He paused, debating whether to tell Al the other thought that had him confused, then decided to hell with it. "I didn't panic straight away. My first thought was that I knew some of the firefighters who were working yesterday, and I hoped they were okay. It was strange."

"That's not strange, Harry. Wondering if your friends were all right makes sense. Are you going to contact them?"

He snorted. "I wouldn't say they were my friends, as such. I'm photographing them for the calendar, and I've met most of the crew from Cam station. Even the ones I could've done without meeting." Harry breathed more easily now, and he settled back against the sofa. "Thank you. I'm sure you have a crazy schedule."

"You don't need to thank me, Harry. You're my best friend."

"I'll let you get back to your appointments."

"You're welcome, Harry. Remember to call me if you need me."

"Yes, sir."

"Don't make me feel old. Have a good day and take it easy for the next couple of hours."

"Will do." He ended the call, knowing he'd told a little white lie. He had a full schedule for himself that day. After advertising for a kids' photoshoot opportunity, he'd received so many people who were interested, he'd set up a second, then a third day to fit them all in. The first round of clients began in two hours and would take most of the day.

He took one more deep breath and strode to the kitchen, sourcing a quick breakfast of scrambled eggs and toast. While he ate, he messaged Zuri with the plans for the day and replied to a message from Joey.

JOEY: *I'm sorry I didn't have a chance to warn you about the news. We've been running around like a dog trying to catch its tail, and it slipped my mind. Sorry.*

HARRY: *You don't need to worry. I saw it, but Al was there to help. It's fine. Stop worrying about me. I have a busy day. It will keep my mind off it.*

It would distract him, although it didn't at that minute, and the food turned to ash in his mouth. He threw the rest in the bin. Circling the room, he turned everything off and unplugged it, testing the smoke alarm before he grabbed his equipment and left the apartment. It was the only way he could settle enough to work without wondering whether he would have a house to go back to.

He drove to work, mind on the firefighters the whole way. When he parked, he pulled out his phone and dialled.

"Paul Thompson."

"Hi, Paul. It's, um, Harry. Harry Jones, the photographer." He slapped a hand to his forehead for sounding like an idiot.

"Hey, Harry. How are you doing?"

"I'm good, thanks."

"Glad to hear it. How can I help you?"

Harry's eye twitched, and he rubbed at it. "This is stupid, sorry, but I wanted to make sure the firefighters are okay, and there are no injuries or anything. I saw what happened on the news."

"Ah, yes. The wonderful world of media. It's not stupid at all, Harry. Everyone is fine. No injuries or fatalities, just a few exhausted crew members. Thank you for asking."

Harry exhaled, the weight lifting from his shoulders as if he was responsible for those men and women out there, saving lives. "I'm glad. I'm sorry to have disturbed you so early."

"It's no trouble. Thank you for caring about them. They mean a lot to me, too."

The words echoed around his head for several hours after Paul had said it, but he realised it was true. Although he'd only met the firefighters a few times, most of them were pleasant, friendly and helpful. There were a couple of them who could use a little calming, but mostly, they were good people.

A bang, a yelp and a tinkle of sound to his right startled him out of his daydream between clients, and he whirled around, his heart racing.

"What's wrong?"

Zuri held out her hands. "It's fine. The bulb blew. It startled me, is all."

Henry inhaled and exhaled, then drifted over to the socket and switched the light off and unplugged it. It was something he'd needed to get used to because it came with the job, but it didn't stop his fingers tingling or him from feeling lightheaded every time it happened.

"Could you get the broom, please?" Zuri rushed off, and Harry stared at the glass on the floor. It must've been a bad batch of lightbulbs to blow like that. Normally, the element inside them severed, but this one had shattered the glass casing entirely. When Zuri came back, he took the broom from her and swept the glass shards. "Could you get the hoover and give it a once over to catch any pieces I might've missed? I don't want anything to get into the little ones' feet while they're here."

While she did that, Harry got the small, three-step stool from the side of the room and climbed to the light. Wrapping his hand in a towel, he unscrewed what was remaining of the bulb and wrapped it in the towel before replacing it with a new one. By the time he'd finished, he was behind schedule, but he'd make it up that evening instead. After another sweep to double-check he'd not missed any glass, they set up, ready for the next fairy to visit their homemade garden.

"Welcome to the fairy garden," Zuri said to the four-year-old girl who clung to her mother's trousers. "Would you like to be a fairy today?"

The little girl nodded, though she still didn't let go of the fabric. Harry wore a gnome outfit to help the girl feel at ease.

"We have the prettiest fairy outfit for you to try. Would you like to see it?" Zuri asked. The girl nodded, and Harry moved to the side, away from the girl, and crouched next to a plastic toadstool. Zuri, the girl and her mother spent several minutes deciding which outfit the girl wanted to wear, then the visitors disappeared behind a curtain.

Zuri clasped her hands together near her heart and mouthed, "Isn't she adorable?"

Harry grinned and nodded. Whilst he didn't want to do this job, he loved the way the children could fall into their "role" when they dressed up, even the shy ones.

"Would you like to sit on this toadstool?" he asked in a soft voice when they returned.

The girl nodded, pulling on her lip. Her mother led her over, but the girl pulled away and stepped closer to him. "You have a funny hat," she said.

"My name is Gnome Harry. What's yours?"

"Mona."

"Hello, Mona. Would you like me to help you get up there?" He pointed at the toadstool, and Mona nodded. He glanced at her mother, who nodded and smiled, then Harry lifted her onto it. He bolted it to the floor to stop any mishaps, but he still made sure she had her balance before letting go.

He fluffed her skirt around her a little more, then stepped away. "I'm going to get my camera so you can see how pretty you look, okay?"

Mona nodded, and Harry grabbed his camera, holding it up and bringing the girl into focus. "Smile for me."

She did, and Zuri was right. She was adorable. When he'd taken a couple of pictures, he showed Mona on the camera screen. Her smile lit up the room.

"I'm going to take some more now, okay. If you want to get down, let me or Zuri know, and we'll help you down, okay? After, we can find some other photos to do, too."

Mona gave a half-smile. Harry took it that she understood and went to work. He never had a set number of photos he took for these sessions because he wanted to ensure each parent got the best results from his business. Sometimes, it took extra time, but the result was worth it. When Mona and her mother left, they were both in high spirits. Harry would take a few days to get the best photos and make them look amazing before contacting them to come back and choose which they liked. He had a free pack, which included a keyring and a photo, and then he had more expensive options, which included more items like a mug, larger photo options, photo frames, canvas bags and more. Obviously, they tried to encourage them to buy the more expensive options, but he would never push it on anyone.

"Thank you for your help today, Zuri. I appreciate it as always," he said while they walked towards their cars.

"You're welcome. I love watching the kids' faces when they see the stage and costumes. It's amazing."

Harry grinned. "They are adorable, aren't they?" He stopped beside her car. "But thank you anyway. I know you can't be here every day, but when you are, it makes life easier."

She lifted onto her toes to kiss his cheek. "You never know, when I've finished my degree, I might join you." She cackled.

"Oh, god, no! Save me! I take it all back!" Harry feigned horror, then waved and deposited his equipment in his car. He hadn't checked his phone, but he'd do that after he'd had his swimming fix. He wanted to enjoy the relaxed feeling for a little longer before he let reality intrude once more.

The pool was cooler than he liked, but he'd warm up once he started swimming. He inserted his earplugs, then pulled on his goggles and dunked under the water, both to check the goggles didn't leak and to get used to the water. He came up for air, then began front crawl.

The rhythm of the strokes and the timing of his breathing cleared his mind. He didn't think about anything other than the feel of the water sliding over his body and the sound of his breathing, made louder by the plugs. He alternated between front crawl and backstroke, then cooled down with breaststroke forty-five minutes later. When he finally stopped, his breathing was laboured, but he felt as relaxed as he could ever be.

He kept the earplugs in while he showered, ignoring the people around him, however awful that was, and dressed without a care in the world. At least that was what it felt like after he'd finished swimming. It was only when he was back in his car and had pulled out his phone that real life came back.

MUM: *Would you like to come around for dinner tonight? Say eight o'clock?*

He didn't want to, but he knew she'd worry about him because of the news. It would be easier to assuage her fears by visiting than over the phone.

HARRY: *I'll be there.*

He drove home, putting his equipment in its place before sighing and locking up again. His mother, Esme, lived a fifteen-minute drive away on the other side of Cambridge in a lovely cottage-style house. It was a lot roomier than it looked, with three bedrooms, two bathrooms, three reception rooms and a kitchen. It was an older house, but Harry had the place rewired a few years ago, and it was looking good for its age.

"Mum!"

"In the kitchen, sweetie."

He wandered down the photograph-filled hallway, smiling when he caught sight of big smiles and family holidays. At the doorway, he paused, inhaling.

"Mmm, pie, if I'm not mistaken," he said with a grin.

"You'd win that bet." His mother peered over her shoulder, mouth curled into a smile he would never forget. Esme was sixty years old and loved being busy. She was part of the local community and held fundraisers and events throughout the year to help different charities and businesses. She'd recently helped Ave Oxford with her fundraiser for the reopening of Nourris Moi, a local restaurant that was, coincidentally, owned by a firefighter's boyfriend. That was a heartbreaking tale Harry rarely thought about.

"How are you?" he said to distract himself from his thoughts.

"Great, thanks, sweetheart. I felt like making a pie today and knew I'd make one too big. I needed someone to help me eat it."

"Oh, I was convenient, was I? Typical." He rolled his eyes and huffed.

"You'd fit in well with the drama club, my dear."

They laughed, and he kissed her cheek. "Shall I set the table?"

"Yes, please."

They worked, with Esme talking about her activities and Harry letting his worries go. He knew they would get around to why he was there when they were eating, but for the moment, he was content to listen to his mother talk. She had a calming effect on him unless she was talking about his anxieties, which she did the moment he'd taken the first mouthful of delicious chicken and vegetable pie.

"How are you after hearing the news?"

Harry chewed at a snail's pace, not wanting to choke, and swallowed. "I'm okay at the moment. I spoke with Al straight after." He chuckled. "He must be psychic because he called me several minutes after I watched it."

His mother's mouth curled at the corners. "He's a good man. I'm uneasy about you doing the firefighter calendar, Harry." She moved the food around on her plate, staring at it as if it held all the answers to her questions.

"I know you are, Mum." He rested his hand over hers. "I'm dealing with it. It wasn't the best idea to take the work on, but I want to expand my client base from the children's photoshoots. I need to do more. This will help."

"But at what cost?"

Harry didn't have an answer for her. "Maybe it will desensitise me somehow. I don't know. The firefighters are pleasant people, Mum. I've made some new friends." It wasn't quite true, but it would help ease her mind.

At his words, her mouth quirked, and she glanced at him. "Any that have caught your eye?"

Bright blue eyes, dark blond hair and a cocky smile flashed through his mind, but he grinned and shook his head. "No. I don't think that's a good idea, do you?"

She kept quiet, then said, "Why not? It might help."

"Having a relationship with someone who I could lose in a fire any day of the week? I don't think so." He sat back, having lost his appetite, and his breathing increased. He rubbed his hands on his jeans.

"They could help you understand fires, learn about them, how to keep everything safe."

Harry closed his eyes. "No."

"Sorry," she whispered.

He inhaled and plastered a smile on his face, though his chest hurt. "It's fine. We're fine." Leaning forward, he picked up his fork. "Tell me about the next fundraiser."

His mother accepted the change of subject and launched into a detailed explanation of her most recent escapades. Harry, though his stomach churned, ate his food, asking questions and appearing interested in what she was saying, while he held himself together by a string. It wouldn't do to break down in front of his mother. She wouldn't let him leave her sight for months if he did. He knew that from experience.

When he climbed into his car after struggling through a bowl of ice cream, Harry pulled out his phone.

HARRY: I need you.

He didn't wait for a response. He drove home and settled in to wait, closing his eyes and clearing his mind.

A weight beside him snapped his eyes open, and he stared at his best friend.

"Come on," Al said, standing and holding out his hand.

Harry gripped his hand and didn't let go.

Chapter 5

Jason

"Are we heading to Crush tonight?" Jason asked Jasmine, staring at the TV in Jason's apartment. "I can't wait to shake off this melancholy that's come over the station since those assholes started the car fires. I wish the police would hurry up and catch them."

"At least the fires have stopped now," Jasmine said. "Maybe they got fed up?"

"I doubt it. If they're in the mood for setting fires, I doubt they will stop without good reason. I suppose if the police are getting close to finding them, they might. I don't know."

"But to answer your question, yes, I want to go to Crush. I have my eye on a guy there, and having you as my wingman would be ideal." Jasmine's mouth curled.

"Why would me being there help your plight?" Jason raised his eyebrows.

"You're cute. If you're with me, I'll know if he's gay because no one turns you down."

Jason wrinkled his nose. "I've had plenty of people turn me down, and you know it." He wasn't bitter about it;

he thought it showed great sense in the men. He could only give them one or two nights, so saying no to that meant they knew who they wanted to end up with. Jason respected them more than anyone else.

"Yeah, but most of the time, they're on cloud nine when they have your attention." Jasmine elbowed him. "You definitely need to go out. You're too sad for my liking."

He pushed off the sofa and strode to his bedroom. "I'm going to get ready, then. Do you have stuff with you, or are you going home first?"

"I'm going home. Order a taxi for seven and pick me up on the way."

He stopped, stood to attention and saluted, saying, "Yes, sir, ma'am, chief!" before ruining it with a grin.

"You finally realise who's in charge. I'm impressed." Jasmine gathered her belongings.

"I'm in charge. You're a stand-in for when I'm tired."

Jasmine said nothing, only pursed her lips and left the apartment. If he was being honest, he wasn't in the mood to go out, but he knew he needed something to take his mind off the craziness of the last few days. Far too many cars had been stolen and set alight for his liking. He drifted to his bedroom, knowing he had an hour before he had to get ready for the taxi. Pulling out his phone, he ordered one for seven o'clock as Miss Annoying had told him to, then climbed into the shower, the heat of which soothed his muscles.

His shift had finished that morning, and he'd slept for seven hours straight after. Usually, he slept for four, then woke early enough to ensure he could sleep the following night. After sleeping for that long, he couldn't guarantee a decent night's sleep that evening. He needed to go out and tire himself out.

With the water pounding his body, his thoughts went to a certain green-eyed photographer. The man was an enigma, more so because he'd stopped Jason in his tracks when he'd been messing around close to the expensive equipment. Jason didn't always think things through, but when he'd seen that panic in Harry's eyes, he'd felt shredded to his soul. No one had ever made him feel that aside from his brother, who was best left out of Jason's thoughts.

He washed and dried, then laid on his bed, staring at the ceiling. He needed to relieve some tension tonight. His cock was hard without even thinking about anyone of consequence, and that was a red flag if you asked him. Finding a guy to help him with the issue shouldn't be a problem.

The text message saying the taxi had arrived came through right after he splashed some aftershave on. He grabbed his coat and jogged down the stairs instead of waiting for the lift. Once he sat in the taxi and confirmed Jasmine's address with him, he pulled out his phone and messaged her.

JASON: *On my way. We're going to slay tonight, babe!*

JASMINE: *If you talk like that, you'll be leaving the place alone...babe.*

Jason snorted. They didn't have pet names for each other because they all sounded romantic or coupley or awful. He slid his phone back into the pocket of his black jeans, which, paired with his light blue shirt and leather jacket, made him look "*tantalisingly tasty,*" according to Jasmine. When she sashayed down her garden path, Jason's eyebrows rose. She was going all out for this guy, whoever he was.

"Wow," he said. "What did the guy do to deserve this treatment?"

She crossed her legs, the light pink, knee-length skirt falling to the sides of her thighs like waves. Her dark pink top had floaty sleeves—he knew that because she had trained him well in female dress codes—which matched the design of the skirt. She reminded him of a raspberry, but in a good way.

"He's a nice guy, Jason. He catches my eye but seems overlooked by other people." She shrugged. "We'll see."

"You look stunning."

She beamed. "Thank you."

"This is the kind of dress you should wear for your wedding."

She laughed, covering her mouth with her hand to hide the crooked teeth he knew she hated. "What wedding?"

"When you get married. I don't mean now. Just whenever you do. It looks great."

She side-eyed him, frowning. "What's got into you tonight?"

Jason looked out of the window. "No idea. Must be this job."

"They'll find them."

"I know." He cleared his throat. "We're here."

They climbed out and thanked the driver, then entered the bar. It wasn't as noisy as usual, but it was only Tuesday. Neither had invited anyone else to their impromptu night out, and they made their way to the counter.

"Charlie, my man! How are things? Is Josh around, too?"

The manager of Crush held out his hand for Jason to shake. "I'm doing good, thanks. Josh is around somewhere. He's helping because we're short-handed tonight. Remember, it's his birthday this weekend. We're celebrating here, of course. Friday, all right?"

"I'll come, but I'll have to leave at a reasonable hour because I have work the next morning. Tonight, though, does that mean we'll get to see your cocktail routine?" He grinned and sat on the stool.

"Maybe," Charlie said. "I'll have to ask the boss."

Jason smirked and turned to Jasmine. "What are you drinking tonight?"

"I'll have a vodka and orange, but remind me of this later, so I don't mix my drinks, okay?"

"I'll do my best, but remember, I'm drinking, too."

Charlie placed a drink in front of her and assured her he would make sure she only had those drinks while she was there. The man had been working at Crush since he was eighteen years old, and the owner, Tom, had been training him because he wanted to take a back seat to the business when he had a family. Both came at roughly the same time. Charlie was in his element, though. He shone every time he was behind the bar and even more when his fiance was with him.

"Do you see your conquest yet?" Jason asked his best friend, pivoting to survey their surroundings. He lifted his glass to his mouth, then paused when he met the emerald-green eyes he'd been thinking about earlier. "What are the chances?" he murmured.

"Chances of what?"

Jason faced Jasmine, leaning his elbow on the bar. "The guy in the black shirt in the booth by the corridor is the photographer for the calendar. I don't think he liked me."

"Why?" she asked, peering over his shoulder.

"Because I almost broke a few things that looked expensive." He held out his hands before she could interrupt. "One of them wasn't my fault. Dean shoved me, and I tripped."

"Well, he's staring at you, and they're not dagger-like eyes. I think you're okay." She nudged him. "And no, my guy isn't here yet."

"Sorry to eavesdrop, but who are you looking for?" Charlie asked, setting fresh drinks where their old, empty ones had been.

"Ethan?" Jasmine said. "I'd like to ask him out."

Charlie grinned and called to Josh when he appeared at the other end of the bar. "What's up?"

"Have you heard from Ethan today?"

Josh frowned but nodded. "Yeah. He's popping in at some point tonight, but he has to tuck Dane into bed first." He glanced at them.

"There you go. If you stick around, you should be able to catch him," Charlie said with a smile.

"What do you need him for?" Josh asked, and if Jason wasn't mistaken, he was looking out for his friend.

Jasmine straightened. "I was going to ask him out, but it looks like he already has someone."

"He's single," Charlie said.

"In that case, I'm going to ask him out."

Josh grinned. "Good on you. Dane is his friend's kid, who loves it when Ethan babysits him. I think they're both kids, to be honest."

Jason clapped. "Yay. Let's get this party started! Not many for you, though, miss, if you're going to make a lick of sense when Ethan gets here."

"But—"

"Nope. Remember what happened last time?" Jasmine cringed. "Exactly. You'll need to drink water in between; otherwise, you'll throw up over him."

"Sometimes, I hate you."

"Sometimes, I hate me, too."

And wasn't that the truth? Jason lifted his second drink, downing some of the smooth orange mixture. Vodka wasn't his drink of choice, but they often drank in camaraderie because it was easier to remember one drink than two when they were both three sheets to the wind.

He glanced across at the booth where he'd seen Harry sitting with four other people but couldn't see him. He wasn't unhappy about that. At least that was what he told himself. Letting his gaze roam around the occupants of the bar, he found a couple of men who could be potential hook-ups but found he couldn't muster up the energy to approach them. Instead, he faced the counter and stared into the mirror behind the bottles.

"What's the matter?" Jasmine asked.

"Nothing, why?"

"You're still moping."

"Am not." He was.

"Hmm. Why not go over and speak to your photographer? He keeps looking at you."

Jason's heart skipped a beat. "No, he's not. He's not even there anymore."

"Ha, I knew you liked him."

Jason rolled his eyes. "I don't like him. I feel bad for nearly wrecking his equipment. It can't be cheap."

"Bloody hell, these fires have definitely got to you. Normally, you would've thrown back a humorous barb at my statement." She rested a hand on his shoulder. "Is that all that's bothering you?

No. "Yes. Isn't it enough?"

"Of course, but you seem...I don't know, sad but a different sad." She waved her hands. "I can't explain it."

"I'm fine." His words trailed off when he met Harry's gaze in the mirror. The man was at the other end of the bar, giving his order to Analise, another bartender. They didn't look away when she went to fill the order, but Jason tilted his head and grazed his teeth on his lower lip. He didn't think the man liked him, but maybe he would be interested in a roll around in the sheets despite that.

"Go for it," Jasmine said, nudging him and knocking his drink over.

The liquid spread across the counter and doused Jason's lap. "Fuck!" He stood, pulling his shirt away from his stomach.

"Shit, sorry." Jasmine grabbed some napkins and tried to dry him off.

Jason raised an eyebrow. "I think I'll get sorted in the bathroom. I might take it off and dry it under the hand driers." He glanced at her. "Will you be all right here?"

She waved her hand. "I'll be fine. I promise I won't go anywhere without letting you know first."

Jason worked his way around the people and down the corridor to the men's bathroom. Once inside, he slipped off his leather jacket and hung it on the hook on the back of the door. He undid the buttons of his shirt and slid it off his shoulders. He remembered hearing somewhere that the stain needed to be washed out before it dried, but he didn't know if that was the truth. He held it under the tap for a few seconds anyway, then tried the hand drier. The feeble attempt at heat made him realise it would take a while.

The door behind him opened, and he glanced over his shoulder. Harry came to lean against the sink closest to him.

"Is it okay?" he asked.

Jason nodded and cleared his throat. "Yeah. I doubt I'll get this dry, but I have to try, especially with how cold it is out there."

"Do you have anything else you could wear?"

"Only my jacket." He nodded to the door.

"Do you want me to grab it? You've got goosebumps."

Jason checked in with his body and acknowledged that the goosebumps had nothing to do with the cold air and everything to do with the closeness of the man beside him. "I'm good at the minute, thanks." They were silent, then Jason said, "Sorry about being clumsy the other day."

Harry frowned at him, then the corners of his mouth turned up, and it changed his face. "It's okay. We all have our days, I'm sure."

"Me more than others. Always a troublemaker." His heart rate increased after his brother's words came out of his mouth. He focused on the heater, moving the fabric back and forth.

"I wouldn't say you were a troublemaker. Maybe the class joker."

Jason peered at him and saw the curve to his lips, and relaxed. "That's me. Always ready with a joke."

"How about being serious for a moment?" Jason met Harry's gaze. "Are you up for a mutually beneficial night?"

If he hadn't been, he was now. His cock hardened at the thought of having Harry above him, but sense prevailed for once. "I don't top."

"And I don't bottom. We're good." Harry stepped closer. "I know it's not good to mix business with pleasure, but there's something about you, even if my instincts are telling me I should run far away," he murmured.

Jason must've taken the fabric away from the heater because the noise stopped, leaving them in silence, but he didn't stop staring at the man. He didn't have any quips this time. This was something he wanted, even if it was a bad idea.

"Yes," he said, his voice croaky.

Harry's gaze dropped to Jason's chest, then lower, and Jason turned to face him, his shirt forgotten. He stared at the tongue that peeped out when Harry swiped it across his lips. He studied the stubble covering his jaw, the tiny scar on his cheek, the curve to his nose, the darkening green of his eyes.

Harry leaned forward, and like a magnet, Jason did, too. Their lips met, and he felt a tingle in them. They were not touching at any other point, but Jason's body was on fire. He whimpered when Harry pulled back.

"Fucking hell," the man murmured, then slammed his mouth down again.

This time, Harry slid one arm around Jason's waist; the other hand cupped his nape, holding him in place. Their mouths devoured each other, licking, sucking and nipping while heat built and built.

"Ahh!" He jerked when his bare back touched the icy wall, but he returned to the kiss straight away. This was like nothing he'd ever felt before. Finally, he skated his hands around Harry's back and gripped the back of his shirt. He wasn't planning on letting go anytime soon.

"Jason, are you still—"

Charlie's voice was like a bucket of cold water over him, and he pulled away, meeting Charlie's amused gaze over Harry's shoulder.

"Sorry. Josh checked upstairs, and there was a clean shirt you could borrow. I'll leave it here." Charlie hung it up on the same hook as Jason's jacket was and left, closing the door behind him.

He glanced at Harry, who had a grimace on his face. "That's what we get for making out in a public bathroom," Jason said.

Harry pulled back, his groin sliding over Jason's as he went, then came back with the same motion, dragging a groan from Jason. "These will not go down easily," Harry said.

"Nope. I could help you with yours if you want?" The idea of having his lips stretched around Harry's cock made his mouth water.

"I don't think that's a good idea."

"Maybe not, but are you sure? I'll make it quick." The more he thought about it, the more he didn't want to wait.

Harry stared at him for several long seconds. "In the cubicle. I'll be there in a minute."

Jason didn't need telling twice. He slid into the furthest cubicle from the door and listened to Harry moving around. Within minutes, the man pushed into the too-small stall, holding Jason's jacket and both shirts. He hung the jacket and clean shirt on the back of the door and dropped the other to the floor.

"Someone will see that."

"I know. That's the point. They know you're in here. They won't think it's unreasonable if someone comes in. You could be changing." Harry rubbed his hands together. "This is a bad idea."

"Your dick says otherwise." Jason smirked.

Harry swapped their positions, bodily moving Jason where he wanted him, which set Jason off. He loved being told what to do. The man stood against the wall, straddling the toilet, then wiped the toilet seat and told Jason to sit on it.

"Not very hygienic, but better than the floor."

"My prince." Jason fluttered his eyelashes, and Harry snorted, the movement taking Jason's attention to the cock he wanted to worship. He licked his lips. "Can I?"

Harry hooked his thumbs in his jeans pockets and nodded. "Have at it."

Jason dragged his lower lip through his teeth and unfastened Harry's jeans, letting the thick, deep purple shaft free. Harry hissed at the same time Jason flicked his tongue over the slit, catching the slightest taste of precome. Never before had he wanted to be perfect at a blowjob. What was it about this guy that set Jason off?

Chapter 6

Harry

The initial swipe of Jason's tongue sent little jolts of pleasure through his body, allowing him to forget about Jason's link to fire. He hadn't intended to proposition the firefighter, especially with Harry's anxiety as it was, but he couldn't resist. He tensed when Jason licked him again, trying not to show how the man affected him, but if the smirk on Jason's face was anything to go by, he already knew.

After gaining relief from Al the previous evening, he had no intention of getting more that night, but when he'd seen Jason without his shirt on again, he couldn't resist him, even if his mouth needed to be used for something other than the snarky quips it usually was.

Jason wrapped his hand around the base of Harry's cock and treated it like an ice cream—long licks and swirling his tongue around the head as if licking droplets of melting cream, which Harry supposed was true because he was leaking like a faucet. Harry clenched his hands into fists inside his pockets and tried to resist reaching for the man, although he couldn't take his eyes off him, especially when he had pleasure-reddened cheeks and lust-darkened eyes.

The bathroom door squeaked open.

"Jason?"

Jason pulled off him and grinned up at Harry, locking gazes. "Yeah?"

"Are you okay? Does the shirt fit all right?"

He coughed. "Yes, I'm good. I'm changing now. If the shirt doesn't fit, my original one will be fine, if a little wet. Thanks, Charlie."

"Okay. I'd hurry if I were you. Jasmine has caught her man, and you might get left behind." Charlie sniggered.

"Duly noted."

They stayed still when the door squeaked again, and keeping eye contact, Jason lowered his head until his mouth covered Harry's shaft. His cock hit the back of Jason's throat, then went further, stopping when Jason's lips reached the hair on Harry's groin. Jason nestled his nose into the hair, then swallowed and lifted off. Electricity sparked through Harry.

"Fuuu—" he finished the word on an exhale when Jason did the move again but faster. The man swiped his tongue under the head and over the slit before repeating the move several times.

Harry's body wound tighter and tighter, and he could barely keep his eyes open until he saw Jason fumbling with his jeans. The sight of the firm, uncut cock sent Harry higher, but the image disappeared when Jason continued laving Harry. He closed his eyes, picturing Jason's cock and what it would feel like to wrap his hands around it, to have it in his mouth. Tingling travelled down his spine, and he removed one hand to slide through Jason's hair and grip.

"I'm close."

Jason made a noise in the back of his throat the moment Harry's tip reached it, and he was done. He bit his lip, tasting blood, and erupted into Jason's warm mouth, slamming his head back against the wall and closing his eyes while the pleasure coursed through him. A brief thought that this felt better than anyone else ever had flitted through his mind but floated away again along with the haze. Harry exhaled as Jason released his cock from his mouth, but Jason pressed his forehead to Harry's stomach and groaned. It was then Harry realised Jason's hand was stroking his cock at speed beneath them.

Wanting to help, Harry slid his hand down the side of Jason's face and tweaked Jason's nipple, then his other hand encircled his own cock, rubbing it against Jason's face. Jason nuzzled into it and groaned again, and Harry felt the contractions in Jason's body the second he released.

They lapsed into silence but didn't move position. Eventually, Jason lifted his head, meeting Harry's gaze, and Harry almost came again. From where he stood looking down at the man, he could see his cock, still semi-hard, near Jason's face and Jason's cock beneath them in the same condition. Jason's eyes were glassy, his lips red and puffy, and a red flush tainted his cheeks. If Harry could've, he would've taken a photo to show people what genuine pleasure looked like.

Harry cupped Jason's jaw. "Thank you," he whispered.

As close as it was, Jason pressed a kiss to Harry's shaft, then took hold of it, carefully returning it to Harry's trousers before doing the same with his own. When they were decent, Jason shuffled back and stood, reaching for the clean shirt. Disappointment curled through him when the perfect body disappeared behind the fabric, then the leather jacket.

Jason ripped some toilet paper off the roll and crouched between Harry's still spread legs, wiping off the mess he'd created off the floor, then threw it in the toilet. Harry stepped away from the wall, and Jason reached behind him to flush the toilet. He went to pull back again, but Harry gripped his shirt, stopping him.

He stared into the ocean blue orbs, not understanding what he was seeing, and dragged Jason down for a kiss. He'd meant for it to be hard and quick, but it turned him around, and he nipped and licked at the bruised mounds for several long minutes.

Jason cleared his throat. "You can say you've slept with a model now." He winked, and Harry flinched, stepping back.

His tongue worried the lump where he'd bitten himself, and he studied the cubicle wall, shoving his hands into his pockets again. "You better get out there. I'll wait a few minutes before I leave." He rested his shoulder against the wall, avoiding Jason's gaze.

Neither moved initially, then Jason unlocked the door and slid out, Harry relocking it after him. He shook his head and leaned his forehead on the door, closing his eyes, listening to the door creak as Jason left. He should've known better. He would be nothing more than a notch on Jason's bedpost, which wasn't a bad thing because Harry could do without the drama of a relationship with a firefighter, especially with his fear of what Jason fought every day. It stung, though.

When he thought enough time had passed, he exited the cubicle and washed his hands, checking his appearance in the mirrors before leaving the bathroom. Undoubtedly, he would get ribbing from his friends about how long he'd taken, but he'd take it with good grace.

"I thought you'd left," Al said.

"Nah. Must've been something I ate." His lie wouldn't fool all of them, and when he glanced at Joey, he knew it hadn't, but he didn't care. If he could pretend while they were still in company, he could get through the evening, but he refused to look in Jason's direction.

"What sessions do you have booked for the rest of the week, Harry?" Al asked, gulping his beer.

Harry lifted his drink, sipping at the lukewarm drink and grimacing. "Tomorrow, I have two sessions with the calendar and three children's photoshoots, then Thursday and Friday, I have the calendar because I want time to go through what I've already taken and pick the best ones."

"How have they turned out?" Joey asked.

Harry's mouth curved. "Fantastic. The props make it easier, but we're taking it outside on Friday, trying to get some less...sterile ones."

"Sterile?" Kade laughed. "I wouldn't call any of those guys sterile."

Kade was Joey's partner. Both were detectives with Cambridge police, and they hung out at Crush as their time off allowed. It might have had something to do with Kade's girlfriend being a bartender.

"Sterile was the wrong word." Harry chuckled. "Staged might be better. I want to see if I can get some more natural-looking photos in their environment instead of in a studio with props."

"Does it matter?" Al asked.

Harry shrugged a shoulder. "Not really. It might sell a few more calendars."

"Most people want to see naked firefighters and won't even acknowledge the background."

Harry frowned at Al. His tone was harsh, and his face was pinched and ruddy. How much had he drunk while Harry was in the bathroom? It wasn't like him to belittle Harry's work.

"Maybe, but if it sells even one more calendar for the cause, I'll be ecstatic."

He glanced at Joey, who raised his eyebrows and shrugged. Al said little more after that, downing drink after drink until Harry lost track of how many he'd consumed. Two hours later, Al stood, gripping the back of the booth, and waved his phone around.

"My taxi has arrived. See ya."

Harry watched Al weave through the throng of people, bumping into several and being set on course again by others.

"Should I go with him?" he asked Joey, staring after his friend.

"It's nothing we haven't seen before, Harry. He'll be fine."

"Yeah, but he was...acting strange tonight, don't you think?"

Harry saw him and Kade exchange a look before Joey said, "He'll be fine."

Harry turned his focus back on his companions and caught Jason's eye. The man's mouth was a firm line, and he could see the man's eyes narrow on him. He averted his gaze and met Joey's. His heart pounded, but he plastered a smile on his face and joined their conversation. He had a sudden fear that he'd upset two people that night, but he had no idea why and what he could do to make it right.

"Mr Jones, we are interested in buying some of the photographs we saw on your website."

Harry stared at the computer screen, listening. "Really?"

"Yes. I work for Addams Advertising, and we've been looking for landscape photos for our new campaign. I think we'd be a good fit for your work." The woman inhaled. "I would like to make an appointment to visit you and discuss our needs and if you might be able to help further."

"Okay, yes. Um, when are you thinking?"

"Is it possible to come tomorrow? I know it's short notice."

"The only time I can spare is between three and four o'clock. Is that any good for you?"

"That would be perfect. I'll see you then."

Harry hung up and stared at the calendar as if it might bite him. There was no way he'd turn her down unless she asked for a price too low for him to make a profit, but it appeared the prices on the website hadn't swayed her. He'd never made an enormous amount of money with the landscapes, which was why he'd taken to doing children and quirky photoshoots, but he loved taking the scenic ones all the same.

"Everything okay?" Zuri asked, startling him from his musings.

Harry blinked at her, then at the people behind her, and stood abruptly. "Yes, sorry. I have my head in the clouds today." He held out his hand to Paul. "I believe we have two sets to shoot today?"

Paul shook hands, tilting his head towards the two firefighters behind him. "Yes, we have Maddox and Layton here now because they'll be heading off to their night shift at six o'clock, and in half an hour, Matias and Nash will join us. They've finished nights and have been sleeping."

"You never know, the sleepy rumpled look might work for them," Harry joked.

Paul snorted. "I'll leave that decision in your hands." He narrowed his eyes at Harry. "Are you sure you're okay?"

"Yeah, I'm fine. Some potentially good news that threw me for a loop. Wasn't expecting it."

"I'm glad to hear it." He paused. "I can't stay today because I have meetings to attend, but Maddox is the watch commander for Green Watch. He'll stay while the photos are being taken. Those boys might need to be kept in line."

His words reminded him of a topic they'd discussed before. "Did you speak with the female firefighters about my idea?"

Paul clapped his hands together, a smile brightening his face. "Yes, I did. They wholeheartedly agreed, and I cleared it with the bosses. Let me know when, and we can sort their photos, too."

"Fantastic. I will."

Harry had originally wanted to include all the firefighters in the calendar, but Paul had told him that the higher-ups wanted just men. Although Harry could understand why, he hadn't wanted the women to feel left out and had spoken with Paul about creating a female firefighter calendar. He hadn't been sure they would accept it, but Paul must've worked his magic. Harry had thought it was a brilliant idea, especially since Cam station was an LGBTQ+ inclusive station. Some buyers might want the female counterparts instead.

"Before you go, can I check the dates for the last photos? You know, the group ones?"

"Sure."

They finalised the dates, then Paul waved and left. The group photos were going to be of the four different Cam crews and then one photo of the watch commanders on their own. That would make the twelve photos they needed for the calendar. Despite this not being his usual photography subject of choice, Harry had enjoyed it. Maybe it was the people.

"Right. Let's get things started. If you could change into the outfits, I'll get the set ready."

"Right-o," Maddox said.

The time flew by while he took the photos, the firefighters listening to him with no problems and doing what they were told. As they were leaving, Matias hung back.

"Is everything okay?"

Matias cracked his knuckles, making Harry wince. "Yeah, um, I wondered whether," he inhaled, "you would like to come out for a beer tomorrow night? A friend is celebrating their birthday at Crush."

"Oh, um..." He hadn't expected that. After what he did with Jason the other night, he should say no, but they weren't in a relationship, were they? And given what Jason said afterwards, he didn't appear to be interested in a repeat.

"You don't have to tell me now if you need to check your diary or something. Or don't feel you have to say yes if you're not interested. I thought I'd ask on the off-chance."

Harry threaded a hand through his hair, knowing his answer. "I'm sorry. It's not because I don't like you. You seem like a nice guy, but I can't...I have this issue with..." He tapped his hands together in a nervous gesture he'd thought he'd grown out of. "I can't…" His eye twitched, and he rubbed it.

Matias held out his hands. "No, it's fine. It's not a problem." Matias's smile faded, and Harry could see the tinting of Matias's cheeks while he shuffled to the door. "Thank you for the photos. I'm sure they'll turn out brilliant." He gave a wave and left.

Harry stared at the door and scrunched up his face.

"I can't believe you passed up on that," Zuri said, nudging him with her elbow. She fanned her face.

"It would never work, Zuri. My anxiety would never leave me in peace if I dated a firefighter."

Zuri cocked her head. "Your anxiety doesn't leave you in peace anyway," she said, slipping her arm through his and squeezing. She rested her head on his shoulder. "We need to work out who you would be comfortable dating and try to find you someone. It's not fair that you're on your own. I want to see you happy."

Harry kissed her hair. "I am, or I will be when I get through this meeting tomorrow."

Zuri lifted her hand and jumped on the spot. "I know. I'm excited for you. Do you know which photographs they like?"

He disentangled himself. "No, she didn't say. Only that they were landscapes. I have loads of those. Some better than others."

"If it's an advertising campaign, they might pay you to take more or different ones unique to them. You could charge an arm and a leg for that."

He picked up bits of equipment and sorted them into the relevant boxes. "No matter what, I won't sign anything tomorrow. I'll get them to give me a contract to look over if they want something different from what I've already taken. I'll need to speak with a lawyer and get them to check it over first."

"Why?"

"Because there are always little bits in contracts that benefit the company and might not benefit me. I want someone to check it over to ensure I'm not being made a fool of. I don't want to end up signing the rights to all of my work over to them by accident."

Zuri exhaled. "Good point. This is something I would never have thought about. I would've signed and cried after the fact."

"You have more sense than me, without a doubt. Don't pretend otherwise." He yawned. "I'm going to close up after this and get to work on the editing of the photos. You can head out after if you like."

Zuri beamed. "Thanks. I could do with nipping to the supermarket for groceries. Mum might forgive me for forgetting the asparagus last week if I bring her some today instead."

Harry laughed. "It's your fault for trying to memorise the list instead of taking it with you."

"I left it on the side! It wasn't my fault!" Zuri pouted and threw some fairy wings at him, then frowned. "Why were these even out?"

Harry withheld his grin. "Layton thought they might look good on Maddox. He wasn't amused."

"When did I miss this?"

"You were on your break."

"I miss all the fun," she muttered.

Chapter 7

Matias

Matias felt his cheeks heat when he exited the studio. He hated asking people out because the rejection stung regardless of who said it. He refused to stop asking, though, because eventually, someone might say yes.

"Everything okay?" Nash asked when Matias reached him at the side of the road.

"Yeah, all good." He rubbed at his cheeks, hoping the flush was not as visible as it felt. He cleared his throat. "What are your plans now?"

Nash yawned. "I feel like I need more sleep, but I'll go to the gym. What about you?"

"I might visit Mum. I've nothing else planned."

"Why don't you come with me? Get your blood pumping." Nash winked.

Matias rubbed the back of his neck and grimaced. He didn't enjoy going to the gym; he preferred running along a pavement and watching the scenery go past, but maybe doing something different would be good for him.

"Sure."

"Gee, don't sound so enthusiastic." Nash rolled his eyes and headed for his car.

"Sorry." He sighed. "I need to go home and get my stuff. I'll meet you there."

"All right. See you soon."

Matias remained standing on the path and wished he hadn't agreed to go. He could easily message Nash and tell him he'd changed his mind, but it was a good thing to get him out of his apartment. He wandered down the street towards his home, which wasn't far from Harry's studio.

He didn't regret asking Harry out, but he should've waited until all the shoots had finished because it meant Matias still had to face him one more time. Many men had caught his interest over the years, but none of them had panned out for more than a short time. He wanted more. He wanted what his parents had. What his sister had. What was so difficult about that?

Letting himself into the apartment he shared with his brother, he shouted out his greeting.

"I'm in the kitchen!"

Alejandro was stirring something on the cooker when Matias entered the kitchen. "Smells good. Whose recipe is it this time?"

"Tia Elena. She gave me her paella recipe."

Matias's stomach growled, and he wavered again about meeting Nash. He shook his head. "I'm heading to the gym, but make sure some of that is available when I get back. I'm starving."

"Have you not eaten today?" Alejandro frowned at him.

"Yes, Alejo. I'm a growing boy. My stomach knows no boundaries."

Despite their Spanish heritage, they only spoke Spanish around their parents and grandparents, except for the odd word here and there. Food, though, was something every member of their family loved. A good thing for him, Alejandro loved to cook.

Matias dragged himself to his bedroom and packed his gym bag, then said goodbye to his brother again. He hooked the backpack over his shoulders and began a slow jog to warm up. He didn't own a car, but he loved running and didn't mind the exercise. He might regret it on the way home, though.

A horn beeped, and Matias jumped. A car pulled up beside him, and he ducked to see inside.

"Do you need a lift?" Harry asked.

Matias's cheeks heated again, and he cursed his pale skin. He was paler than his more tanned siblings. "It's okay. I'm heading to the gym."

"I don't mind."

Matias hesitated, but in the end, he agreed and climbed in, giving Harry the gym's name. "Thanks."

"No problem." Harry cleared his throat. "Look, about earlier..."

"Honestly. It's fine, Harry. I won't chase after you to get you to change your mind. You're either interested, or you're not."

A flush invaded Harry's cheeks. "If you weren't a firefighter, I would be."

Matias frowned. "Why?"

Harry's hands clenched on the wheel. "I have issues and...I need to stay away from people who lead dangerous lives. I can't explain."

Matias didn't understand, but it wasn't his place. "It's fine. Honestly."

"I'd love to be friends, though?" Harry glanced over at him with a wince. "I know that's the standard brush-off, but..."

Matias chuckled. "Friends, it is."

They spoke a little more before Harry pulled into the car park.

"Thanks for the lift."

"You're welcome. I'll see you soon."

Matias waved goodbye and watched until Harry was out of sight. He'd not expected Harry to be averse to dating firefighters. It was a shame to think he was out of the running because of his job. He'd thought he'd seen Jason show some interest. Maybe he'd mention the conversation to him and make sure he didn't get embarrassed by the same brush-off that Matias did.

He grimaced and turned to the gym entrance. Here goes nothing.

Chapter 8

Jason

PAUL: Don't forget you need to meet us at Harry's studio at 4 p.m. this afternoon for the last photo shoot.

Jason had rolled his eyes and replied that he'd be there. He'd forgotten about the final shoot; otherwise, he might have reconsidered the hook-up with Harry the previous week. He snorted. Who was he kidding? He wouldn't have changed that at all. It had been fucking sexy. Looking up and seeing Harry watching him with the droopy, pleasure-filled gaze had Jason's cock valiantly trying to rise again, even though it had released seconds prior.

He changed position, trying to think of something else before his erection made itself known inside a bakery for the occupants to see.

The photoshoot. Yes, he'd be there because he'd promised Paul he would be. His last photo would be with Dean, Scott and Niall, but he didn't know what the props would be, and he was sure his ideas wouldn't be welcomed. He grinned.

"What would you like?" the assistant asked, smiling.

"A caramel latte and the pancake stack to eat in, and ten cakes to go. I don't mind which."

"Okay." She pressed on the screen a few times, then said, "That will be twenty-two fifty, please."

He held out his card to the reader, waited for the beep, then returned it to his wallet, sliding the leather pouch back in his pocket. "I'll be over there." He pointed to a table, and the assistant made a note. He moved to a table by a window and sat, pulling out his phone again to bring up a card game. He played several games until a girl of no more than nineteen brought over his breakfast-slash-lunch-slash-afternoon snack.

"Thank you. This looks delicious." Jason sent a lopsided grin in her direction and withheld his chuckle when she fumbled the plate and cup.

"Do you need anything else?" she asked. Her voice was as shaky as her hands, and she couldn't look him in the eye.

"No, thanks. Just the cake box when it's ready." He winked at her and focused on his food.

Nothing beat pancakes for any meal of the day, preferably covered with syrup. Many people had bemoaned his ability to eat an absurd amount of sugar and yet stay slender enough to do his job. Even if he developed a rounded stomach, he wouldn't give up his pancakes. He cut into the tower and sliced a triangle from the entire stack as if he were cutting a cake. He swiped it through the syrup and shoved it in his mouth, groaning when the sweet, tacky flavour burst onto his tongue.

While he chewed, he studied his surroundings through the window. People rushed past, their coats pulled up around their ears against the falling rain and chilly breeze Jason had escaped by entering the café. Cold and blustery days were to be expected at the beginning of November, but it didn't make anyone happier about it. Jason, on the other hand, loved rainy days. He didn't care if he was out in the rain and soaked to the skin because everything about the rain was amazing, although he could concede that icy rain might have had its downfalls.

Christmas was only six weeks away, and he seriously needed to consider what he was buying for Jasmine and his crew members. There was no expectation of buying anything for his crew, but he liked to share the Christmas spirit and make people laugh when they had to work, which they would this year. Jason didn't mind it, but those with families always had a tough time.

Draining his coffee, he set the cup on the table and picked up the previously delivered box of cakes, which they'd helpfully put into a bag for him, and his large bag of uniforms he needed for the photo shoot. He hoped there was something in there for everyone because he didn't know what they liked. The wind belted him when he exited the bakery with a wave and a thank you to the employees, and he flicked his collar up and hunkered down for the walk to the studio. It was only five minutes away, but it gave his mind the chance to come up with various ways of greeting Harry. He could go for his usual joke and say, "Where's a bathroom when you need one?" but he didn't think that reference would go down well, considering their circumstances. His best idea was the normal, "Hello. How are you?" but it felt...bland, though why it unsettled him, he didn't know.

Before he could decide, he was at the door. He opened it and heard a distant chime from the upstairs studio, letting the occupants know someone had entered the building. It wasn't safe leaving the door unlocked, in his opinion, but it was something to have a bell. The stairs were sturdy but steep and narrow, and he climbed them at an angle to stop his shoulders from brushing the photos on the walls. He wouldn't want to damage any of them.

"Jason! Nice of you to join us," Niall said with a grin.

Jason pushed his coat sleeve back with numb fingers and glanced at his watch. "I'm not late. What are you complaining about?" He placed the bag on a table by the drinks machine. "I have sustenance for those who would like one." He pulled out the box and opened the lid, the scent of sugary goodness wafting to him.

Moving aside, he removed his coat and stepped back when Dean, Niall, Scott and Paul all headed for the box.

"Leave some for Zuri and Harry!" he called, hanging his coat on the hook by the door. He'd learnt his lesson about leaving it lying around on the floor.

He had yet to look at Harry, but he could feel eyes burning into his back; therefore, he spun around with a smirk on his face, which died the second his gaze met Harry's. Harry lifted his chin and licked his lips as if he were steeling himself for the upcoming meeting. Jason could see his

Adam's apple bob when he swallowed, and for a moment, he wished he could see that happen when Jason had his cock in the man's throat.

Jason rubbed a hand over his face and exhaled. This was going to be a long session.

"What made you bring cakes?" Paul asked, biting into an éclair before pausing. "What did you do?"

The tone of voice and slumping of his boss's shoulders made it known that messing up was a regular occurrence for Jason. Amazingly enough, though, Jason hardly ever messed up on a call, which was a great thing but strange. Why he couldn't bleed some of that confidence into his personal life, he didn't know.

"I haven't done anything! Can't I bring something nice for you?" He kept his gaze on his crew and didn't flick his eyes over to watch Harry. His crew was too observant to miss that kind of tell.

"Hmm." Dean narrowed his eyes. "No funny business, Mr Townsend."

Jason saluted. "Aye, aye."

They finished the cakes, although Jason noted Harry didn't take one, then Harry called them over to change their clothes. Harry's idea for the group shot was to stage a nearly naked rescue. With there being four of them in this photo, it needed to be a small scene, and when Harry detailed the idea, Jason felt excitement fluttering in his stomach.

Each of them took turns in the changing area, small as it was, until they were dressed in their yellow trousers and helmets, then Harry positioned them where he wanted them. Niall climbed a ladder that had been bolted to the ceiling and floor and hung off it. Dean stood a step behind him on the floor, resting both forearms over the handle of an axe that was laying across his shoulders. Scott held a hose across his waist that was wrapped around one of his legs like a snake and dropped to one knee, and Jason held onto a pole, again fixed ceiling and floor, his helmet in his hand.

He tried to forget about Harry having his hands on him and positioning him the way he wanted him because it would easily translate into something his mind could grab onto as a fantasy for later.

"Perfect. Stay like that for me while I focus the camera," Harry said, stepping away and crouching. "Okay, let me see those smiles."

Jason gave his usual smirk and removed his hand from the pole, instead resting his forearm against it. Every time Harry asked them to reposition a little, Jason did. At one point, he put his helmet on and tilted his head down until his eyes were only visible underneath it. Harry cleared his throat and requested for them to swap positions, and Jason found himself with the hose between his legs.

A quip was on the tip of his tongue, but when he met Harry's gaze, his mouth dried up. The banked heat from earlier had seeped into the edges of Harry's eyes, and Jason had an overwhelming need to throw himself at Harry's feet. Instead, he stared at the floor until Harry called for them to smile.

Despite it being an hour-long session, the time flew by. While Scott and Dean redressed, he and Niall stood with Paul and Harry at the computer, watching Harry's fingers move across the keyboard and mouse.

"I know it looks plain now, but I had the green screen set up behind them. To give you an idea of what I'm planning, if I add a few special effects...you get this."

He stepped to the side, and Jason stared, mouth gaping.

The photo, which he'd honestly thought wouldn't look very good alongside the others the man had taken, had been transformed. Whereas before they were on a plain background, Harry had added in a raging fire behind them and smoke drifting across the front of them. It looked amazing, and he told him so.

"Thanks. I'm going to try other effects to see if something else works better, but you'll get to choose the final ones yourself." He aimed the last comment at Paul, who nodded.

"These are going to look great," Paul said. "And they'll be ready in time for Christmas."

"Yes. These are the last photos I needed. I'll be working on them over the next week to ensure they're as good as they can be, then I'll send them to you for your final choices. The calendars should be ready by the end of November."

"Great work, Harry. And you, too, Zuri." Paul clapped Jason on the shoulder. "If you don't need me anymore, I'll head back to the station. Paperwork calls my name."

"I'll be in touch, Paul."

"Take care, and make sure you pop round for dinner one evening; otherwise, Quinn will have my hide."

Harry flushed but nodded. "I will."

Paul left after several goodbyes, and Jason and Niall swapped places with Dean and Scott after bidding them goodbye.

"What are your plans after this?" Niall asked through the curtain that separated them.

Jason grinned—though Niall couldn't see it—knowing the response he'd get from his next words. "I'm going Christmas shopping."

"Seriously? It's not even halfway through November yet."

"What can I say? I'm a rule breaker."

Niall scoffed. "Well, I'm done. I'll catch you at work in a couple of days. Have a good haul, Jason."

"See you soon."

It was only when silence descended that he realised he was now the only firefighter left in the building. At least they had Zuri to stop any uncomfortable conversation between them. He finished dragging on his jumper and stepped free of the curtain, his trousers packed into the bag. Paul had graciously offered to bring everyone's helmets and take them back to the station with him. It saved them from having to carry extra items.

He paused when he saw Harry waiting at the coffee machine with his arms crossed.

"Everything okay?" he asked, drifting closer.

Harry nodded, rubbing his eye, which Jason noticed he did whenever he was uncomfortable with the situation. Jason stopped several feet away, not wanting to make him any more unhappy than he already seemed. The thought that Harry didn't want Jason around hurt more than he'd realised it would, and he swallowed down the need to joke about something to break the mood and instead thumbed over his shoulder.

"I'll go. Sorry it took me so long."

He had reached the door before Harry stopped him.

"Wait."

Jason didn't turn around, just stared at the closed door, waiting.

A hand slid into the back of his hair, rising until he gripped and turned his head to the side. Jason didn't have the chance to process the expression on Harry's face because their mouths fused. Harry bit at the mounds and forced his tongue between Jason's lips, opening him up for his exploration.

Jason heard a thud, but his mind was involved in the actions of the man devouring him. He was pliant beneath the man's ministrations until Harry stiffened, and not in the way Jason expected. Harry pulled away, breathing hard, frowned, then stared around the room.

"Wait." He held up a finger, then moved around the room, switching off and unplugging equipment.

Jason's mind was fuzzy, but something about Harry's movements seemed off. He tried to figure out what it was. It wasn't until he was close by again, unplugging the coffee machine, that Jason realised Harry was afraid.

"What's worrying you right now?" Jason asked in a soft tone, not wanting to startle Harry. "I can go if you don't want me here." He didn't want to, but he would.

Harry paused when he reached for the final plug, then continued. "I don't like leaving everything plugged in while I'm not here."

There was a tremor in his voice and sweat beaded on his forehead. Jason couldn't reconcile the explanation and Harry's body language projected a fear of something, but it wasn't his business. If Harry didn't want to tell him, he didn't have to.

"I'll go," Jason said, picking up the fallen bag—that must've been the thud he'd heard.

"No!" Harry inhaled and exhaled before finishing in a careful tone. "Not if you don't want to."

Jason rubbed a hand across his mouth, for once unsure about what to do. "I want to stay with you, but you don't seem..." He trailed off, not knowing how to explain.

Harry straightened and focused solely on Jason, the earlier banked fire now blazing in his eyes. "This is what we're going to do. I'm going to gather my things together, then you are going to follow me home. When we get there, you will listen to my instructions and follow them to the letter. Do you understand?"

Jason cocked his head. "I don't mind being told what to do, but I'm not into the BDSM scene. Are you?"

"No, but watching you fall apart because I said so has been plaguing my dreams for days."

A shiver ran down Jason's spine. "I understand." His words answered Harry's earlier question.

Harry nodded once. "Wait there."

"I have to fetch my car from a few streets away because I couldn't get a parking space closer. Shall I fetch it and meet you outside?"

Silence reigned for several seconds until Harry nodded again.

"I'll be right back."

Jason didn't want to be away from Harry for longer than necessary; therefore, he raced down the stairs. He wished he could figure out what it was about the man that sent all Jason's usual bravado sinking to the floor in submission. He didn't mind, but he enjoyed having a choice. With Harry, his body took over from his mind, and Jason could do no more than follow its lead.

When he reached his car, he shoved the uniform in the boot and climbed in, spending several precious minutes calming himself before starting the engine and driving to the studio. As luck would have it, a car pulled out of a parking space right outside when Jason drove up. He parallel parked and waited, wiping his palms on his jeans. He wasn't due at work for the next thirty-six hours, and if his destiny was to spend it in a sexual haze, he wouldn't mind.

Harry exited the building, carrying several pieces of equipment and bags, and Jason hurried from the car to help.

"Let me..." Jason gathered several things from Harry's hands, allowing the photographer to lock the door without dropping anything.

"Thanks." Harry led the way to his car, opening the boot and the passenger door. "Anywhere they'll fit, please."

The unsure and quiet man had returned, and Jason tried to figure out the two sides of the one man. One was quiet, shy, almost withdrawn. The other was confident about taking charge. Which one was true?

"Thanks. I don't live far from here. It's not..." Harry covered his eyes with one hand and exhaled. "Follow me."

Jason wanted to push for what Harry had been about to say, but he didn't. Instead, he did what he was told and followed Harry to his home. It took about ten minutes, then they were pulling into the underground car park. The building appeared to be several apartments, or maybe flats was a better choice of word. They didn't appear big, but the building itself looked well-maintained.

He climbed out to help Harry carry his equipment again, and they headed for a lift. Harry pressed his floor, and they ascended in silence. Jason wanted to break it, but he wasn't sure what to say. They stepped out of the lift into a plainly decorated but clean hallway, and Jason followed him down to the first door on the left. When they stepped into the flat, Harry stayed quiet, and Jason closed the door and shuffled after him. He couldn't decide if Harry wanted him here or not.

The living room was small, but they had managed the size well to fit in enough furniture to make it feel like a home. Jason placed the bags on the floor where Harry pointed and opened his mouth to compliment the place. But before he could, his mouth was otherwise occupied.

Jason's eyelids fluttered the second Harry took control of the kiss, pushing him backwards until he hit the wall with a thump. He took no prisoners, licking, biting, sucking, all the while moving Jason's head wherever he wanted it. Jason could do nothing but hold onto Harry's hips to stop from sinking to the floor in a puddle of goo.

When Harry pulled away, Jason's mouth followed, wanting more. Harry wouldn't let him, and he thudded his head back, panting, and met the man's gaze.

"Strip," Harry said.

Chapter 9

Harry

Harry sounded a lot more confident than he felt. He knew he wouldn't need to check the plugs because he already unplugged them when he'd left the house that morning; therefore, he wouldn't make a fool of himself as he had back at the studio. What he wanted more than anything was Jason on his back with Harry pounding the tension out of himself.

His phone beeped, but he ignored it, instead focusing on the man who was pulling his jumper and T-shirt over his head. The garments dropped to the floor, and a tanned eight-pack stole Harry's attention. His mouth watered at the sight, and he promised himself he could lick his way across the mounds and valleys of those muscles in a few long minutes. First, he needed Jason to do what he was told.

He crossed his arms and quirked an eyebrow at the firefighter, who hastened to kick off his shoes and unbutton his jeans. Despite Harry's attention remaining on the skin being exposed, he also focused on the man's eyes. Jason's deep blue orbs held many words that he seemed to keep a tight lid on, and Harry wanted to hear all his secrets. He wanted to listen while Jason fell apart. He wanted the man babbling incoherently when he came.

Harry inhaled through his nose, trying to keep control of his emotions. "Better. Follow me."

He whirled around and exited the living room, rounding the corner straight into his room. The room was spotless as always, and Harry strode to his bedside table, where he plugged in and switched on the lamp.

"Shut the door and lie on the bed on your back."

He wasn't sure how far Jason would allow him to go with the ordering, but he'd keep it up until the man showed his disapproval. Jason followed his instructions, though his forehead creased.

"What's wrong?" he asked, sitting by Jason's side, the bed tilting with his weight.

Jason inhaled. "What's that smell?"

Harry's cheeks heated. "Cherry." When Jason lifted his eyebrows in question, he continued, "I like the scent and the taste. Cherry sweets, cherryade, cherry air freshener... It's nice."

"It is. I didn't realise how intoxicating the scent was." Jason closed his eyes, and Harry watched his chest rise and fall.

Harry wanted to touch, but he knew once he'd started, he wouldn't want to stop. He stood, undressing while Jason watched; it was only fair, after all. He kept his briefs on but laid the rest of his clothes over the back of a chair in the corner of the room before returning to the man he needed to spend his time exploring. Standing at the bottom of the bed, he tried not to gape at the perfection he saw. Legs that went on for miles, muscles standing out in stark definition, a flat stomach only marred by the hills and valleys of his abs, a chest heaving with every breath. And his eyes...the ocean blue had deepened to a darker, needier colour, and his eyelids had lowered to half-mast.

"Hold the headboard."

Unable to wait any longer, Harry crawled from the bottom of the bed, taking his time, touching, kissing and rubbing his lips against all the skin he came across while he made his way up Jason's body. Even the man's knees were sexy as hell, though Harry did unintentionally find a ticklish spot behind them, which he filed away for future reference. He ignored Jason's groin, flicking his tongue into each dip of his abs, painting his ownership for the night over the hills.

Jason wasn't quite incoherent yet, but he was trying hard to remain still after Harry had told him not to. His head thrashed on the pillow whenever Harry touched a sensitive area, and Harry noted every one of them. He'd use it to his advantage later that night.

The moment Harry fixed his mouth around one of Jason's nipples, he felt a thrill go through him at the breathy moans and lust-filled groans falling from Jason's lips. Harry lowered his body until he lay against Jason, the man's cock squeezed between their bodies. He licked and sucked the nubs, alternating between that and using his fingers, and rocked his body side to side, giving Jason a brief sensation, but not enough to allow him to come.

"Please, please, please," fell from Jason's lips, music to Harry's ears.

Harry raised his head, watching Jason's face while he slid his body upwards, dragging his cock between them until Harry's hard shaft pressed against Jason's balls. Harry could imagine what it would feel like if they didn't have any fabric between them. With their height differences, Harry couldn't reach Jason's mouth in the position they were in. Reluctantly, he lifted his body and crawled to fit their mouths together.

Harry braced himself on his forearms over Jason's body, their skin sliding against each other. When he couldn't take any more and Jason's entire body trembled, Harry dragged both of their underwear off and threw them in the general direction of the chair. He reached for the bedside table drawer, putting the hand-pump full of lube on the top, then grabbing a condom. Sitting back on his heels, he held it up, rotating it in his fingers.

"Do you want to fuck or be fucked?"

Jason's eyelids fluttered, and his nostrils flared. "I don't top, remember? Fuck me."

Harry's mouth curled, having already discerned the answer. He pumped some lube into his hand, the scent of cherry filling the air, and returned to his place between Jason's thighs. He dropped the condom close by and rubbed the lube onto both hands. It was overwhelming, but he had plans. One hand he wrapped around Jason's cock, stroking with unhurried movements despite feeling the opposite. With the other hand, he pressed a finger to Jason's pucker, massaging in circles until he felt it relax, then he pushed forward.

"Oh, fuck, yes!" Jason's head rolled on the pillow, his back arching and his hands clenching around the slats in the headboard. Harry wondered whether the wood could take the strain, then didn't care. He'd replace it if necessary, but nothing would stop him from witnessing Jason's complete surrender.

Working his finger back and forth until it slipped in easily, he pressed two inside, Jason's movements increasing in intensity after Harry stroked his cock faster. He could see the twitching begin in Jason's abs and dropped his hand to the base, squeezing to withhold his release.

"No! Oh, fuck!" Jason gasped and glared at Harry, who leered in return.

"You'll come when I say you can come."

Harry continued to pump his fingers, adding a third, then stroked Jason's dick again, twisting his hand below the head to drag across the nerves there. Knowing someone gifted him in the dick department, Harry pushed four fingers into Jason's ass, rotating his hand to stretch him, all the while stimulating Jason's cock to distract the man. When he saw Jason twitch again, he stopped and removed his fingers.

"Fucking hell!" Jason panted, arm muscles flexing and releasing, together with the clenching of his fingers against the slats.

Harry ripped the condom open, rolling it on and slathering it in cherry lube, and leaned over Jason. "Ready?"

"Why did it take so long for the photographer to fuck his partner?" Jason said through gritted teeth. Harry raised an eyebrow. "Because he was busy imagining what it—fuck!"

Harry slammed forward, making Jason take every inch of him in one thrust. The instant he sank balls deep, he lowered to his forearms, sliding his hands under Jason's shoulders and cupping them. Jason's legs lifted and curled around Harry's waist, locking ankles at his lower back. That action made them closer in height, and Harry lowered his mouth to Jason's, licking and tangling their tongues while he waited for Jason to adjust.

"You feel bigger in my ass than you did in my mouth," Jason said as his body relaxed.

Harry grinned. "I'm sure there's a joke you could make with that comment."

"Maybe, but my brain isn't working well at the moment."

"You're still far too coherent for me."

With those words, he canted his hips and withdrew a small amount, pushing back in again. Repeating the move several times, his mouth curved into a smile when little mewls of noise escaped from the man beneath him. Harry kissed him once more and lifted to his hands, giving himself more room to move.

"Hold on."

It was the only warning he gave before he withdrew fully and slammed back inside. His hips pistoned, increasing in speed until all he could hear was the slap of their skin, the swearing from below, and their gasps and groans. It was music he could listen to and get aroused from every time.

Harry changed position, resting back on his heels and holding Jason's legs, then pounded his ass. Jason's cursing turned to cries of agreement, and Harry knew he was hitting the spot deep inside Jason.

"That's it. Come for me," Harry said, hammering into him.

Jason erupted immediately, his shouts ear-piercing but sexy as hell as he coated his stomach and chest. It sent Harry over the edge seconds before he expected to, and he ground his dick into Jason's ass, holding himself deep as he emptied into the condom. Harry dropped his head to Jason's chest, his cock twitching again when his eyes focused on the sight of his dick stretching Jason's ass.

Jason's arms dropped to the bed, his eyes closed, and his chest heaved, but he had never looked more beautiful. Maybe it was because he wasn't cracking jokes.

Harry withdrew in slow motion, wanting to extend their pleasure enough to try the patience of a saint despite how sensitive he knew they both were. Although saints wouldn't...Never mind. He stared at Jason's gaping hole, trying to close, and couldn't resist adding a finger to feel him again. Jason jerked and moaned. Harry removed his finger and leaned down, licking around the entrance, soothing it and tasting the cherry lube—the whole reason he chose the flavoured option. He lifted his gaze to Jason, finding the man's focus already on him, his hands gripping the pillows, his mouth wide.

Harry finished with a last lick, then removed the condom and tied it off, throwing it to the floor before licking up every drop of Jason's release coating his skin. He may have spent several long minutes "cleaning" the man's nipples, too. Finally, he leaned down and kissed his lips, a soft brush of thanks.

They needed to clean up, but Harry found himself reluctant. Instead, he lay beside Jason, dragging him against his side with his head on his chest, and wrapped his arms around him. He didn't try to understand the reasoning, but he couldn't resist the impulse. It was too strong. He had never done this for other guys he'd brought back, and whenever Al had helped him, he would leave once Harry had relaxed. They never cuddled like this.

"You're thinking loudly," Jason said.

Harry kissed his head and tightened his hold. "Sorry." He exhaled. "We should get cleaned up."

"We should, but I don't want to."

Harry's shoulders relaxed, and he kissed his head again. "Then sleep."

It must've been the magic words because, within seconds, Jason's hold slackened when sleep claimed him. Although Harry wanted to join him, his mind was mixed up and going a mile a minute. He couldn't be interested in this man, could he? The class clown. Someone who hid behind his jokes.

That was the crux of the matter. Harry had figured out that Jason hid his unease behind humour, and Harry wanted to find out more about him, but he couldn't. No one could rely on him. He'd hurt many people before; he couldn't get into a relationship. Sex he could do. Anything else, no.

He exhaled towards the ceiling and reached for the lamp, switching them into darkness. It took a long time for sleep to come, especially because it was only early evening, but the next time he opened his eyes, he was alone in bed.

Weak light tried to lighten the room, but Harry knew Jason wasn't there. He rolled, facing the side of the bed where Jason had been, and noticed a piece of paper. He unfolded it.

Thank you.

That was it. It annoyed Harry that he was more troubled about Jason's disappearance than he should be. He couldn't have a relationship. Why should he care Jason hadn't been there to wake up to?

He dropped the note back on the bed and flopped onto his back, staring at the ceiling. It was Saturday, and he had plenty of work to get done, including several photography sessions calling his name. He sat upright, rubbing his face. When he opened his eyes again, he noticed the condom had gone, and so had his underwear. He glanced around the room, his boxers rested on the chair with his other clothes, and when he checked, the condom was in the bin. He hadn't expected Jason to tidy up after them. He paused. He also hadn't expected his anxiety to disappear. Usually, he was meticulous about tidying up, not wanting to chance anything that could start or encourage a fire to be left on the floor. Last night, he hadn't been worried about that.

Harry rubbed his forearms. He needed a shower.

"Hey, Mum," Harry said, struggling through the doorway with the food his mother had asked him to bring. He'd ended up doing the entire shop for her instead of the few items she'd asked for because he'd argued that he'd already be there, and why not? Joey and Clemency brought up the rear with several more bags because they'd pulled up at the same time he was emptying the car. More fool them.

"We're here, Esme!" Clemency said, pushing past him to sashay down the hallway to the kitchen.

"Ooh, come in, come in. How was your trip to Paris?"

His mother's voice carried from the back of the house, and he grinned at her exuberant greeting, following the sound. The scent of cooked meat, stuffing and potatoes filled the air, becoming stronger the closer he drew. When he entered the kitchen, Esme, Clemency and Naomi were deep in discussion about the fashion industry and Clemency's recent trip to Paris. He made a note to ask his sister about pooling money to pay for a trip to France for their mother; he was sure she'd enjoy it.

Esme came over after several minutes, embracing him and kissing his cheek. "How have you been, sweetheart?"

Harry smiled. "I'm good, Mum."

"Could Al not make it today?"

Harry's smile dimmed a little. "No, he had other arrangements."

"That's a shame." She returned to the oven. "Dinner will be twenty minutes."

Harry and Joey went to the living room, their experience having shown that his mother wouldn't allow them to help.

She wouldn't let Clemency or Naomi help either, but they would sit and talk to her. Esme loved cooking and hated being waited on.

"What is Al doing today?"

Harry shrugged. "No idea. I saw him yesterday for a couple of hours, then he left and said he wouldn't make it today."

He didn't know what was wrong with Al. He'd been cheerful and talkative one minute, then Harry had told him about the calendar and what happened with Jason, and within half an hour, Al had left. It was almost as if he didn't want to hear about Harry's sex life, which was fine, except Al expected him to listen to his own.

Joey squinted at Harry. "What's going on with him lately?"

Harry cocked his head, staring at the detective. The tone he'd used was the one Harry heard when Joey was trying to get information out of them. "I don't know, but it seems like you think I should."

Joey held out his hands. "No. I'm curious. He rarely misses Sunday dinners, and he's seemed a little out of sorts lately."

Despite his concern, Joey's gaze never left his. "If you have a point, Joey, make it."

Joey's expression dulled, and he rested his chin on his hand. "I think he likes you as more than a friend, Harry."

Harry sniggered. "Don't be stupid. We've been friends for years. He doesn't think of me that way."

Joey sat forward. "How often has he offered to 'help' you?" Harry opened his mouth to talk, but Joey held up his hand again. "From what I've observed, it's gone from every other month to every week. Granted, you don't take him up on the offers more often, but his actual *offers* have increased."

"What difference does that make? He's trying to help."

"He is, but I think he's also trying to show you he's there for you. That you can lean on him. That he won't leave you."

Harry stared at the fireplace, memories flicking across his mind while he thought about Joey's words. Actions and moments where Harry thought Al was being friendly when he could've been wanting more. Harry couldn't make sense of the truth of the memories because he didn't know if what Joey had said now tainted them.

He rubbed his twitching eye. "No, he can't. I can't have a relationship, Joey. You know that. He knows that. It's ridiculous."

"It's not ridiculous, Harry. It's worrying. Especially because I know you don't feel the same for him."

Harry dropped his head on the back of the sofa, trying to understand this new knowledge—if it was even true. Had their sexual moments meant more to Al than they had to Harry? Harry had been pleased and sated, but he hadn't felt... His heart rate increased, and he tried to stop the words from forming in his mind, but it was too late. He hadn't felt like he had when he'd been with Jason. No, he wasn't in love with Al.

But he felt something for Jason, and *that* was a problem.

Chapter 10

Jason

When Jason had awoken wrapped in warm arms, he hadn't wanted to move, but they'd made no promises about sleepovers or seeing each other again. He did what he always did and slipped out of the apartment, though this time, he left a note. Sitting in his car in the underground car park, he kicked himself. Thank you was insignificant compared to what they'd shared that night, as far as he was concerned.

Harry had a phenomenal amount of potential with his business. From what he'd overheard Paul and Harry talking about, a company had contacted Harry about a contract for advertising photos. If the contract was good, Jason hoped Harry would accept because his work was amazing. He didn't need Jason hanging around and bringing him down.

"Oh, please, god, bring back the cocky joker we all know and love!"

Dean dropped to his knees beside Jason's chair and raised his hands above his head, then lowered to the floor, then over his head again. Jason sipped from his cup with raised eyebrows, waiting until he was done before spearing him with what was, hopefully, a glacial expression.

Dean twisted, shouting over his shoulder, "Niall! It's not working. If anything, it's getting worse! Bring help!"

Jason withheld his chuckle. If they wanted to make a show, he'd let them.

Niall came through the door, dragging Scott with him, who held a bag—a first aid kit if Jason wasn't mistaken.

"Help has arrived!" Niall called.

Scott shook his head but sank into a chair beside Jason. "Oh, dear. What do we have here? Have you lost your mojo, Jason?" The words were said in monotone and in a "he wished he was anywhere but here" tone that Jason snorted into his cup.

"It's working! We knew you could do it, Oh Wise One!" Dean said.

By this point, there were several other people around the room, witnessing the craziness that was his friends.

Scott opened the bag and retrieved a stick decorated with ribbon. With a sigh and a roll of his eyes, Scott waved the "wand" and said, "I insist that the bad mojo releases you from its clutches. Find some other victim and leave this man alone."

At the absolute absurdity of seeing Scott waving a magic wand around, Jason lost it. He rested his head on the table in uncontrollable laughter. This was a moment he wished he had Harry with his camera. All Scott needed was wings, and he would've looked perfect for a pantomime.

Someone handed him a tissue when he recovered, but every time he looked in Scott's direction, it set him off again. It had been a long, long time since he'd laughed like this.

"What's happening?"

Despite the words being spoken in a hushed tone, he heard every word. Harry. He glanced up and saw the man standing in the doorway with Paul, who had a grin on his face.

"They're cheering Jason up."

Jason tried to contain his grin, but once he caught Dean's expression, he snorted again, covering his face with his hands. "Please, god, don't let the alarm go yet," he said. He inhaled and exhaled, blowing out his cheeks, and regained some control. "Whoever persuaded Scott to do that...I owe you." A chuckle escaped again, but he held his breath and thought about something else.

"Why does he need cheering up?" The whispered words reached his ears.

"We don't know, but we know he's been quiet for all of our shifts this week," Dean helpfully supplied the answer.

"Oh." Harry licked his lips and held up an envelope. "If it would help, I've brought photos."

Paul clapped Harry on the shoulder, and they left the room, but not without Harry staring at Jason for several seconds. When he disappeared, someone wrapped their arm around Jason's shoulders.

"Is that why you've been quiet?" Niall whispered in his ear. "Did something happen between you?"

Jason sipped his coffee, wishing the alarm would sound, then slapped himself mentally for wishing for a fire.

"You don't have to tell me anything," Niall continued, sitting in the seat Scott had vacated. "I pined for someone for months, then when we finally hooked up, it blew my mind, but they didn't feel the same way. I'm hoping that's not what you're going through because it sucked."

Jason shook his head and dropped his voice. "We hooked up. Twice, but..." He didn't know how to explain. "He doesn't need me."

Niall cocked his head. "Is that him talking...or you?"

Jason averted his eyes from the knowing expression. He couldn't say more. Hardly anyone knew his history, but he found himself talking, "All I ever bring is trouble. He doesn't need me bringing him down. I fight fires because of the shit I did as a teenager. If it wasn't for Paul..." Jason ducked his head. "No one needs that."

He swallowed hard and stood, the joviality of minutes ago once more gone.

"Jason?" He glanced at Niall. "You know where I am if you need to talk."

He nodded once, then exited the dining hall, following the corridors and steps until he breathed fresh air. He leaned back against the wall of the station and dropped to a crouch, closing his eyes. It was warm for mid-November and seven o'clock at night, too. Thinking of the time had him frowning and glancing towards the interior of the station. Why was Harry here at this time of night? And come to think about it, why was Paul?

He shook his head and let his mind go blank, shoving everything aside and wiping his mind free. He didn't know how long had passed before his legs shouted their disquiet about his position, and he stood, holding onto the wall for support. Locking his knees, he stretched, then jumped when someone slammed him back against the wall.

He met wide emerald-green eyes and tensed.

"What are you doing?" Harry asked.

Jason tried for humour. "I'm striking a pose to keep those fires away." Harry crossed his arms, and Jason noted the envelope had gone. "Why are you here so late?"

Harry's cheeks tinted. "I finished the photos and wanted to bring them in. I didn't realise the time until I was already here. Paul was about to leave when he saw me."

Jason catalogued the dark circles under his eyes and couldn't help but reach out and smooth his finger over the pinched crease between his eyebrows. Harry's eyes darkened, and Jason licked his lips, ready to close the distance when a shout made him aware of where they were. Harry's eyes widened again, and he stepped back, but Jason couldn't let him go. He grabbed Harry's arm, pivoting them around the corner of the station and slammed him against the wall, following straight away and covering his lips with his own.

Harry moaned into his mouth, sliding his arms around his back and gripping his jacket. Jason cupped Harry's jaw, tilting his head to go deeper, but he grunted when Harry swapped their positions and held Jason against the wall with his body. Jason spread his legs, lowering himself to a similar height to Harry and letting him have his way, gripping at Harry's back.

When he felt lightheaded, he pulled away, gasping for air. They rested their foreheads together, and Jason watched Harry's eyes close. Jason caught a shine behind Harry, and he tensed his arms and squinted at it. Harry went to move, but Jason stopped him.

"Wait. We have a visitor." Jason smiled and nodded over Harry's shoulder. "Foxy's back."

"Foxy?"

"Our mascot."

Harry glanced over his shoulder. All Jason could see was the tip of the fox's nose and two bright eyes watching them from the bushes.

"Is he friendly?" Harry asked.

"I wouldn't take him to a barbecue, but he's all right. Dean's got closest to him, but he's sat a few feet from me before, watching."

Harry turned back to Jason, staring into his eyes. "What are we doing, Jason?" he whispered.

Jason didn't answer him. He couldn't because he had no idea. Harry bowed his head and pulled back, despite Jason trying to stop him. The alarm blared through the station, making Harry jump. Jason leaned forward, kissed Harry with everything he had in him, then raced into the station, climbing into his boots, then the engine and checked the computer.

"Shed fire. Marlowe Road. Looks like it's spreading fast as it's surrounded by hedges and fences."

They peeled out of the station, Jason glimpsing Harry's wide-eyed expression from the side of the road. He couldn't think about him now. He needed to focus. With a heavy heart, he pushed Harry from his mind.

A rhythmic pounding sound pulled him from his sleep, and Jason repeatedly blinked to keep his eyes awake. When the sound continued without stopping, his eyes flew open, and he scrambled from the bed in all his naked glory. He unlocked the door and flung it open, only to receive an armful of thrashing man. Jason braced himself while the person beat his fists against Jason's chest, but he couldn't understand what was happening.

He inhaled, ready to tell the person to get off him when he scented cherries. Harry. What was Harry doing?

"Hey? Hey! Harry? What the fuck is going on?" he said when Harry didn't reply, just continued to flail in his arms. Jason wrapped his arms around him and let him continue, glancing to the doorway and seeing Ford standing there.

Ford held out his hands, palm up, and shrugged. "He banged on the front door, then mumbled that he needed to see you. I pointed to your door, and he started banging when he couldn't open it. Sorry."

"It's fine. I don't know what's wrong, though."

As if the words had penetrated Harry's mind, the man slumped into Jason's arms. Jason stared at Ford, silently asking for help while rocking Harry side to side.

Ford stepped closer. "It might be some sort of anxiety attack. It's like what my sister used to do. Until she exhausted herself, we couldn't get any information from her about what had started it all. If it is, hold him. He'll come back soon."

Jason swallowed hard, scared for Harry, terrified for himself and his ability to look after another person, but he nodded and steered Harry towards the unmade bed. He sat on the bed, pulling Harry with him. He was pliant in Jason's arms, and Jason leaned against the headboard and held him.

He hadn't known Harry had anxiety issues, although as his mind wandered through their interactions, several things Jason had put down to being uniquely Harry made more sense if he did. Or maybe it was nothing to do with anxiety, and Harry had an OCD thing about it. Jason didn't know, and he hated not knowing. He preferred to have all the information at hand to make an executive decision about the best course of action. It served him well as a firefighter, and he needed that now, but the only one with the information he needed was currently tucked into his arms.

Jason started mumbling random things interspersed with "Shh" or "You're okay."

He hadn't looked at the clock when he'd first woken; therefore, when Harry stirred, Jason didn't know how long they'd been sitting that way. Enough that Jason's legs were numb, though.

"Hey, you. Are you okay?"

Harry stared at him, eyes red-rimmed, lips puffy, nose running. "Why didn't you..." He broke off into a coughing fit, and Jason reached for the bottle of water on his bedside table and handed it to him.

Harry drank half of the bottle, then gripped it, refusing to meet Jason's eyes. "Why didn't you tell me you were okay?"

Jason frowned. "What do you mean?"

Harry lifted his head. "You ran headfirst into danger and didn't tell me you'd made it out okay."

His mouth dropped open. Harry had been worried about him. Jason exhaled and wrapped Harry back into his arms, kissing his head. "I'm sorry. I didn't think what it would mean to you to see me racing out of there. I didn't think..." He paused, then inhaled and continued, "I didn't think you'd worry about me."

Harry pulled away and stood, throwing his arms wide. "You ran headfirst into a fire! Of course, I'm going to worry about you, you stupid asshole! Then you finish your shift and drop into bed while I worry the fuck about whether you made it out alive! I'm not inhuman! I have feelings! I haven't slept since you left. I couldn't take it anymore and had to check if you were okay."

Harry seemed to run out of steam; his shoulders lowered, and he covered his eyes with his hands. Jason wasn't sure whether he should reach out to him again, especially with how angry he was with him.

"I'm sorry. I've always been told I'm an insensitive asshole. A troublemaker. Not worth anyone's time. I didn't think you'd care."

Harry lifted his head and glared at him. "You are a fucking idiot."

He turned and exited the bedroom, leaving Jason staring after him. The front door slammed several seconds later. Jason leaned down, resting his elbows on his knees, and stared at his hands. He closed his eyes, memories resurfacing of his brother's hands grabbing him and shaking him while calling him all the names Dillon could think of and more. Harry had proven how stupid Jason was. Jason needed to let him go.

You're worthless.

You're pathetic.

You're a waste of space.

Jason stood on trembling legs to close and lock his door, then climbed back into bed, not intending to get out of it for the next four days. With Dillon's voice cursing him, he pulled the cover over his head and fell into a fitful sleep.

"Get your ass out of bed!"

The words had him flinging his cover back and sitting upright. "How did you get in?"

Jasmine waved her hand. "I opened the door." She covered her nose. "You need a shower. Desperately."

Jason glanced at the clock, which had the date on it, too, and groaned. "Leave me alone, Jas. I need sleep." He pulled the covers up again.

"From what I've heard, you've been asleep for three days. Not even moving to get food. I think it's time you got up and had a proper meal."

"I have work tomorrow. I need sleep."

"If you don't get your ass out of this bed by the time I return, I'm calling Paul. *And* Dean. *And* Scott *and* Niall *and* Valerie. And whoever else I can think of."

The door closed, and his shoulders loosened. He dozed, then heard his door open again. "For god's sake, Jas. Leave me alone."

His mattress upended him onto the floor, sprawling amongst the covers, which was a godsend in some ways because he was naked.

"What the fuck!"

He pushed the covers from his face and glared at the six men and two women standing before him. Jasmine hadn't been joking when she said she'd bring in the cavalry. Jason dropped his head into his hands and listened while Paul told everyone to wait in the living room. The door closed, and Paul dropped beside him on the floor.

"What's wrong?"

"I'm not worth your worry, Paul. Leave me to it." His hands slipped from his face when he fell forward. "Ow!" He rubbed the back of his head and glared at Paul. "What was that for?"

"For thinking that I don't care about you." Paul's mouth was a thin line. "Not only are you one of my men, which makes you family, you mean a lot to me in your own right. I saw how you were as a teenager, Jason. I know some of what you went through, but if you could see yourself now, see how I see you, you wouldn't say stupid stuff like that. The man you are today puts that teenager to shame, and I'm glad of it. The man you are today is worth my worry, your friends' worry, and your roommates' worry." He paused. "I'll ask again. What's wrong?"

"Harry came looking for me. Ford thinks he was having some sort of anxiety attack or something. I don't know. He shouted at me for not telling him I was okay after racing out the other night." When Jason glanced at him, Paul looked confused. Jason's cheeks heated. "We've hooked up a few times. When he came in to give you the photos, we kissed, but then the alarm went off, and I had to go. He was mad at me." Jason swallowed hard. "I didn't think he'd care."

Paul exhaled and slid an arm around Jason's shoulder, pulling him close. "You'd be surprised how much that man cares even when he tells himself not to."

"He called me an idiot."

"You are!" Paul hollered. "But not in the way *you* think. You're an idiot for thinking we wouldn't have an intervention for you. You're an idiot for pushing people away. You're an idiot for not going after what you want." Jason frowned at him, and Paul snorted and shook his head. "Harry."

His boss stood, and Jason felt a weight lift from his shoulders. Yes, he wanted Harry, but he couldn't have him.

"Get yourself showered and dressed. We're going to Ave's for dinner."

At the thought of the woman's cooking, Jason's stomach growled, and he clamped a hand over it.

"You have twenty minutes before we leave without you." Paul left the room, closing the door behind him.

Yes, he wanted Harry. He really wanted Harry, but how could he have him when he always brought trouble with him?

Chapter 11

Paul

Paul exited the bedroom and closed the door behind him, facing a living room full of people with worried expressions. He inhaled. He couldn't tell them everything Jason was going through—that wasn't up to him—but he could explain a little.

"He's fine. A little down, but nothing Ave's cooking and a little social interaction won't fix. He has some things to work through. Give him a breather, but don't treat him any differently than what you usually would. If you handle him with kid gloves, he'll fall further."

"Is he hurt?" Dean asked.

"Not physically. As I said, he has some things to work through. If he wants to talk about them, listen, but otherwise, leave him be."

Valerie clapped her hands together. "Let's get this show on the road! Ave's here we come!"

Paul snorted.

"Does Ave know we're coming?" Scott asked.

Paul glanced at the man, wishing he would stop pretending not to care about the people around him. "She does. I rang her before I left the house. She already has a feast cooking."

Scott gave one of his rare smiles and headed for the door. "I'll wait in the car."

Paul squeezed his shoulder and turned when the bedroom door opened. Jason appeared with a towel around his waist.

"I'm going to have a quick shower."

Paul nodded, and Valerie shouted, "Make sure it's long enough to get rid of the stench. Eau de boys' locker room doesn't work for you!"

The crew jeered, and Jason lifted his middle finger, then locked himself in what Paul assumed was the bathroom.

"You can wait in the cars if you want," he told them.

"And miss the chance of scoping out his apartment? No way." Dean and Valerie wandered around the room, pointing and chatting about the photos and knick-knacks they found.

By the time Jason was ready, Dean was the only other person waiting in the apartment.

"Where did the rest of them go?" Jason asked.

"They're waiting in the cars. Come on. Let's eat."

Ave welcomed the crew with open arms when they entered her house. "Come in, come in, come in. George is watching the food, and the boys are in the garden despite the cold weather."

Although she didn't make it obvious, Ave hugged Jason tighter and whispered something in his ear. He nodded in return, and the corners of his mouth quirked up. Paul was sure Ave would get him out of his low mood in no time at all.

"Dinner will be another fifteen minutes. Why not head out and play with the boys for a bit? You can build up your appetite." Ave winked at Paul.

"Are you sure that's a good idea, Ave," Paul said. "They're hungry enough already."

"And there's enough food in that kitchen to feed an army. Go on. Go."

She ushered the crew outside, except for Paul, who mostly got a pass when it came to mothering. Although even he was on the receiving end some days.

Ave faced him when the door closed behind the crew. "How is he?"

Paul tilted his head back and forth. "He's been better. His demons are calling. Or I should say his asshole brother's voice is calling. If I'd known what Jason had been going through before..." Paul shook his head.

"It wasn't your fault, Paul. You did what you could with the information you had. Nobody could expect more."

"I know. I feel like I let him down, though." Paul stared out of the window, watching the adults and young boys race around the garden.

"You were one of the few people there for him. If it wasn't for you, he wouldn't be the man he is today."

But if he'd seen the signs beforehand, he could've stopped the pain Jason had been going through earlier than he did. He kept those thoughts to himself.

"Set the table for me, Mr Big-Station-Commander-Boss-Man."

Ave nudged him with her elbow, and his mouth twitched. There was a reason they all went to Ave when they needed cheering up. She knew how to bring them out of their heads and back to the present. Paul put it down to the foster parent in her. After fostering many children over the years, she had a knack for sure.

Once everyone had washed up and sat down, they all grabbed each other's hands.

"My family grows every year, and I love that. It makes me realise that this world, with all its flaws, can also provide some amazing opportunities for love, family, friendships and more. I'd like us to remember how important every one of us is to every other one of us. We may not show it every day. It may be invisible. But it's there. Looking around the table, I see lives being lived, chances not being wasted and help being given when it's wanted or not." She winked at Jason, who grinned. "Thank you."

"Thank you," everyone said.

This was something Paul had taken from Ave. Neither of them was remotely religious, but as Ave had told him many years ago, it shouldn't stop them from being thankful and reminding those around them of the love that was sent their way.

Chatter rose, and Paul beamed. Jason would be fine once he'd found his feet again, and looking at him now, it wouldn't take him long.

Chapter 12

Harry

Harry hadn't slept well for several nights. Ever since *that* night. When Jason had screeched out of the station in the fire engine, Harry's heart thought it would burst. He'd watched the news, trying to find out information about any fires that had broken out to see what the result was, but nothing helped. By the time it reached mid-morning the following day, he had been a wreck. He needed to see Jason, but he hadn't had his address, so he'd done something he had always promised himself he wouldn't. He'd used his friends to get what he wanted.

Harry pulled out his phone, dialling. "Joey, I need you to do something for me."

"Are you okay?"

"No, not at all. I need you to look up someone's address for me."

Joey said nothing, but Harry could hear his breathing on the other end of the line. "I can't do that, Harry. You know I can't."

"You have to, Joey. I need to see him and check that he's okay. Please, Joey."

"Tell me what happened?"

"I don't have time! I need to check that he's okay, then I'll leave. I'm not going to become a stalker or anything. I just... Please!"

Joey sighed. "What's his name?"

"Jason...fuck! I don't know his surname. He's the firefighter." A chuckle sounded. "Shut up, Joey. This is serious. He went out on a call while I was there yesterday, and I need to check that he's okay. I've not heard anything. I'm worried sick."

"All right, all right. Hold on, though I don't need to tell you I had nothing to do with finding this information."

Harry could hear tapping and assumed Joey was at his computer. His own fingers tapped against his leg while he waited for the information that would hopefully clear his mind. Sweat poured down his back, and he tried to calm his breathing, knowing he'd end up in a car accident if he drove like he was.

"Here it is." Joey rattled off an address. "I need you to be careful, Harry. I'm worried about you."

"I'll be fine after I know he's okay. Thank you."

He ended the call before Joey could give him any more warnings. He grabbed his car keys and ran out of the door, hoping to get it cleared up fast enough for him to get to work. The instant he knocked on the apartment door, he couldn't remember if he'd switched off the car engine or not. He didn't care. He needed to check on Jason. There was no answer, *and he banged on it. Repeating the action until someone who wasn't Jason opened the door.*

"Can I help you?"

"Jason. I need to see Jason."

"He's asleep."

"I need to see him. I won't be long. He was working last night and went out on a call and..." Harry kept talking, but he had no idea what he said. His focus was on getting to see Jason, and he could feel himself getting more and more worked up the longer it took to see him in the flesh.

Eventually, the man led him to a door. Harry tried the handle, but it wouldn't open. He banged on it. Tears streamed down his face, and he was mumbling something even he couldn't understand. When the door finally opened, he fell into Jason's arms and sobbed while slamming his fists against his chest.

He couldn't remember anything between that and when he shouted at Jason for being an idiot and stormed out. He hadn't left the engine on, but he *had* left the keys in the car and his phone on the front seat. He'd caught a break that no one had stolen, either.

After reaching home, he'd filled the bath and soaked for a while before he felt centred enough to work. Zuri had fretted over him, but he couldn't get out of the funk he'd landed in. Joey, Al and Clemency had all been to see him, but he'd refused them all.

Telling himself Jason was a colleague, a friend, a co-worker, an acquaintance didn't mean jack-shit. In his mind—or his heart, he hadn't figured that out yet—Jason meant something to him, and that meant he cared about his well-being. It took everything in him to stay away from the man after leaving him sitting on his bed. He'd been angry and hurt that Jason hadn't thought about him.

Even now, four days after the incident, he couldn't seem to pluck up the courage to call Paul and ask about the photos. No doubt, they were laughing at his craziness, and he didn't want to witness that. He'd spent much of his free time at the pool, trying to swim away from his problems.

The day dragged on when he wanted nothing more than to curl under his duvet and hide away from the world, and even when the studio closed, he found he couldn't settle. He unplugged everything but sat by the window, staring into the darkening sky, and watched the city lights come on.

He didn't know what time it was when he heard the bell for the front door. He'd been sure he'd locked it. Panic began worming its way through him, but he found he couldn't move. The footsteps grew closer. His hands clenched the arms of his chair, and his breathing increased. He could feel sweat beading down his back and the side of his face. His mind focused on what he could feel and hear because there wasn't a lot he could see with the lights off.

The steps stopped outside the door, then Harry jumped when a knock sounded, and the door opened.

"Harry?"

Air whooshed out of him, and he dropped his head between his knees to counteract the lightheadedness, linking his fingers behind his neck.

"Harry!"

The footsteps started again, crossing the distance between them at speed until Jason dropped to his knees in front of him. All Harry could see were his knees, but he could feel Jason's hand resting on his back and stroking his hair.

"Talk to me, Harry. Are you okay? I didn't mean to scare you. Fuck! I didn't even know if you were still here, but when I found the door unlocked, I panicked. Harry? Please talk to me."

Harry couldn't, but he released his hands, resting one on top of the hand Jason had on his head. The other hand gripped a fistful of Jason's jacket at his side. When his breathing eased, he raised his head and pulled Jason closer, wrapping his arms fully around the man and tucking his face into his neck. Despite everything that had happened, Harry felt safe.

"I'm sorry about everything," Jason whispered, his hand making a soothing journey up and down Harry's back. "I'm sorry for being an idiot. I'm sorry for not thinking about you. I'm sorry for being a fool and a joker." He exhaled, the air ruffling Harry's hair. "It's all I know how to be, other than unintentionally causing people pain and suffering."

There was something to unpick there, but Harry didn't have the mental capacity to do it at that moment.

"I'm sorry for being a hysterical mess," Harry said into Jason's neck. "I have triggers. I have issues. I'm not a calm, sensible human being."

"Calm and sensible are overrated."

Harry snickered, the mood lightening. Pulling back, he cupped Jason's face, the streetlights sending shadows across it. "I'm sorry for the other day."

"No. You don't need to be. I should've considered the effects of seeing me racing out of there. I should've messaged you."

"And I should've called instead of racing around to your apartment and waking everyone up."

Jason pressed a kiss to his forehead. "How did you know where I live, anyway?"

"My lips are sealed." Harry rolled his lips inwards.

Jason grinned. "Oh!" He reached down and plucked something off the floor beside them, the crinkling noise loud in the silent room. "I brought you a gift."

Harry lifted it into a shaft of light, seeing a cluster of flowers wrapped into a small bouquet.

"I was told purple hyacinths were for saying 'I'm sorry,' but I don't know if it's true," Jason said.

"They're beautiful, thank you." He leaned down to smell them, closing his eyes as the sweet scent filled his nostrils.

"Can I take you home?" Jason asked.

Harry stared at him, mapping the details of his face. "What are we doing, Jason?"

"I have no clue," he whispered, "but I can't stop, whatever it is."

Jason leaned in, taking his time before their lips touched in a kiss soft enough that it brought tears to Harry's eyes.

"Take me home."

Jason kissed him once more, then stood, pulling Harry to his feet. "Is everything off?"

"Yes. I need to grab my equipment."

"Why do you take it home to bring it back tomorrow?" Jason asked.

"It's thousands of pounds worth of equipment. Even though I'm insured for it, I don't want it to go missing because my business would suffer. I prefer to take what I can with me. It's stupid, I know, but..." He shrugged.

"It's not stupid if it eases your mind. What do you want me to carry?"

Once they packed up, they descended the stairs, and Harry locked up.

"Despite me asking you to take me home, I'll drive myself and meet you there, if that's okay? I'll need my car tomorrow."

Jason's mouth curled at the corners. "I assumed you would. I'll see you there."

He dropped a kiss on him, then tucked his hands into his pockets and moved to a car down the street. Harry knew this because he stood and watched him until Jason waved at him, then he climbed into his car. The journey went quickly, and he reached it a couple of minutes before Jason.

When Jason pulled up, he got out muttering, "Damn traffic lights."

Harry snorted and locked his car, shifting the stuff on his shoulder when he pressed the lift button. They rode in a silence that was neither uncomfortable nor charged.

Exhaustion clouded his body, and he assumed a similar thing of Jason.

"Were you at work today?" he asked, unlocking the apartment door.

"Yeah. It's been a long few days."

Harry frowned and placed the items he carried onto the table. "Why?"

When Jason didn't answer, he glanced over and saw Jason staring at his hands. A wave of something washed over him, and he hurried over, wrapping his arms around Jason's waist.

"What happened?" he said into Jason's chest.

"Can we go to bed first? To sleep."

Harry peered up at him. "Of course." He grabbed Jason's hand, dragging him to the bedroom, and undressed him. Leaving the briefs in place, he tugged on his hand and pointed for him to lie down. Once Harry had tucked him under the covers, he undressed and nipped to the bathroom. When he slid under the covers beside Jason, the man opened his arms, and Harry rested his head against the warm, solid chest, feeling the racing heartbeat.

The silence continued until Jason heaved an exhale. "My parents died when I was thirteen. My brother, Dillon, had turned eighteen the previous month. It meant I could stay with him instead of being sent to a foster home. Unfortunately, Dillon wasn't pleased with this outcome because it stopped his plans for joining the Royal Marines." He sniffed. "His verbal abuse started after realising he'd have to put his career on hold. By the time I turned eighteen, physical abuse was a normal part of our daily lives. Dillon said he was teaching me to be stronger. To withstand what life threw at me. To become a better person."

Harry couldn't imagine what he had gone through. To start with that at thirteen, when he'd lost his parents, was inhumane.

"Before he left, I began getting into trouble with the police regularly, graffiti, stealing, breaking and entering, that kind of stuff. I got in with the wrong crowd, and we started setting fires in small places, places we didn't think would harm anyone. Then the leader decided he wanted to go bigger."

Silence lingered, but Harry didn't want to push him.

Jason snorted. "I got caught by an off-duty firefighter. He changed my life."

"Who was it?"

"Paul." Jason's heart had calmed by this point. "He taught me better ways of dealing with what I'd been through. He helped me to get therapy and, when I reached eighteen, put me through firefighter training."

"What about Dillon?"

"He knew nothing about it. It's how I wanted it. The day I turned eighteen, Dillon left me with a parting gift, and I've never seen him since."

"Gift?" Harry wasn't sure he liked the tone Jason had used.

"He broke my wrist, telling me he was saving me from getting drunk and being arrested because I was a troublemaker and unworthy of people's time."

Harry sat upright. "That fucking asshole! I'll kill him! I don't care if he's a fucking marine; he's a dead man."

Jason's laughter broke through the angry haze that had descended over Harry. "Thank you. I appreciate that, but I haven't seen him in seventeen years."

Harry nestled back into Jason's arms. "I'm sorry for what you went through."

"Thanks." He ran a hand up and down Harry's arms. "The reason I explained this was because the last few days have been difficult for me." He cupped Harry's chin and stared into his eyes. "Before I explain, you need to understand this wasn't your fault. I don't blame you for anything. All right?" Harry's heart pounded, but he nodded. "I let you down, and it took me straight back to being in that house with my brother."

Harry's heart broke, and tears brimmed in his eyes, wanting to fall, but he held back because what right did he have to feel upset when it *was* his fault?

"Therapy had helped me all those years ago, but every once in a while, something happens, and I'm right back to square one. I'm a troublemaker. I'm worthless. Both are a repeated refrain that doesn't want to leave. I might not have seen my brother in seventeen years, but he has been with me every step of my life. Your words, although not meant to hurt, opened up a wound that has festered for too long."

At that, Harry's tears overflowed. "I'm sorry," he said, trying to get away from him, but Jason's grip on him tightened.

"You don't need to be sorry. I need to find a way to deal with this, once and for all."

"You shouldn't want me in your life. I'm not worth it!" He struggled to get free. "You need to leave before I hurt you, too."

Jason manoeuvred them until Harry was beneath him on the bed. "You won't hurt me."

"I hurt everyone!"

"No, you don't."

"No one is safe around me!"

Jason rested his thigh over Harry's, though Harry was running out of steam.

"You're a good man, Harry."

"I killed my father and brother!"

The second the words had escaped, Harry went slack, tears streaming from his eyes as sobs wracked his chest. Arms wound around him, but he couldn't lift his arms to reciprocate because he was exhausted. He lost sense of time but eventually became aware of the cover above him and a warm body beneath him. The rhythmic beat of the man's heart centred him. His throat felt tight and raw, his eyes were scratchy and his nose stuffy, but most of all, his entire body ached. It was as if he was one complete bruise, which he supposed was an apt description.

Although he felt warm, he didn't want to move. The serenity of the moment was too complete to break with what he knew would be questions he didn't want to answer. He wanted to bask in the tranquillity before being slammed back down to earth.

Chapter 13

Jason

Jason felt his heart break in two when Harry fell apart. He hadn't expected it, but he wouldn't leave now. No one could hear what Harry had said and listen to his breakdown without feeling something for him. Jason wanted more information from Harry before he came to his conclusions about what he'd shouted out. He didn't believe for a moment that the man above him could hurt anyone, especially two people close to his heart. There had to be more to the situation, and Jason was staying around to find out what it was. He couldn't leave if he tried.

The sobbing eased in small increments. Jason manoeuvred onto his back while still holding on to Harry, even when Harry's body went lax. He didn't think the man was asleep, but even if he was, Jason would hold on to him, helping him settle, reminding him he wasn't alone.

Jason heard his phone beep, but he refused to reach for it. If it was urgent, someone would ring him. The weight of Harry on top of him was nice. Harry's head fit beneath his chin as if that space had been made especially for him. He could smell the sweet scent of cherries, and he wondered whether Harry owned every cherry-flavoured and scented toiletry made. His mouth curved at the thought. When Christmas came around, he would have to find something Harry didn't have.

Jason closed his eyes and turned that thought around and around, realising he wanted Harry to be in his life through Christmas, if not longer. For some reason, the idea didn't spook him as it had before.

"Sorry."

The words, though whispered, made Jason jump, but he squeezed his arms, then loosened them again, showing he was listening.

"You have nothing to be sorry about."

"I have a lot to be sorry about. Breaking down on you is the least of it." Harry exhaled, the heat of his breath coasting across Jason's skin.

He held onto Harry and rolled them to their sides, facing each other, but close enough for Jason to keep Harry in his embrace. He twined their legs, rested their foreheads together and closed his eyes.

"There is something about you, Mr Jones, that I can't ignore. If you asked me what it was, I wouldn't be able to explain it, but it's there, nonetheless. I want whatever you can give me. Whatever you're *willing* to give me. I want to be here for you when this happens. I want to be who you turn to when you need someone to catch you when you fall." Jason snorted, opening his eyes and brushing his thumb against Harry's cheek. "I have never entertained these thoughts with someone else. I don't know what it is about you, but you keep me coming back for more."

He leaned forward, rubbing his lips against Harry's in an almost-kiss.

"There's something about you, too." Harry's eyes seemed to sparkle in the light, making the green glow, and it mesmerised Jason.

Jason quirked the corner of his mouth. "Well, I didn't come here today expecting an exchange of confusing emotions. I expected to grovel at your feet."

Harry's smile was watery but there all the same. "You still can if you want to."

Jason chuckled. "Maybe later. I'm comfortable here." Silence reigned until Jason said, "Do you like films?"

"Um, sometimes. If I'm in the mood for them. I'm usually working on photographs in the evening and only listen to music."

"What music do you like?"

"Anything but pop music."

Jason snorted. "Any reason for that?"

"Nothing specific, but I'm sure it has something to do with every boyfriend Naomi, my sister, has ever brought home. She has a thing for musicians. Most of the ones she chooses are supposed pop musicians, but their version is...not something I like. I guess it's made me steer clear of pop music in general."

"That's a shame. You should tell Naomi to get better taste in boyfriends, then you can get back to liking it again. There are some decent songs in the charts at the moment."

"You're a music dork, too?"

"Dork?" Jason laughed, rolling to his back when his sides began to hurt. "Oh, my god. I've not heard that term for years! Dork! I'm going to use that for someone else. Love it." He wiped his eyes with his fingers, then rolled back to Harry, who sported a smile. "Sorry. Yes, you could say I was a music dork, too. They're my jam."

Harry pinched the bridge of his nose. "You're an idiot."

Jason settled. "I keep getting told that." He dropped a kiss on Harry's forehead and spread his hands on his back, rubbing up and down.

Harry's eyes closed. Jason didn't think it would take long for them to fall asleep; therefore, it surprised him when Harry began talking.

"My father and brother died in a fire I caused when I was seven."

Jason could hear the tears Harry withheld in his voice, the thickness in his throat, and he couldn't stand it. He ran his fingers through Harry's hair, trying to soothe him.

"My brother, John, was two, and he'd always suffered from colic. When Dad wasn't at work the following day, he would sleep with John in the downstairs guest bedroom to give Mum a full night's sleep. I couldn't sleep, so I went downstairs to get a glass of milk. My parents trusted me to do that without causing a mess, and I'd done it many times." He sniffed and swallowed. "I tripped on the rug in the kitchen and fell into the cooker. I caught myself before I could spill any of the milk and checked the cooker to make sure it was okay." He closed his eyes. "It looked fine.

I couldn't see anything wrong with it, and I went to bed. Mum woke me and told me we needed to get out. We ran to Naomi's room, and Mum picked her up. We ran down the stairs and out the front door."

Jason could hardly keep himself in check. He wanted to comfort Harry but didn't know if he wanted him to.

"It was only when we stopped across the road and turned to watch the house burning that I realised Dad and John weren't with us. When I asked Mum, she shook her head and cried, holding Naomi and me closer." Harry's tears overflowed. "I kept asking her where they were, but she never answered. It was later that day she told me that the fire had blocked their escape from the guest room, having started in the kitchen, right next to where they were sleeping." He coughed to clear his throat. "I killed them because I fell into the cooker and hadn't understood that the knobs were wrong."

Jason gripped him, whispering nonsense into his ear when Harry broke down again. To have such a burden resting on his shoulders must be such a struggle for him. The longer they lay there, the more Jason frowned while he thought over the story Harry had told. If it had been something to do with the cooker, he would've expected there to be an explosion of some kind if it involved gas. He didn't know the circumstances, and he might be missing some information from Harry, but from what he had been told, it didn't make sense.

Harry fell into a fitful sleep, and Jason held him close and followed him. He woke up several times throughout the night when Harry moved. Jason let him reposition himself, then wrapped him in his arms again.

His alarm woke him the next morning, and Jason groaned, burrowing himself further into the pillow. An elbow in his side had him lifting his head and squinting at the man beside him.

"Turn it off. Please, turn it off," Harry whispered, putting a pillow over his head.

Jason grunted but fumbled for his jeans, bleary-eyed. Pulling out his phone, he silenced the offending object and swung his legs over the edge of the bed. He rubbed his face hard, trying to wake himself, then stood, pulling on his jeans.

"Where you going?"

The words made Jason chuckle. Not quite a proper sentence, but enough to get his point across. He knelt on the bed, pressing a kiss to Harry's neck and shoulder. "I'm going to work. Can I come to see you tonight when I've finished?"

Harry hummed, and Jason took that as agreement, although he'd send a message later to double-check. No taking things for granted when he hadn't included words, and especially when it was six o'clock in the morning.

He dressed as quietly as he could, then slipped out of the room, shutting the door behind him. Checking he had everything he'd arrived with, he slipped into the kitchen and tore off a slip of paper from the fridge, scribbling a note for Harry to see when he woke. He glanced around the place, figuring out where the best place to put it would be, which wouldn't spark any of Harry's anxiety. He put it on the bathroom door with some tack he'd found. Hopefully, it would be an innocuous enough place.

He did a quick check of the flat, making sure Harry hadn't missed any plugs or anything, knowing if Harry found them when he woke, he'd have a bad day. When he passed the desk, his eye caught on some firefighter photos. He lifted one, grinning at Matias's pose. Jason didn't think that had been one of the options given to Paul. Maybe Harry had caught some candid photos of them all. He bet the others would love to keep theirs. He'd have to remember to ask Harry. Putting it back in its place, he froze, seeing his face looking back at him. He moved a few other photos until he was staring at the one he'd thought Harry had taken when Jason had been suggestive with the hose.

The face staring back at him didn't look like him. His eyelids lowered, his face flushed, his mouth a little open, holding onto that hose as if his life depended on it. Was this what he looked like, or was it a trick of the camera?

Exiting the flat, he strode to his car, frowning. The photo had shown him a side of himself he hadn't seen before, and he wasn't sure if it was a good look or not. Those thoughts plagued him on the drive home to shower and change before work.

"What's up with you?" Scott asked several hours later. "You look like someone's pinched your joke book."

"Hardy-har-har. I'm fine." Jason couldn't decide if he was all right or not. He couldn't understand why a photo of him had thrown him for a loop. It wasn't as if he hadn't seen himself in photos before. What was special about this one, and why couldn't he get it out of his head?

"I'm glad he's not on cooking duty today. There's no telling what we'd end up with," Valerie said. She ruffled his hair as she passed by. "It's better when he's in Romeo-mood."

Jason grimaced. "Romeo-mood? Dare I ask?"

Valerie dropped into a chair opposite him and grinned. "It's what I call your 'I'm looking for a hook up' mood."

"And why do you prefer me like that?"

"Because you're adorable." Valerie blew him a kiss.

Adorable? He didn't think he was, but he would be the last person to disabuse her of the notion. "Thanks. I think."

"Really, though. What's wrong?" Valerie leaned her elbows on the table. "Scott's right. You seem down today."

He didn't know what to tell them because he didn't know the answer himself. Contentment had flowed through him when he'd left Harry in bed, but it had stumbled when he'd seen that photo. What was it about the photo that had...unsettled him? He didn't even know if that was the right word. Harry should be his concern, not a photograph, which reminded him of something he needed to do.

He stood, his chair scraping behind him. "I have to speak to Paul." He wandered off without saying more, focused on his destination, clenching and releasing his hands. The events of Harry's past had nothing to do with him, but he needed some help. At least, Jason thought he did.

Knocking on the door, he waited until Paul told him to enter, then sat in the visitor's chair, leaning his elbows on his knees.

"It's unlike you to be worried about saying something. What's happened?"

Jason swallowed. "There are some things I can't tell you because I was told in confidence, but do you know anything about the fire from when Harry was a child?"

Paul cocked his head, staying silent while studying Jason. He squirmed but tensed his muscles to keep him from moving. Whatever Paul had been searching for, he must've found it because he leaned back in his chair.

"I do."

Jason clenched his jaw. "Are you able to tell me what happened?"

Paul pressed his lips together and rubbed his face. "Shouldn't you be asking him?"

"He's told me what happened, but..." Jason didn't want to say anything about Harry blaming himself. Was he worried they'd confirm what Harry himself thought?

"You want to know from someone who isn't close to the situation."

"I want to know from someone I trust to tell me the truth. His story is...heart-breaking."

Paul nodded. "It is. Many people suffer from things they have no control over. It's why we do our job, isn't it? To help those who have no experience."

Jason agreed, but he didn't know what that had to do with Harry's story. "No one can control fire."

"Quite right." Paul tapped his thumb against the top of his desk. "Harry was seven when the fire broke out in his home. His father and brother remained in the house because Harry's mother, Esme, couldn't reach them. The fire covered the only entrance to the guest room. She ran with Harry and Naomi."

"What caused the fire?"

"A faulty wire in a portable heater. From what Esme told the firefighters at the time, they'd been meaning to get it fixed, but they hardly used it. As we know, though, it doesn't matter whether it's used. A faulty wire is a fire waiting to happen."

Jason's heart pounded, taking his breath, and he dropped his head into his hands. It wasn't Harry's fault. Had no one told him how it had started? Would they think to tell a seven-year-old? It certainly had never crossed his mind to let others know. Maybe they should change the rules or something because Harry had been beating himself up for years about something that wasn't his fault. An arm came around his shoulder.

"Are you going to tell me what happened now?"

Jason sniffed. "I think I need his permission first. He's...taken on a lot of responsibility for things that he didn't need to. I need to speak to him, and if he says it's okay, I'll explain."

Paul tightened his arm. "Okay, but know I'm here if you need me. If *he* needs me."

"Thank you."

"And bring him around for dinner one day. Soon."

Jason stood, turning in Paul's arms and taking the offered hug. "I will."

Paul let him go and rounded his desk. "You're good together."

Jason snorted. "I don't know if he'll put up with my personality for long, but thanks."

"You'd be surprised. He's stronger than he thinks he is."

"I know, but it's what he thinks that matters."

Paul nodded. "True. You can try to persuade him otherwise, though." He winked.

"I will do what I can."

Jason left and descended the stairs, thoughts going around in his head. Did no one realise what Harry was dealing with? How come his therapist had mentioned nothing to him? Harry had mentioned finishing his sessions with his therapist, but when was that? Are they likely to have told him the results of the fire or just dealt with whatever Harry told them? Did he tell them anything?

Lots of questions, and only Harry could answer them. Jason was glad to have the next twenty-four hours off because he wanted to speak with Harry without interruptions.

"Jason, did you hear about those car fires?" Dean called from the other end of the equipment room.

"No. Did they catch who was doing it?"

Dean nodded. "It was a bunch of nineteen- and twenty-year-olds. They thought it would be hilarious to steal the cars and send us on wild goose chases around the city. The police don't think they've caught all of them, but the rest aren't telling."

Jason inhaled and shook his head. So close. He'd been close to doing that exact thing himself when he was that age. He still remembered the fight he'd started with the leader of the group he'd hung around with. Jason hadn't wanted to take part, but Mitchell had threatened to point the finger at Jason, and he hadn't wanted to get into trouble. What he hadn't realised was Mitchell had planned on throwing Jason to the wolves, anyway. No matter what had happened that night, they would've found Jason and accused him of the crime. It was a lucky break that Paul had found him first.

The last he'd heard about Mitchell was that he was serving ten years in prison for armed robbery. Jason pinched the bridge of his nose, thinking of what his life could've been like.

"Earth to Jason."

He blinked and refocused on Dean. "Sorry. Got a lot on my mind at the moment."

"I can see that. You need to work off the tension. Come on, duties await."

Jason groaned but followed Dean. Despite Jason being the crew commander, he didn't take it seriously enough to ignore others when they told him jobs needed doing. He wasn't far enough up the chain of command to ignore orders, even when they came from someone technically lower ranked than he was. Jobs needed doing. It didn't matter who did them, provided they got done.

Once his shift ended, he'd return to Harry, and they'd have the talk Harry needed to hear. Hopefully, then he'd begin to heal.

Chapter 14

Harry

When Harry had woken to an empty bed, he believed he'd dreamt the whole thing, but the note on his bathroom door proved him wrong.

I'm sorry I couldn't stay to wake you up. I would like to see you again tonight if I can. I know I asked earlier, but I wasn't sure if you were coherent enough to understand my question. Lol. Message me and let me know if I can visit and what time is best for you. I'll even bring takeaway (if you tell me what you like). Have a good day. J.

Harry smiled and continued into the bathroom, switching on the shower and standing under the spray when it was warm enough. While the heat of the water warmed his body, he closed his eyes and thought about what had happened the previous evening. He hadn't planned on blurting out his problems, but when Jason had admitted to being hurt by Harry's words, he'd fallen down his rabbit hole and pressed the present away in favour of the past. It hadn't been as bad as usual. Maybe having Jason there and telling the story aloud helped him keep one foot in the present. He didn't know, but he had nothing to hide from Jason now. Not only had he word-vomited his secret, but Jason had also witnessed his anxiety attacks. If he still wanted to visit, who was Harry to scare him away?

He ate some toast, made sure his equipment was ready to go and that he had the photos and memory sticks he needed for the day's sessions. Pictures from the firefighter shoot laid across his desk, and he grinned at the candid shots he'd caught when the guys were messing around. He planned to send those to the fire station so the crews could have them if they wanted them. He picked up the photo of Jason and stared. The slight curve to Jason's mouth belied his serious expression, and anyone who looked at it would know he was a mischievous little shit. He might give the photo to Jason later.

Pulling out his phone, he shoved the last bite of toast into his mouth and sent a message to the man.

HARRY: *I'll be home by five. You're welcome to visit after that. I love any takeaway except Thai. For some reason, it doesn't agree with me.*

He hesitated over the end of the message and whether to add anything further but left it as it was. There was an extensive discussion needed that night because Harry was still undecided about having a relationship with a firefighter. His anxieties might get the better of him, and he didn't want to put that burden on Jason.

Harry gathered up his things. By the time he arrived at the studio, his smile was wide, and he felt lighter than he had in months. The studio was struggling for light because of the cloudy weather despite all the windows in the place, but Harry knew the lights would make up for the abysmal UK weather.

His first session that morning was with his best friend. Clemency had requested some photos that weren't taken by the photographer her modelling agency had provided, and although the agency had agreed she could source new ones, they had told her they would not pay for the sessions, only the photos they wanted. Harry had told Clemency the session would be free, but she wouldn't hear of it and would only book a session if he'd taken payment upfront. Interfering friend that she was.

Clemency was bringing her own clothes. All Harry needed to do was make her look like the goddess she was, which shouldn't be hard.

The bell went, and his heart jumped before settling again. The same thing happened each time.

"Hello-oooo! Anybody here?"

Clemency's voice came through loud and clear, even before she entered the studio. "Hey, you! How are you?"

"I'm doing good. I bet you're still buzzing from Paris, aren't you?"

Clemency closed her eyes and pressed a hand to her chest. "Of course!" Harry hooted his laughter. "There were shops and cafes and shops. Oh, it was wonderful. If I could afford to move to Paris, I would."

"And London?" Harry asked, plugging in the lights.

"Meh. Same old, same old. There is talk of another visit to Paris and maybe even Venice." She clapped her hands together and pressed them to her mouth. "I'm excited."

"And that's why you wanted these photos."

"Yes! The photos the agency has of me are fine, but I don't think they capture *me*. The essence of who I am."

Harry raised his eyebrows. "And you think I can?"

"I know you can because you've done it before without even trying, silly boy."

"Clemency, I'm five years older than you. Stop trying to pretend I'm younger."

She huffed. "It's that youthful skin of yours. I'm envious."

Harry waved her towards the changing room. "Go, change. Leave me in peace."

She tossed her hair, worthy of Miss Piggy, and slipped into the changing area, laughter floating back.

Harry threw a hard-boiled cherry sweet into his mouth and started up the computer. His phone rang.

"Hey! How are you?" he asked.

"I'm all right, thanks. Been busy," Al replied.

"That's good." Harry hadn't spoken to Al for a while. Joey's words floated through his head, but he brushed them aside. If Al wanted Harry, he would've said something.

"Can I come over tonight?"

Harry stopped the automatic agreement before he spoke. Usually, he wouldn't decline to have friends over. "I can't tonight."

Al went quiet, and Harry considered changing his plans. He didn't want things to get strained between them, but he wanted to see Jason, too.

"Okay." A bell rang. "I have to go. My next client is here."

"Ring me when you have a break. We'll sort a night out."

"Yeah," Al sighed. "Bye."

The phone disconnected before Harry could reply, and he stared at it. There was no way Al wanted a relationship with him. Nothing pointed to that conclusion, but he couldn't wash them away because he knew how good Joey was at his job. He was a detective, after all.

"Ta-da!"

He jumped and swung around, his phone falling to the floor. "Shit! You startled me."

Concern clouded Clemency's features. "Are you okay? I thought you'd heard me."

He picked up his phone, checking for damage. "I spoke to Al, but he didn't seem in a good mood."

"He hasn't been in a good mood for a few weeks now. No idea what's wrong with him, and he's certainly not telling." Clemency picked a piece of lint off her top.

"Joey thinks he's in love with me."

Clemency tilted her head. "Yeah, I can see how he would think that. I don't know. Maybe."

Harry exhaled. "If he is, it might be a problem."

"He'll have to get over it. Just because you've been bumping hips doesn't mean you're his."

He heckled her over the choice of words, then sobered. "I don't want to upset him."

"I don't think you'll have a choice. If he wants you for himself, he's got a shock coming." He frowned at her. She jutted her hip. "You're in love with someone else."

"What! No! What? No, I'm not. Who?"

Clemency tittered, the tinkling sound echoing in the large studio space. "What's that phrase? 'You protest too much' or something."

Harry's heart raced at the implications of Clemency's words. He wouldn't say he was in love with Jason, but there was something about him. As the man's words from the previous evening stated, "*I don't know what it is about you, but you keep me coming back for more.*"

"Let's get on with these photos," he said.

"Nothing like changing the subject, but I'll allow it." She winked and sashayed her way to the stage.

They spent an hour taking photos and checking how they turned out before their time ended. There were several photos Clemency said the agency would like, and he marked them as the ones to work on first. Any others he could finish if he had time left.

"Right, Harry. I'm heading off. Thank you for this." Clemency bustled over to him and drew him into a hug.

"You're welcome. I'm glad I could help. I'll get the touch-ups done, then email them across to you the moment they're ready."

She bussed a kiss on his cheek and waved. "You're a star. Thank you, sweetheart."

Harry had an hour before his next appointment, so he turned everything off except his computer and sat down to touch-up the photos from the previous day. He tried to get them done the day he took the photos but depending on how many he took, depended on how long it took him. If he had a busy day, he also struggled to fit it in. Yesterday hadn't been bad, but he'd been distracted and hadn't done what he should have. Now, things were better between him and Jason—although not settled by any stretch—he could concentrate easier.

By the time Zuri entered the studio, holding out a mug of hot chocolate from the bakery across the road, he'd managed to finish one set of photos and had only Clemency's to go through. He knew he wouldn't get those done that night, especially if Jason turned up, but he would make it a priority the following day.

There were six appointments booked in for that day, each one half an hour long with half an hour in between to give him time to go through the photos with the parents to let them choose the ones they wanted him to work on. Some photographers worked differently, checking the photos before giving the parents a choice, but that seemed backwards to Harry. Why work on photos they might not pick? It seemed like a waste of time to him. This worked best for him, and that was all that mattered.

Zuri ran out for lunch at around midday, leaving Harry pulling his hair out with a parent who couldn't decide. His next appointment was in ten minutes, and he hadn't had the chance to do any touch-ups to these.

"I don't know. They're good, but I can only afford one."

"Okay, let me print out some thumbnail pictures, and you can take them home and decide, then call me later today to choose. I won't be able to work on them until you decide."

He clicked around his screen and held out a piece of paper to her. He only did this in extenuating circumstances because someone had once cancelled all photos with him and printed some from the ones he'd printed for them to decide from. He'd learnt from his mistakes for sure. Now, the pictures were small enough that they couldn't be blown up and reprinted without severe pixellation, but big enough they could see the detail they needed to.

"Thank you. I'll call you later today. I'm sorry for being a pain."

"Don't worry about it. I know the decision is difficult. Take your time."

He ushered the woman and her child out of the studio in time for the next appointment to arrive. He exhaled and rolled his head on his neck before smiling at the newcomers.

"Good afternoon. I hear we have a superhero in the studio." He grinned at the four-year-old boy.

Even though he didn't have time for his lunch when he should've had it, he took a few minutes after the superhero to wolf down his sandwich. When his last photo shoot finished, he packed up, checked he'd switched everything off and drove home. He arrived at twenty past five and deposited his equipment in its space next to his desk. The memory sticks he placed next to his computer to persuade him to do some work the following morning. It depended on how long Jason was hanging around.

Hungry, he grabbed a banana from his fruit bowl and ate it while he made a cup of tea. He wasn't expecting Jason for another hour because he didn't finish his shift until six o'clock and had to pick up the takeaway. Harry jumped into the shower to waste some time, but when it took only fifteen minutes, he rolled his eyes and sat at his desk, trying to get some work done before Jason arrived.

The doorbell jerked him from his screen, and he glanced at the clock. Six-thirty on the dot. How did he manage that?

Harry saved his work and opened the front door. "Hello."

Jason smirked from his lean against the doorframe. "Good evening. I have something you might enjoy."

Harry raised his eyebrows. "I'm sure you do, but do you have food?"

Jason brought a bag from behind his back and grinned. "Of course. What else did you think I was talking about? Get your mind out of the gutter, Mr Jones." Jason lifted his nose and walked past Harry to the kitchen.

Harry shook his head, his mouth twitching. "My mind only goes that way because you start it."

"I have no idea what you're talking about. I'm innocent."

"Yeah, innocent until proven guilty, which would happen quicker than a murderer standing over a dead body holding the murder weapon."

Jason opened his mouth and inhaled, eyes widening. "How dare you!" He ruined it by bursting out laughing. "You're right."

Harry leaned his hip next to where Jason emptied the containers as if he lived there. "What did we end up with?"

"Indian. I passed one on the way here, but I wasn't sure which you'd prefer, so I got extras that can be reheated another day unless you're super hungry." Jason eyed him. "You look famished if I do say so myself."

Harry withheld his grin. "Really? I don't understand why. I've had plenty to eat today."

Jason nudged Harry until his back was against the counter, then manoeuvred between his legs. "Are you sure? Maybe it's something only I can help with." His hands caressed Harry's hips and waist.

"Hmm, maybe." Harry slid his arms around Jason's neck, threading his fingers through the hair at his nape. "Do you have the medicine I need to get better?"

"I believe I do."

Jason lowered his head and fastened their lips together. Harry closed his eyes when Jason's tongue started a leisurely exploration of his mouth. He paid no attention to how long they kissed, only the feel of Jason beneath his hands and mouth. The scent of him filling his nose—something fresh, yet a hint of smoke lingering. That thought had Harry pulling away.

"Everything okay? You're trembling." Jason rubbed his hands up and down Harry's arms.

"Yeah." He tried for a smile. "I can smell the smoke. It's fine."

Jason backed up. "Sorry. Can I borrow your shower?"

Harry frowned. "Haven't you already showered?"

"Yes, but I can try to get rid of the scent. I can't always manage it, but I can try."

Harry's shoulders lowered at his kindness. "You are welcome to shower if you want to, but you don't have to. I can manage. I wasn't expecting it, that was all. I'll be fine now."

A crease developed in the centre of Jason's eyebrows. "Are you sure? I don't want to make you feel uncomfortable."

"Nah, I'm good. Let's eat." He turned to the counter and grabbed two plates from the cupboard. "What did you get?" Jason explained the choices, and Harry chortled. "A couple to choose from then?" he said when the list grew to eight dishes.

Jason's cheeks darkened. "I didn't want to get something you didn't like."

Harry kissed his cheek. "I'm messing with you. Thank you. It will be delicious, I'm certain."

They ate and spoke about Harry's day. Jason appeared to avoid talking about his work, even when Harry asked about it. When they finished their food and had settled on the sofa with a drink, Harry pointed it out.

Jason's face contorted. "I don't want to make you uncomfortable by talking about the calls I've had to attend. I wasn't sure if it was better you didn't know or better you did." He cleared his throat. "There is something I want to talk to you about, though."

"What's that?"

"I know you're possibly going to be mad at me, but I spoke to Paul about the fire."

Harry didn't need to know which fire because it was obvious. Several feelings went through him—sadness that he'd found out the little details Harry had left out, relieved that it was all out in the open, and anger that Jason didn't believe his version of events. He drank some more of his tea, not saying anything until he'd got a handle on his emotions.

"And?" he said finally.

"It wasn't your fault."

Harry rolled his eyes and shook his head. "That's the only thing you have to say about what you've found out?"

"I haven't read the report or anything. I asked Paul for the basics because what you'd said didn't sound right."

"You thought I was lying?" Harry stood, rounding the sofa until he could pace behind it.

"No! Never. I meant that the circumstances of the fire didn't sound right. If the cooker had caused the fire, there would've been an explosion of some sort because of the gas, but there wasn't. It wasn't the cooker that set the fire. It was faulty wiring in a heater."

Harry couldn't hear him. His breathing increased, his hands shook, and his head spun. He rested his hands on the back of the sofa and was partially aware of Jason gripping hold of him. He came back to himself, staring at the ceiling with something soft at his back. His lips were dry, and his head felt sluggish. Rolling his head to the side, he saw Jason sitting on the floor next to the sofa, holding out a glass with a straw. Harry frowned. He didn't even think he owned a straw.

"Take a sip. Nice and slow."

Harry did what he was told, enjoying the cool liquid in his mouth before letting it wet his throat. "What happened?"

"I think you had a panic attack," Jason said. "I'm sorry. I didn't mean—"

Harry laid a hand on Jason's arm. "It's okay. It happens." His eyelids fought to close, sleep dragging at him. "Stay."

"Are you sure?"

"Hmm."

Chapter 15

Jason

Yet again, Jason found himself dealing with Harry's anxiety attack, and yet again, he was the cause. He had no issue helping Harry at all, but he needed to stop being the issue. Dillon was obviously right about him. He clenched his jaw against the threat of tears, covered Harry with a blanket he'd retrieved from the bedroom and relaxed against the beanbag by his side, watching the tension slipping from Harry's face in his sleep.

Harry's phone jerked Jason from his staring, and he scrambled to stop it. The name on the screen had him pausing. *Joey Kirkland.* Jason knew him. He was a detective Jason had spoken with on several fire investigations. Was he friends with Harry? The phone stopped, then started again.

"Hello?" he said, creeping to the doorway, hoping he didn't disturb Harry.

"Who is this?" The voice was hard and sharp.

"It's Jason Townsend. Sorry, I saw your name and thought it best I answer in case you got worried."

"Where's Harry? What happened?"

"Harry's here. He's fine. He had a panic attack again, and he's now sleeping it off."

Joey exhaled loud enough for it to be heard over the line. "What happened?" he repeated.

"We were talking about the fire from when he was younger. I gave him some new information, and he struggled with it."

"New information?"

Jason worked his jaw. "Apparently, Harry believes it was his fault his father and brother died because he'd knocked the cooker when he'd been getting a drink that night. No one told him that the fire started from a faulty wire." He didn't mean to sound accusative, but why had no one told him?

"He didn't know?" Joey's voice rose.

Jason felt mollified that Joey hadn't kept the knowledge from him. "No. He still believes it was his fault. When I explained, he had a panic attack." He wandered into the kitchen to make a cup of coffee; he needed to stay awake for several more hours, anyway.

"Harry doesn't do well when news comes to him out of the blue. When there have been incidents I've been told about, I try to contact him first to let him know what happened, and he can stay away from the news reports."

Jason closed his eyes and dropped his head back. "And I gave him a shock of news. Fuck!"

"No. It's better coming from someone than from seeing it in the news. Not that this information would be, but you get my meaning. Maybe you could have slowed your delivery of it, but because he's close to this, he would've still reacted the same."

They were silent, Jason moving around to make his drink until he asked, "Did you need Harry for something?"

"I was checking up on him because I'd not heard from him today. Clemency said he'd been a little out of sorts when she'd seen him this morning."

"Clemency?"

"One of Harry's friends. There's me, Clemency and Al who hang out as often as we can get together."

"I wondered how you knew each other." Jason sipped his coffee.

"We all went to school together."

"Ah, okay."

"He's mentioned you a couple of times," Joey said.

Jason raised his eyebrows. "He has? I don't know if that's a good thing." He snorted.

"It's good because it wasn't in a bad context. From what I could gather, he found you confusing. Something he needed to figure out." He paused. "Looks like he figured it out."

Jason could hear the smirk in his voice. "Yeah, looks like."

Joey cleared his throat. "Don't hurt him, okay. I know there will be bumps along the way but, unless you're certain this is what you want, don't go down this road. He's had enough shit happen to him."

Jason wanted to bristle and argue about Joey's words, but he stopped and thought about what he'd say if someone hurt one of his friends. It would be along the same lines. "I want this. I don't want to hurt him, and I hope I don't, but I can't make promises. No one can. All I can say is I will try to do everything I can to make him happy."

"That'll do, firefighter."

Jason chuckled. "I'll tell him you called and get him to give you a ring in the morning."

"Thanks. Get some rest."

Jason hung up the phone and grabbed his coffee, stopping to lean against the doorframe and watch Harry sleep while he finished his cup. Though he told Joey he was all in, he second-guessed his decision. Not because he didn't want Harry, he did. Jason could promise to be careful, but there were many risks involved in his job. Was that something Harry could put up with? Especially with how safety-conscious he was.

Jason chewed on his lip and returned to the kitchen. He made himself another coffee, then settled back onto the beanbag with his phone. Unwilling to disturb Harry's much-needed rest, he chose a movie on his phone and put the subtitles on.

He woke when he felt a hand running over his head, the darkness only permeated by the weak streetlight shining through the centre of the curtain Jason had left open for this exact reason. Rolling his head to the side, he winced when his neck protested, but he ignored it and glanced at Harry, who was smiling at him.

"Hey. How are you feeling?"

"Good, thanks."

Harry's voice was raspy, and Jason leaned forward for the cup of water he'd refreshed before he'd settled in to sleep. Handing it to Harry, the man drank it all.

"Thanks."

"You're welcome." Jason cupped his cheek. "How are you really?"

Harry's mouth curled at the corners. "I'm okay. I'm sorry for checking out on you last night."

"You don't need to be sorry. I should've warned you before telling you."

Harry blew out a breath. "It's hard for me to believe. I'm not saying I don't believe you," he rushed to add, "but it's hard to forget what I've spent so long thinking about."

Jason slid his hands down to grasp Harry's. "I can understand that. I'm sorry about how I told you. I hadn't thought about the consequences and ploughed ahead as I normally do. I suppose I could blame my job because I have to make split-second decisions, but I'm also impulsive and grab for what I want. And I wanted you to stop blaming yourself, without thinking about how to do that safely."

Harry leaned forward and kissed him. A brief peck of his lips, but Jason felt it down to his bones. They rested their foreheads together, and Jason closed his eyes, enjoying the moment.

"We both have things to deal with," Harry said. "I think…"

When Harry didn't finish, Jason peered up at him. "What?"

Harry inhaled. "I want us, Jason, but I'm scared. I'm terrified you'll die in a fire. I'm afraid I'll be left alone again.

I'm scared of dying in a fire myself. I'm worried about many things, but for the first time, I want to stop letting it control me. I want to attend therapy sessions again, and I think you should do the same."

Harry's eyes dropped when he said the final part, and Jason realised Harry was worried he wouldn't want to do it. Funny thing, though, the moment Harry started talking, Jason had thought it sounded like something he should do. He wasn't sure how it would help, but if it would, it was enough reason for him.

"I want us, too. Let's do it."

Harry raised his head, almost clocking Jason on the chin. "Are you sure?"

"Yes. It can't make us any worse than we are, can it?"

Harry winced. "I guess not, although I'm going to take that as a compliment."

Jason sniggered. "Sorry, you know how my brain works."

Harry rubbed his thumb against Jason's cheek. "I'm glad you can see the light side of things."

Jason kissed him, a press of lips together, then withdrew. "Bed?"

"Definitely. My back's aching."

"You're not the only one. Falling asleep on a beanbag is less comfortable than people say it is."

"Bet your ass is numb," Harry said, sitting upright with another wince.

Jason grinned. "Nah, it'll be fine." He stood and groaned. "Fuck, maybe not. Although it's more my hips than my ass."

"Come on. Let's get some more sleep, then at least one of us will be functional in the morning."

Jason slid his arm around Harry's shoulders. "I can have a lie-in. I'm on nights tomorrow."

Harry groaned. "I can't. I have an appointment at ten and have some photos to edit before that. I'll leave you to sleep, though. You can let yourself out when you wake up."

"I can head home if it will make things easier for you?"

Harry silenced Jason's words with a kiss. "No. You're staying."

"Your wish is my command."

They cuddled in bed, with Jason as the little spoon, and he thought about what they'd discussed. He wasn't sure therapy would help him, but at the same time, he wanted to help Harry. If that was the way to do it, then he'd do it without fail.

Jason arrived at the station with a spring in his step. He felt lighter than he had in days, maybe even weeks. The idea that he felt happier in a relationship—something he'd never thought was possible because of his troublemaking tendencies—made him shake his head in disbelief.

"What's up with you?"

Jason pivoted around, coming face to face with Scott's shocked face. "Nothing, why?"

"You're like an eager recruit. What did you do?"

Jason snorted and held up his hand. "I've done nothing." He swung around and headed for the changing area, greeting those he passed. It was true. He hadn't done anything yet. He hadn't been sure if he wanted to tell the crew about his and Harry's plan but then realised it would be better if he did. If for whatever reason, something happened because of a session he'd attended, they needed to know. But he'd tell them in his own way. He grinned.

"There! Look! That's what I'm talking about! You only have that look on your face when you've done something or are about to do something." Scott pointed a finger at him, a worried expression on his face. "Dean! Valerie! Niall! Quick!"

Jason burst out laughing, holding onto the locker for support. "You're an asshole, you know that, right?" he said between breaths.

"Takes one to know one."

"I never said I wasn't."

The door flew open, and three people came rushing through.

"What's wrong?" Dean asked, panting.

"He's chirpy." Scott pointed a finger at him, waving it up and down.

Dean stared at Scott as if he was an alien. "I ran from the other side of the fucking car park because I thought there was a problem. He's always happy!"

"This is different. He's up to something."

Jason sat on a nearby chair, holding his sides. "God, I needed that. Thanks, Scott. I do have news, but let's wait until we start the shift, and I'll explain it all."

Valerie narrowed her eyes at him. "You better not be dying because I'll kick your ass."

"I'm not dying."

"Good."

Jason got ready for the shift, a smile permanently on his face. He wouldn't mention Harry's agreement to have therapy because he'd not asked if he could share that or talk to Paul about the fire situation. It would have to wait for another day, but he could talk about his plans.

When they waited in their ranks while Ian went through the motions of the start of the shift, Jason prepared himself for the potential outcome of his announcement.

"Does anyone have anything to add?" Ian asked, checking behind him to see Paul shake his head.

Jason raised his hand. "Yes, please."

Ian raised his eyebrows but nodded for him to go ahead. "I wanted to let you know I will be starting therapy sessions soon. I don't know if it will have any bearing on my work, though it shouldn't, I wanted you to be aware." He aimed the last words in Paul's direction.

Paul gave a smile and a nod but said nothing. Ian tilted his head. "Is this something you will share with us, or a general heads up?"

Jason hadn't thought about that. "Um, I don't know, to be honest. I haven't thought that far ahead. We...I'm looking into therapists. I'll let you know once sessions start, but I don't know if it's something I'll be able to talk to you lot about or not."

"Let's play it by ear then," Paul said.

No one said anything else, and they finished the meeting and dispersed to their jobs. Jason felt another weight lift from his shoulders. Therapy might be a good thing, after all.

Dean caught up to him. "Jason, if you—"

The alarm blared through the station, and Jason raced for the engine. "House fire. Glenvale Drive. No other information."

He jumped into his boots and climbed into the cab, Scott gunning the engine the instant the doors were closed. Jason's heart raced. The adrenaline rush was always ready in the wings for when they attended scenes. More information came through as they got closer. No occupants in the house, thankfully. It made their job a little easier. There was a crowd of people when they arrived, and Scott set about sending them further back. They worked the scene as they usually would until a woman's screech rent the air.

Jason hurried over. "What's the problem?" Though his heart already knew.

"My mother is in there! She's eighty-two! Did she get out?"

Jason's breath caught. He hadn't sent anyone in to check the property because he'd been told it was empty. "I don't know."

He raced back to the scene. "Niall! Valerie!" He waited until they were near. "Suit up. There might be someone inside."

Valerie's eyes widened, and she grabbed the equipment they donned to go inside ablaze. Niall followed suit, and Jason checked them over before sending them in. His head hoped they'd find her in time but observing the orange flames reaching for the sky, his heart knew if she was in there, she was gone.

He waited with bated breath while information continued to come through the radio until Valerie's voice said, "We have her."

Jason closed his eyes and dropped his head, able to tell from her voice that the outcome wasn't good. He swallowed hard and continued with his job, staring at the woman they carried from the house and placed on a stretcher. The paramedics enclosed her inside the ambulance, but her daughter's screams blistered the air. This was the worst part of their job. Losing people in a fire was never a good thing, but the feeling of being responsible never went away.

Jason stepped back as if someone had physically struck him when the thought registered. *The feeling of being responsible never went away.* He understood what Harry had been feeling all this time because every victim Jason had ever recovered from a fire felt like Jason's fault.

Therapy was looking better every minute.

After they had secured the scene, they rode back to the station in silence. Jason pulled out his phone and stared at it for several long moments before unlocking it.

JASON: *I'm fine. See you soon x*
Then he dialled and lifted it to his ear.

"Joey Kirkland."

"He's going to need you," he said without preamble. "We've pulled a body from a fire. I'm sure they'll be reporting it soon if they haven't already."

"Understood. Are you okay?"

"Physically, yes."

"Take it easy. I'll keep you updated with Harry."

"Thanks."

He stared out of the window, watching the world go by. So many people having no idea what had happened that night.

"It wasn't your fault," Valerie said.

"No, but it doesn't stop the pain of knowing her life could've been saved if I'd told you to check the building."

"It's not something we usually do, Jason. You weren't to know."

"Maybe it needs to become something we do regardless of if someone said the place is empty. Think how many more we might save."

No one said anything else, and when they pulled into the station, Paul waited for them, even though he should've been at home already.

"If anyone would like to talk through what happened, I'll be here for a few more hours, and a counsellor is on her way. I know this is something that happens regularly. I want you to talk through it. We've made this station an amazing place to work, and I don't want your mental health to be affected any more than it needs to." Paul stepped to Jason, clasping his shoulder. "You made the right call. You weren't to know. You followed procedure."

"Maybe that procedure needs to change?"

Paul nodded. "Maybe you're right. Get yourself sorted. We'll talk."

Jason nodded, pulling his phone from his pocket.

HARRY: *Thank you. Stay safe x*

Chapter 16

Harry

He knew something bad had happened because Joey came to see him instead of calling. When he opened the door, his first thought was that something had happened to his mother by the sadness on Joey's face.

"Breathe, Harry. Everyone is fine."

It took him a minute to realise he was sitting on his sofa with his head between his knees. He didn't remember getting there.

"Are you feeling better?" Joey asked.

"A bit. At least until you tell me why you're here. Not that I'm not pleased to see you." He tried for a smile.

"Jason asked me to let you know of an incident they called them to today. There was a fire, and an elderly lady died."

"Jason's okay, right?"

"Yes, he's fine. Upset but physically fine."

Harry thought about how Jason would likely react to losing someone on his watch, so to speak. Despite Jason's joker facade, he felt things intensely.

"I need to call him." He scrambled to stand, patting his hands over his body to locate his phone.

"Calm down, Harry. Let's get you a drink first."

Joey disappeared into the kitchen while Harry found his phone on his desk where he'd left it. He saw a message from Jason saying he was fine, and he replied. He wanted to call, but if Jason was struggling, the last thing he needed was Harry fawning over him to the extent Harry wanted to. He sank back onto the sofa and rested his head against the back, closing his eyes.

"Here. I've made you some tea. I thought coffee might make you feel worse."

"Thanks." Harry sat forward, accepting the cup. "Jason messaged to say he was fine. I replied to the message, but I won't call him. I don't think it will help. Not while he's working."

"I agree. I'm sure he'll see you tomorrow."

"I have a late start tomorrow. I might wait at the station when his shift finishes."

He could tell Joey wasn't sure if it was the best idea, but he said nothing about it.

"Can you tell me what happened?"

Joey crossed his ankle over his knee and ran a hand over his head. "They were told no one was in the house and didn't send anyone in. The neighbours hadn't realised the owner's mother had moved in the day before. As far as they knew, the house was empty because the owner was at work."

"That's terrible." Harry knew what the person would be feeling. It was something Harry dealt with even twenty-eight years later. Jason would feel the loss as if they were family; he was that invested in his job. One thing Harry struggled with was that he knew Jason would put himself in the path of danger to save someone else. What Harry needed to decide was could he live each day knowing Jason might not return?

His hands shook, and Joey removed the cup.

"I don't know if I can do this, Joey! One day he might be there, and the next, he might not."

Joey pulled him into his arms, surrounding him with the scent that was uniquely Joey. Harry knew about Joey's lifestyle and had always wondered what it would be like to be cared for by a Dom, but he realised it was what Joey always did. He cared about his friends and family with everything in him, in the same way he would with a sub.

The tangent his thoughts went off on helped calm him.

"I need you to think about something, but I need you to try not to panic about it. I'm trying to give you perspective, but I don't want to make things worse."

Harry pulled back and tucked his legs into his chest, then nodded, bracing himself for another flush of anxiety.

Joey lifted his leg onto the sofa and faced him. "What you described—not knowing if he would be there one day—that's what we all deal with. Yes, more because of his job, but my job is similar. It scares every person in this world that their loved one will leave them one day. I am. The thought that you or Clemency or Kade would wave goodbye one day and I'll never see you again scares the shit out of me. But I would prefer to have you in my life; otherwise, I would've missed out on a lot of joy in my life."

Harry could see the emotion behind Joey's eyes and knew he was telling the truth. He didn't know if he could be as strong as Joey.

"One thing I don't think you realise is that you're already living like that."

Harry frowned. No, he wasn't. He wasn't in a relationship with anyone... His eyes widened.

Joey nodded. "You have people around who you care about, Jason included. There's no changing that. Instead, you need to learn to deal with the what if part of life."

Harry's heart raced, but he nodded. "We've already decided to speak to a therapist. We both have issues that need dealing with. This is one more thing to add to the list of discussion topics."

Joey patted his hand. "I'm glad. You deserve to live as peaceful a life as you can." He reached to drain his cold coffee if his expression was anything to go by. "How about a film?"

"Don't you have somewhere to be?"

"I'm exactly where I need to be."

Harry sniffed to withhold his tears, turning to face the TV while Joey chose what to watch. He lost himself in the film, letting his thoughts go.

Joey left when the film ended after checking Harry didn't want him to stay overnight.

"I'll be fine. I'll sleep like the dead after this, anyway."

They both knew he was lying, but Joey didn't call him on it. Once he was alone, he stared around his hallway as if it was a strange place. He felt jumpy and out of sorts, which his therapist would tell him was to be expected, considering what had happened. He wanted to contact Jason but didn't want to mess up his shift. The man needed his head in the game if he was to stay safe.

Harry chose a shower to distract himself. The warm water helped his muscles unclench, although it wouldn't be for long. Every time he found his thoughts turning in that direction, he redirected his mind to something more pleasant, like the evening he'd spent in Jason's arms. That had been the best night's sleep he'd experienced in years.

With his body sufficiently prune-like, he dried off, dressed and made himself another cup of tea. The news was off-limits, but he could watch another film. It was the best he could do. He got up several times to refill his tea but finished several films during the early hours of the morning.

At seven the following morning, he contemplated going to the station like he'd told Joey he would, but he wasn't sure if it was the best choice for Jason. Maybe he needed a breather. He might prefer to be alone to deal with it. Harry didn't know, so he messaged him instead, then waited for Jason's reply.

HARRY: *I'd like to see you, but I don't know if you need to be alone. If you want some company, let me know.*

When he didn't receive a reply even after Jason's shift finished, Harry tried not to feel upset about it. He contemplated trying to sleep but knew he wouldn't be able to. After making some toast and another tea, he sat at his desk and stared at the photos of the firefighters. He'd grown close to some of them during his time doing the shoot, and he'd enjoyed getting to know them, which he'd not done for a long time. The last time he'd "made new friends" was when he'd hired Zuri, and that had been difficult for him, although easier because it was work-related. They didn't socialise outside of work. Before that was Joey, Al and Clemency, and he knew them because they had gone to school together. He wasn't built to make new friends. But the firefighters had somehow wormed their way into his life without him even realising it, especially Paul and Jason.

The longer he looked at the photos, the more he realised he wanted to give them to the firefighters as a gift. He doubted it was often they got photos of them in firefighter gear, even half-naked. Maybe he could frame them.

A knock sounded, and his heart leapt. Scrambling to the door, he flung it open and almost cried when a dishevelled and tired-looking Jason stepped inside.

"Are you okay?" he asked, closing the door.

Jason stared at him and shook his head. "Not particularly."

"Come on. Shower and bed."

"I had a shower before I left."

Harry cupped his jaw. "I know, but I want to take care of you."

Jason didn't reply. Harry gripped his hands and tugged him towards the bathroom. He wasn't uncomfortable about the scent of smoke because he was becoming used to the smell, but he couldn't think of a better way to help Jason relax. Although he had some massage oil in the bathroom. He could give him a back massage to help him sleep.

Switching the shower on, he undressed Jason with careful movements, not wanting to startle him when he seemed focused on something far from where they were. Harry didn't mind, but he wanted Jason to be here and now and not somewhere in his nightmares. When they were both naked, he pulled Jason under the spray and washed him in slow strokes of his hands. He avoided his groin, to begin with. A release would benefit Jason because he needed to be reminded of the present before he could grieve for what had happened.

The thought had him frowning, but he focused on his actions. He remembered several times when he'd released and began crying, almost as if the cover had been removed from the camera and he could see the light again. It helped him, though he hadn't realised it at the time. Hopefully, it would help Jason.

After thoroughly washing his lover's hair, back and front, Harry dropped to his knees. He used his hand and soap to stroke the man's length repeatedly, watching it lengthen and thicken. Jason whimpered while he stroked, and Harry glanced up, witnessing the pain cross Jason's face, though he knew it had nothing to do with being physically hurt. This was all emotional. Harry continued with his hand, but his tongue joined in, flicking across the slit and around the head. He rested the head of the dick in his mouth, not encasing the shaft entirely, and fluttered his tongue over the nerves at the same time that he stroked.

Jason braced his hands on the tiles and Harry's head, a heavy presence but not clinging. Harry kept up his ministrations, and within seconds, Jason released into his mouth with muted groans. When the contractions eased, Harry pulled off and washed Jason's groin, careful of the newfound sensitivity. Harry stood and met Jason's gaze.

"I..." Jason didn't finish. Instead, tears overflowed down his cheeks.

Harry cupped his jaw and kissed his lips. "Bedtime."

He helped him dry off, Jason crying the entire time. Harry tugged him into the bedroom and tucked him under the covers, sliding beside him. He pulled him into his arms and held him. The tears continued but escalated in severity until Jason sobbed into his chest.

Harry held him until he fell into a fitful sleep.

The ringing of a phone woke Harry, and for a second, he wondered where he was, which was stupid when he realised he was at home. The thing that threw him was the warm body beside him; he had yet to become accustomed to that sensation.

The phone rang again, and he swung his legs over the bed and stumbled to the living room for it. He'd left it on his desk if he remembered correctly. He grabbed the phone and answered without checking the screen.

"Hello?"

"Oh, thank god! Where are you?"

"Zuri?" He glanced at the screen and confirmed her voice. "What's the matter?"

"It's ten-thirty, and you're not here, Harry! I thought something had happened to you!"

He could hear the noise of cars in the background. "Ten-thirty?"

"Yes." She paused. "Are you okay?"

"Not really, no. Um, okay. When's our first appointment again?"

"Eleven."

He wrinkled his nose. "I'm not going to make it. There was an incident last night, a fire. I'm with Jason."

"Oh, the woman who died. Okay, don't worry. I'll wait here until the clients get here, then I'll explain we need to reschedule. You only have two shoots today. Can you access the schedule and call the other person to rearrange it? Or you could send me the details, and I'll do it for you."

"If you wouldn't mind, Zuri. Sorry. Things are a bit..."

"I know. Don't worry. It'll do you good to take a day off, anyway."

Harry snorted in agreement. "I'll send the details over in a few minutes."

"Okay. Take care of him and yourself."

"I'll try."

"You better, or I'll be round there kicking your ass."

He would've laughed at the idea of the tiny woman doing that, but she was a black belt in karate, and he knew she could do it. "Speak to you later."

After the call ended, he checked his phone for messages, finding several he would need to respond to. First, he sat down at his computer to check the schedule, then took deep breaths when he found the computer still turned on from earlier that morning. He'd never turned it off when Jason had arrived. His heart raced, and he placed his hands at the back of his neck and rested his elbows on the desk, breathing into the space between. Counting his breaths worked to bring down his panic. He wiped the sweat from his forehead and sat back. Nothing had happened. Everything was fine; that was what he needed to remind himself.

Opening the scheduling app he used, he texted the details for both appointments to Zuri. She might be able to catch the first person before they turned up. It was strange for him to have an entire day stretched out ahead of him, but excitement flowed through him when he thought of spending it with Jason.

He peered through the bedroom door on his way to the kitchen, watching the rise and fall of the man's back, then closed the door to allow him to sleep. More tea was necessary, maybe coffee even, but he didn't want to add caffeine into the mix of his already jittery state yet.

When his tea was ready, he settled in front of his computer again and answered the messages on his phone.

JOEY: *How are you?*

HARRY: *I'm fine. I didn't go to the station this morning. I messaged Jason instead, and he turned up at my door. He's sleeping now.*

He didn't want to give information about Jason's mental state because it wasn't his place to say anything, but he wanted to reassure Joey in case anyone asked. The next message was from Al.

AL: *We need to talk.*

HARRY: *We will, just not today. Things are difficult at the moment. I'll explain another day. I'll let you know when I'm free.*

After he sent that, he winced. He sounded harsh and dismissive when he hadn't meant to. Al would be well within his rights to bite Harry's head off for those words, but he'd worry about that another day. The last message was from his mother.

ESME: *I've not heard from you for a while. Is everything okay? Message me when you can. I know you're busy.*

HARRY: *Sorry, Mum. Things are weird right now. I'm looking after someone today because they've had a troublesome night. I'll call you later. I promise.*

Harry stared at his computer screen, watching the slideshow of photos that made up his screensaver. He nudged the mouse, and the screen flickered to life. He studied the schedule for that day again and swore when he realised what day it was. He was supposed to be meeting with Leticia from Addams Advertising the following morning. They'd booked the appointment when his lawyer had given him the go-ahead after he'd checked the contract over. The company was more than generous with their offer; therefore, Harry had signed it and mailed it back to them. For their first official meeting, he should've had some photos ready to show her, but he'd been focused on other things this past week that he'd not sorted any out. While Jason was sleeping, he would go through his computer and find anything that might work with the brief they'd given him. If he couldn't find anything, he'd have to spend the afternoon or evening taking photos.

His phone beeped again.

MUM: *Can I help with anything? I can bring some food over to save you from having to cook.*

He paused with his automatic refusal at the end of his fingers. It would make things easier if he didn't have to stop and cook for them, and if he ended up having to go out to photograph, they would have a decent meal inside them.

HARRY: *Are you sure you don't mind?*

MUM: *Of course I don't. I'll bring over a picnic-style lunch and some food you can reheat for dinner on my way to shopping. It's not a problem. I'll see you soon.*

HARRY: *Thank you.*

MUM: *You're welcome, sweetheart.*

With one less thing to worry about, Harry set about going through the thousands of photos he had saved on his hard drive. Although this was easier than finding something new to use, it would take more time, but time was all he had that day. At least until Jason woke.

Chapter 17

Jason

Jason woke to silence. He rolled onto his back, then stopped when he noticed an audible clicking sound, though he couldn't place what it was. Rubbing his hands over his face, he inhaled, wondering what time it was. From the light coming through the gaps in the curtains, he wasn't late for work, so that was a bonus.

He sat upright, sliding his legs over the edge of the bed. He saw the red glow of numbers on the bedside table and huffed. He wasn't used to having a visible clock in his bedroom; he usually used his phone. It was three o'clock, and his stomach grumbled. He should get himself up and ready for home because he was back at work that evening.

Sighing, he found his clothes piled on the drawers and got dressed. He needed to prepare himself for speaking with the counsellor again tonight. They had briefly spoken the previous night, but Jason had requested to meet with her again tonight. He'd explained that he wanted to see Harry and make sure he was okay, then he'd rest easier. Amanda, the counsellor, had agreed and allowed him to leave after a few basic questions—he assumed to find out his mental state. He must've passed because she'd let him leave.

He exited the bedroom and aimed for the noise, which he'd figured out was the click of a computer mouse. Harry sat at his desk, chin in his hand and a frown on his face. Jason's mouth curled at the look of concentration.

"Hey," he said in a soft tone, not wanting to startle him.

Harry whipped his head around, scrambling to get up from the chair. "Hey. How are you?"

Jason opened his mouth to answer as he usually would, then noticed the concern in Harry's expression and stopped to think about his answer. "Tired, but okay." It surprised him it was the truth. "I'm sorry about—"

"No! You don't need to be sorry. I'm glad you came to me. I wanted to come to the station, but Joey didn't think it was a good idea."

"I'm glad he got hold of you. I didn't want you seeing what happened on the news."

"He came round, and we watched a film. I didn't realise you'd asked him to."

"I rang him when we were heading back to the station after I messaged you. I didn't want you hearing it from someone else."

Harry stepped closer, lifting his hands and resting them on Jason's chest. "Thank you." He pecked his lips. "Are you hungry? Mum brought round some sandwiches and some roast chicken to heat for dinner."

"Either is great, thanks. I have to nip home before I go back to work tonight. I need to change my clothes."

"Okay. I'll do the chicken. You will have a good meal inside you before working hard again."

Harry slid his hands free and stepped to the side to walk around Jason, but Jason caught him before he could get further. He wrapped an arm around Harry's lower back and a hand to the back of his head and kissed him. It started soft and slow, but at the first tentative lick of Harry's tongue, Jason tilted his head and deepened it. He hadn't realised how he'd needed this. Needed Harry. He concentrated on the feel of the man and let everything else slide away. Nothing else mattered except for Harry.

When air became necessary, they pulled away, panting. Jason dropped his head to Harry's shoulder, and contentment seeped through him. His stomach intruded, making them both laugh.

"Come on. Let's feed you."

Jason followed Harry into the small kitchen and watched him potter around, making two plates of food and nuking them in the microwave. He hadn't had a roast dinner for two weeks, which was too long if you asked him. The Duck & Waffle called his name, too. It had since his last visit to the place, if not longer when he'd last eaten pancakes. His two favourite meals would disown him if he wasn't careful.

"Pancakes," he said.

Harry glanced over his shoulder. "Pancakes?"

"Do you like pancakes?"

"Yes. Blueberry is my favourite, though I don't make them often."

Jason leaned against the counter and crossed his arms. "Can I take you out for pancakes this weekend?"

Harry lifted the plate from the microwave and set it on a towel, then put the second plate in. When the whirring of the microwave began again, he turned to Jason. "I would love to go for pancakes." He cocked his head. "Would you like to go into the countryside this weekend?"

"I don't have any plans."

"I need to take some photos. Some landscapes. I told you about the new contract with Addams Advertising?" Jason nodded. "Well, they need some from me. I've been searching through what I've already got, and I have some to show for it, but I think I need more." He twisted back to the counter, still talking. "I have a meeting with Leticia tomorrow, which I had forgotten about, and I need to show off my best work."

"Your photos are amazing. You don't need to worry, but yes. I would love to come with you." He exhaled. "I'm meeting with a counsellor tonight," he said when they'd settled down with their plates.

Harry stared at him as if his face held all the answers. "That's good."

Jason focused on his plate. "I think I might ask if she has space to see me regularly."

"If you're comfortable with her, it would be a good idea."

"Do you want me to ask if she could see you as well?" Jason didn't look at Harry, wanting to give him space to decide on his own without giving away his own feelings about the situation.

"Would that be a conflict of interest?"

He glanced up at that and frowned. "I don't know. I can ask. If she says it's fine, do you want me to...?" He trailed off and waved his hand around, trying to get across what his words couldn't.

"Sure. If she has space, I'd gladly meet with her. You can give her my number."

They spoke about Harry's work for the rest of the meal, and Jason helped clean the dishes before it was time for him to leave.

"Thank you for everything," he said, winding his arms around Harry's waist.

"You don't need to thank me. I'm happy I could help."

Jason kissed him. "Can I come around tomorrow afternoon? After I've slept."

Harry nodded. "Ah, hold on." He pulled from Jason's arms and disappeared into the living room. Jason followed, waiting at the door. "I'm at the studio until four, then will be home after that."

"Okay. Shall we say five o'clock? I'll bring food."

Harry teased, "You don't have to bribe your way into the house with food. I can cook for us."

"I know. I didn't want you to have to work all day, then cook. Okay, how about you come over to my place after work, and I'll cook for you instead?"

Harry beamed. "Deal."

Jason pulled him in for a kiss before stepping away. "By the way, I think I know how you got my address." He winked and opened the front door.

Harry's cheeks pinked, but there was a smile on his face. "Not saying a word."

Jason grinned. "I could always get *Joey* to investigate my suspicions."

Harry tried to withhold his smile, but he couldn't. "He did nothing."

"I won't tell a soul." Jason blew a kiss, closed the door, unable to stop from smiling, and strode down the corridor to the lift.

Ford and Ulrich greeted him when he entered the apartment.

"Hey, man. I was expecting to see you this morning. Where have you been?" Ulrich grinned, showcasing his bright white teeth. Ulrich had told him many times in the past how his smile and teeth were conversation starters with women and men.

"I've been at Harry's. We lost someone to a fire last night." He breathed through the nausea, taking his mind back to Harry's flat and how comfortable he felt there. Not that he felt uncomfortable here, but there was something about Harry's place, or maybe Harry himself, which settled Jason.

"Oh, man. I'm sorry to hear that. Is there anything we can do?" Ford asked.

"No, but thanks." He coughed. "What are your plans for the week?"

"We're at work tonight, like you, then I plan to spend tomorrow afternoon, evening and hopefully all night with someone who I pick up from a bar somewhere in this town," Ulrich said.

"Your usual weekend," Jason said.

"Yep."

Ford snorted. "I'm going home to see dad after a couple of hours of sleep. It's his birthday this weekend."

"Oh, shit, yeah. Hold on." Jason stepped into his bedroom and rooted around in his wardrobe for the bottle of port he'd bought for Ford's dad. They'd been roommates long enough that Ford's dad was a regular visitor, and Jason got along well with him. He rejoined the others. "I bought this for him. Sorry, it's not wrapped."

"You didn't have to, but I'm sure he'll appreciate it. Thanks." Ford glared at Ulrich. "You even think about touching it, and I'll make sure a woman never says yes to you again."

Ulrich's eyes widened, and Jason rolled his lips inwards. It was good to be around his friends.

"What about you? You've got an entire weekend off," Ulrich said with a gleam in his eyes.

"Harry's coming over for dinner tomorrow night. At some point this weekend, we're having pancakes because I've not had them for ages, and we're going to the countryside for Harry to take photos for his new job."

"Sounds like you have it all planned out. Good for you," Ford said, clapping him on the shoulder.

"Thanks. On that note, I need to get ready."

Jason left them to their food and shut himself in his bedroom. He discarded his clothes and wrapped a towel around his waist while he picked out his uniform for that night's work. He showered and dressed, calling out his goodbye before leaving the apartment again.

The second he was back at work, he felt a little more centred and human—not to the degree he was in Harry's presence but near to it. He dropped in to see Paul before the shift started and was pulled into a hug.

"How are you?"

"Better than I was." Jason gave a half-smile. "What time is Amanda here?"

"She's here now. Attend the shift start meeting, then go straight to the other office."

"Thanks."

He jogged down the stairs, getting himself ready for the night ahead and feeling more upbeat than he had. Dean caught his attention when he placed his boots by the engine, ready for the meeting.

"What's up?" he asked when Dean came up to him.

"Are you all right?"

Jason smiled at the concern everyone showed for him. "Yeah, I'm good. Although you'll have to pick up my slack tonight because I'm meeting with Amanda after this."

"Not a problem."

"Red Watch!" Ian's voice rose above the conversation, and they settled into a row before him, going through the plans for the shift and the duties that needed attending to. When Ian dismissed them, Jason put his boots next to his door of the engine and told Ian he was going to see Amanda.

He knocked on the office door, and she called for him to enter. Dr Amanda Bagworth had a round face, with blue eyes and a wide smile that made you instantly at ease. She wore her blonde hair in a bob with a fringe and metal-framed glasses, and she had a rounded figure.

"Good evening, Jason. Nice to see you again." She rose and offered her hand, which he shook.

"Nice to see you, too. Although I wish it was under different circumstances." He dropped into a chair opposite her.

"Yes. Unfortunately, my role as a counsellor is not one that usually comes about because of joyful events." Her mouth curved at the corners.

"I can imagine. Before we start, I'd like to ask if you could continue our sessions outside of work." She tilted her head, and he inhaled to explain. "I have a few issues I need to deal with, as does my..." He paused because he and Harry had not confirmed titles, but from where he stood, they were boyfriends. "As does my boyfriend. If you have space, we'd both like to start sessions."

Amanda's eyebrows rose, but she opened a folder in front of her and put her pen to her lip, tapping it. "I have sessions available, but I might not always be able to accommodate your shifts unless we book far in advance. Is this something you're wanting to continue for a while?"

"I think it's going to take longer than a couple of sessions to sort through, yes."

"All right. Let's book you in now for your next one, and I'll contact..."

"Harry Jones."

"And I'll contact Harry about his."

"Thank you."

They settled on the following Monday because he was off, then she asked him about the previous night.

Jason averted his gaze, dropping his chin to stare at his fingers while they curled and stretched.

"Go as fast or slow as you need to, but tell me what happened."

"Procedure states that if a property is deemed empty, it does not need to be inspected while the fire is still burning. I've never second-guessed that process until last night because it saves firefighters' lives. Not putting them in harm's way more than they need to be." He transferred his gaze to the window, though he couldn't see a lot from it. "How can anyone be certain that no one is in the house unless they had evacuated from it?"

"That is an accurate statement, but as you said, it would put more lives in danger if firefighters had to investigate every building fire."

"Where do you draw the line?" he asked.

"What line?"

"The line between keeping firefighters safe and keeping the public safe?"

"It's a good question, and one you can speak to Paul about, I'm sure. You could bounce ideas around and see if there were ways to mitigate the dangers."

Jason stood, drifting to the window, and leaned his shoulder against it, arms crossed over his chest. "I know people have said the woman was of a good age and had lived a long life, but what if her fate was to live to one hundred?

Or older? My actions took away potentially twenty years of her life."

"What if her fate was to die in a car accident the following day?"

Jason stared out at the drizzle, raindrops sliding down the windowpane. "I don't know how to feel about her death."

"What is your body telling you? Or your mind? Or your instincts? Throw some words out for me without thinking about it."

"Pain. Guilt. Sadness. Hatred. Anger. Worthless." He snorted without humour. "How's that for words?"

"Enlightening." She cleared her throat. "Tell me about the hatred."

"I hate myself for deciding not to enter the property. What right do I have to juggle with people's lives? I'm not worthy of the role I have."

"Why do you think Paul gave you the position?"

He glanced at her with a frown. "I don't know."

The corner of her mouth lifted. "Yes, you do."

He clenched his jaw and returned to the window. His chest felt tight, and he swallowed several times to remove the lump in his throat before answering, "He thinks I can do the job."

"He believes in you. He trusts you."

"Maybe he shouldn't."

"He knows you're capable," she said. "Why would he put someone who couldn't do the job in charge of four other men? Because he believes in you."

Jason sniffed, the memories of the previous evening coming back to him in a slideshow.

"He believes in you."

He remembered the time when Dean almost fell into the River Cam while trying to save a man from a car that was hanging over the edge of the river.

"He believes in you, Jason. Maybe it's time you started believing in yourself."

"It's a hard thing to do when I've been told I'm worthless since I was thirteen years old."

"Then it's something we can work on." He heard her rustling around.

"Tell me about Harry. Or I should say, tell me about your relationship with Harry."

Jason grinned. "Don't let him hear you call it a relationship. He might run the other way."

She giggled. "What does he do?"

"He's a photographer. He did the photos for the calendar. It's how I met him. They look fantastic."

"I can imagine they do. Did you ask him out?"

Jason's cheeks heated. "Not in so many words."

Amanda gave him the once-over. "This is going to be juicy. What did you do?"

"No, I can't tell you. He'll kill me."

"You don't have to. Let's talk about—"

"I gave him a blowjob in the bathroom at a bar." Jason held his hands over his eyes, unbelieving that he threw their first encounter out there for her.

"Interesting. Any reason for the bar and not somewhere more...private?"

Jason exhaled and returned to his seat. "He has his own issues, which you'll no doubt find out about. He wanted nothing to do with a firefighter, but we thought one hook up wouldn't hurt." He snorted and shook his head. "How wrong could we be?"

"Things are going well?"

Jason tilted his head from side to side. "Up and down. We have a lot to work on, but we've both admitted to wanting to see where this takes us and agreed we needed your help to do it."

"That's a good sign. Working on a relationship strengthens it in the long term, but you still need to be honest with each other. Which brings me to what happened when you were—"

The alarm sounded, and Jason shouted goodbye and raced from the room. Despite his misgivings about his position, he refused to let his crew down. He would do the best he could and hoped it was good enough.

Chapter 18

Harry

For the first time in a long time, Harry couldn't wait to finish work. He had something to go home for, or at least, somewhere to go to and someone. Zuri had asked him about the previous day, and Harry had given some information but hadn't wanted to say anything about Jason's breakdown. It wasn't up to him to say, after all. He'd received a phone call from the therapist, too. Jason had given her his number, and they'd booked him in for a session the following week in between two clients on a quiet day. He wasn't looking forward to it, but it was the start of his road to recovery, she said. He'd have to make sure Jason was all right when he saw him. The session might have been hard on him.

"Do you have plans this weekend?" Zuri asked, packing away after the last clients.

Harry grinned, remembering the plans he and Jason had made. "I am going to Jason's for dinner tonight, then this weekend, we're going out of the city to take some photos for Addams. I have some that worked, and she was pleased with what I showed her, but I know I can get some shots that might work better for them."

"When is your next meeting?"

Harry packed his bag. "We don't have another face-to-face meeting planned, but we have a video call in two weeks. I told her my plans for the weekend. I think she's hoping there will be more photos for them."

"I can't believe they're paying you per photo. I thought they'd pay for a bulk set or something."

"I suppose they want their adverts to be as diverse and different as they can make it." He shrugged. "I don't know what they're being used for, but providing I get paid, I'm not complaining."

"Amen to that."

When they had finished setting the studio to rights, ready for the following Monday, Harry waved goodbye to Zuri, and he threw everything in his car and headed for home. He didn't want to assume he would stay overnight and didn't want the equipment to be left in his car. If he ended up staying over, they could swing by his place before continuing. For once, he didn't have any appointments on Saturday. He didn't know why he didn't, but he could imagine Zuri had either re-arranged things or had not booked anyone in that day to give him a rest. It was the kind of thing she did.

Despite knowing he'd turned everything off at his flat, he did a quick check through because it was the first time in a long time he'd be away from home overnight. If he would be, that was.

He shook his head at how his thoughts were going in circles. It had also been a long time since he'd been excited about spending time with someone other than friends or family.

He climbed into his car, and his phone rang. Checking who it was, he settled it into the holder and pressed the speakerphone.

"Hi, sis."

"Hey, stranger. I feel like I've not seen or heard from you for a while. How are you?"

"I'm good, thanks. How's..." He trailed off, having forgotten her boyfriend's name.

"Gone. Next question." She tittered, though it sounded strained. "Mum tells me you have a new boyfriend."

Harry wanted to roll his eyes but kept them on the road instead. "I do, yes."

"Are you bringing him for dinner on Sunday?"

He hesitated, having not thought about it. "Um, I don't know. I'll ask him."

"I doubt Mum will let you live it down if you don't."

Chuckling, he said, "True, but he's had a rough few days, and Mum knows it. If he's feeling up to it, maybe he'll come. Otherwise, I'll see you there."

"It'll be a good time for me to get you back for forgetting all my boyfriends' names." Harry could see in his mind how Naomi would roll her eyes.

"You're not with them any longer. What does it matter? When you have someone worthy of you, I'll remember their name."

"That'll be never then because, according to you, no boyfriend will ever be worthy."

"Damn right." He grinned and pulled into the car park for Jason's building. "Anyway, sorry to cut the conversation short, but I need to go."

"Hmm, plans with your fancy man?" She snickered.

"*Goodbye*, sis." He hung up.

Harry pulled the keys from the ignition and grabbed his phone before exiting the car. It took a few minutes to get to Jason's door, but he vibrated with energy when he knocked. The twitch in his eyes was absent for a change. A thought disappeared when Jason appeared in front of him, followed by the scent of something spicy.

"Hey." He didn't know what else to say now he was in front of the man.

Jason cocked his head. "Come on in."

Harry stepped inside, past Jason. Despite having been there before, he hadn't been in the best state of mind and had not taken in any information about the layout or decoration of the place. The hallway opened into the living room, which held a corner sofa, a large screen TV and a four-person dining table. He could see the door leading off the room into the kitchen. Glancing to his right, he saw four doorways leading off the hallway, which he knew were bedrooms and a bathroom. They had used the compact layout well, and the natural light would be amazing during the day given the number of windows the living room had. The apartment couldn't be cheap to rent.

He flushed when he realised he'd been studying his surroundings and ignoring Jason. "Sorry. I didn't see a lot of it last time."

Jason chuckled. "You mean when you broke down my door?"

"I did not!" Harry looked away. "Okay, maybe I would've if you hadn't opened it, but I *didn't*."

Jason stepped closer, cupping Harry's nape, and rested their foreheads together. Harry went cross-eyed trying to see Jason's expression and, in the end, closed his eyes. "I'm glad you're here," Jason whispered.

"Me, too."

Jason pressed their mouths together, sipping from each of Harry's lips several times, and Harry dropped his head back and let him. The slow, sensual kiss sent Harry's head spinning, and he clung to Jason's arms. When Jason pulled back, Harry whimpered—actually whimpered—at the loss. Sounds and smells made their way back into Harry's consciousness, and he regained his balance. The smirk on Jason's face made him roll his eyes.

"Yes, your kiss is mind-blowing. Get over it." Harry pretended to pout.

Jason beamed. "Thank you for the compliment." He massaged the back of his neck as if he was uncomfortable with the praise. "I made chicken cacciatore with new potatoes, carrots and cabbage. I hope that's okay."

"Sounds delicious. You didn't have to go to all this trouble."

"It's no trouble," Jason said, entering the kitchen. "I enjoy cooking, and although I do it a lot, I don't get many chances to eat with someone else." Harry frowned at him in question. "My roommates work different shifts than me, and we rarely see each other. When I cook, I make enough for them as well, but I seldom get to see them eat it because I'm either asleep or at work when they do."

"I bet they love you for cooking for them."

Jason grinned. "They do. It works well because it means I don't have to clean the bathroom."

Harry frowned again. "What does cleaning the bathroom have to do with cooking?"

"We share the chores around the apartment mostly, but because neither of them cooks, they agreed to clean the bathroom between them and let me do the cooking instead. It's a win-win situation for me."

Harry snorted. "I can imagine. You got the best end of that deal."

"Tell me about it."

Jason puttered around the kitchen, stirring one pot, poking a fork into another. "It's almost ready."

"Let me set up the table," Harry said, stepping into the kitchen and reaching for a drawer.

"They're here." Jason pulled open a drawer and passed Harry two sets of cutlery. "Do you want some wine with dinner? Or I have beer, juice, milk, tea, coffee, and other stuff. Ford and Ulrich drink some weird crap."

"Beer would be nice, thanks."

Harry grabbed two bottles of beer from the fridge and set up the table. When he'd seen where the seats were—in a similar place to where they were in Harry's flat—he'd paused, not sure which seats to use. In the end, he wanted Jason close to him and set them at a ninety-degree angle to each other. If Jason didn't like it, he could change it.

Returning to the kitchen, he leaned against the doorframe, watching Jason's sure and steady movements when he removed a dish from the oven and served up the meal. The smell of tomatoes, onions and herbs was stronger, and it made his mouth water. Harry could cook, but he relied heavily on easy meals like frozen pies he could shove straight into an oven. He rarely created something from scratch. He could follow a recipe like most people, but he would never have that flare of...whatever it was that people who *could* cook had.

"It's ready."

"Is there anything you want me to take to the table?"

Jason picked up the plates. "You could grab a couple of glasses of water, please."

Harry stepped to the side to let Jason exit the kitchen, closing his eyes at the aroma wafting past him. He patted his stomach and searched for glasses before washing his hands and filling the glasses with cool water, and taking them to the table. Jason hadn't changed the place settings and had chosen the seat that faced the wall instead of the one facing the window. Though it was dark, Harry could tell the view would be amazing in the daylight.

He dropped into his seat and smiled at Jason. "Thank you for this. It smells delicious."

"Let's hope it tastes it. I've not made this recipe for a while."

"I'm sure it's amazing." Henry forked some into his mouth and closed his eyes, the flavours bursting onto his tongue. He tried to figure out which herbs Jason had used, but he'd never been good at that either. "It *is* amazing."

"Thank you." Jason ate some and nodded his head. "It could've used a little more salt, but it's good enough."

"If this is your version of good enough, I need to taste what you think is divine."

"Pancakes."

Harry paused with his fork halfway to his mouth. "Pancakes?"

Jason nodded, finishing his mouthful. "Pancakes are divine. No matter what they serve them with, pancakes are the most divine food on the planet."

Harry chewed, digesting that bit of information. "I guess we're having pancakes for breakfast tomorrow?" His eyes widened when he realised what he'd said. "Not that I think I'm going to be here for breakfast. We could meet up at a café or somewhere, not here, then eat our fill before going out for the day. Or I could bring you something after I've gone home for the evening. I didn't mean that I would be—"

A finger rested against his lips, and Harry closed his eyes as his cheeks heated.

"You're cute when you ramble." Harry's eyes flew open. "I would love for you to stay over, but I am also content if you wish to go home. The choice is yours."

Harry licked his lips, flicking his tongue against the tip of Jason's finger as he did. Jason's eyes darkened when he removed his hand. "I'd love to stay," Harry whispered.

They ate while keeping the conversation going until every bite had disappeared. Jason picked up the dishes, and Harry followed with the empty beer bottles and glasses.

"I'll wash because you cooked," Harry said, nudging Jason away from the sink.

"We have a dishwasher."

Harry shook his finger. "I'll do it."

Jason held up his hands and stepped back. Harry concentrated on washing each of the items used to create the wonderful meal. Halfway through, Jason came to stand behind Harry, pressing light kisses and small bites to his neck and shoulder while pulling Harry back against his erection. Harry accentuated his movements and rubbed against Jason as often as he could, and if the muted groan coming from behind was anything to go by, Jason was struggling to keep his composure.

"Do you ever bottom?" Jason asked.

Harry's heart pumped, and he hesitated. It wasn't something he'd ever enjoyed. He'd tried with several past partners, but each time he'd not been able to climax, not even getting completely hard. He wondered if this would be an issue for Jason. "No. Well, I have before, but it does nothing for me."

"Thank god!"

Harry howled at the heavy relief in Jason's words. "Why?"

"Because I can't top. I've tried before, and although I orgasmed, it wasn't the same. I prefer someone else to do all the work."

Harry leered. "Oh, that's the reason, is it?" He drained the water and twisted in Jason's arms, sliding his own around the man's waist, despite having wet hands. He'd be out of his clothes soon enough. He pulled Jason's T-shirt up, sliding his wet hands up his spine and receiving a shiver in response. Harry loved being the one to elicit these tells from Jason, the small shivers, the muted moans, the arching of his body. It all culminated in sending Harry higher.

"I think it's time for bed," Harry murmured. Jason dropped his head to Harry's shoulder. "Come on. Let me show you how much I loved your food."

Jason grabbed Harry's hand, leading him from the room towards his bedroom. Harry hesitated in the hallway, noticing things still switched on. He glanced at Jason, who waited for him.

He licked his lips. "Is everything safe?" he whispered, feeling his anxiety racing to the surface.

Jason's face softened, and he stepped closer, wrapping his arms around Harry. "I promise everything is as safe as it can get, but if there's something that will make you feel more relaxed, tell me, and I'll do it."

Harry stared around the living room, his eyes cataloguing everything that could go wrong. Then he peered at Jason, seeing the truth in his eyes. He was a firefighter. He would know better than anyone else. Could he take that leap of faith in Jason?

"Let's go to bed," he murmured in a shaky voice.

Jason kissed him. "If at any point it gets overwhelming, let me know, and we'll sort it."

Harry nodded and followed Jason into his bedroom, shutting out the rest of the apartment. It helped a little. What helped more was the skin Jason showed. He'd pulled his T-shirt over his head and the expanse of tanned, toned muscle had Harry hungry for something different than dinner. A different kind of dinner.

"Take them off," Harry ordered. He stared at Jason's movements, watching every tooth on the zip open as if in slow motion. He swallowed hard but couldn't resist dropping to his knees. He'd wanted Jason to be the one on his knees in front of him, but he could already taste Jason in his mouth, and he wanted the real thing. He pushed Jason's hands away and divested him of his clothes in several seconds. Harry's eyes catalogued every inch of skin on the naked man, and it was all *his*.

Focusing on the shaft standing to attention with its red, swollen head, Harry licked up the pearl of precome on the tip, spreading it around his mouth before lifting his eyes to Jason's and wrapping his hand around the base.

"Stand still. If you move, I stop."

Jason's Adam's apple bobbed, but he nodded.

Harry leaned forward, and starting at the base, licked the length. He curved his tongue around the side, trying to get the dick as wet as possible. After reaching the head each time, he swirled the fluid from the tip and began again. After one final swipe, he paused at the nerve bundle, repeatedly flicking over it and watching Jason tense his entire body and shake with the need to move. Harry knew men could come from having those nerve endings stimulated continuously but finding out if Jason was one of those men was for another day.

After a strong shudder from Jason, Harry took pity and swallowed the cock, taking him into the back of his throat.

"Ah, fuck! Harry!"

Harry took no prisoners, using every learnt tool at his disposal to take Jason as high as he could without sending him over the edge. He wanted Jason as close to the edge as he could get. Backing off again had Jason cursing, and Harry smirked. Patience wasn't something he thought Jason enjoyed, but he would love the result. He'd have to deal with it.

"On the bed, ass in the air."

Harry rose to stand, holding Jason steady until he stumbled over to the bed. The man unceremoniously dropped onto the bed before rearranging himself with slow movements. Harry was sure he spent several long minutes humping the duvet, but he'd let it slide.

He climbed onto the bed behind Jason and, without advertising his plans, buried his face between Jason's ass cheeks and licked his pucker.

"Holy fucking shit!" The cover muffled the rest of Jason's words, and Harry smirked, then refocused.

He firmed his tongue and pressed it against Jason's rosebud, not trying for entry yet, but letting him feel what would be happening. He kissed the area, sucking on it and getting it wet. The pucker relaxed marginally, and Harry pressed his tongue against it, sliding further in. The more it relaxed, the further Harry's tongue went until he was fucking Jason like that.

Chapter 19

Jason

The sensation of Harry's tongue in his ass sent Jason spiralling to the edge once more.

"Holy fuck! Ah!"

He didn't know whether to push closer or pull away; it was *that* good. He gripped a fistful of the covers in each hand and buried his face in the fabric. He bit down on the cover, trying to muffle his pleas. He could feel the heat of Harry's hands spreading his cheeks wide, and Harry went to work between them. Jason was struggling to catch a coherent thought, but he supposed it didn't matter. He lifted his mouth free of the fabric and dragged in much-needed air. He whined when Harry pulled away, wanting him to do more, to take him harder, to fill him up.

"Where are your supplies?"

It took Jason several seconds to figure out what Harry had said, the blood rushing in his ears as loud as the sirens on one of his engines. He pointed to the bedside table, and Harry left him. Jason's body moved as if reaching for his lover. He took several deep breaths, trying to regain his equilibrium. It worked for a short time, then Harry slapped his ass, and a fiery sting spread across his cheek.

"Let's get you ready, shall we?"

Jason inhaled through his nose and repositioned so that he was braced on his forearms and his fingers linked beneath his forehead. The position provided him with a way to push back. He heard the click of the tube, a telltale sound that most of the adult population would understand, even if it had nothing to do with sex. He tensed, waiting for the cold sensation to appear, but it didn't. He relaxed marginally, only to jerk and hiss when the lube touched his skin.

"Sorry, I tried to warm it up."

Jason couldn't reply because he was focused on the fingers Harry pressed against his pucker. He took a deep breath and exhaled in a steady stream to relax his body, giving Harry access. Harry spent several long minutes preparing Jason for his cock, and then Jason heard the crinkle of a wrapper. Jason held his bottom lip between his teeth and braced his body, sighing when Harry pressed against him.

"I wanted to make this last, but I may have to do that next time," Harry said. His voice was low and gravelly and sent tingles of awareness up Jason's spine.

"Don't wait. Do it now. Take me, Harry."

Harry must have taken him for his word because, the next second, he buried as far inside Jason as he could go. He didn't wait either. Jason gripped the duvet again and braced himself while Harry slammed into him over and over. He could feel his climax drawing near. After all, he had been nearly there several times that night.

"Stroke yourself. I want to feel you come."

Jason slid his hand down and wrapped it around his weeping shaft, sounds of pleasure escaping his lips, more so when Harry firmed his grip on his hips and pulled Jason back when he thrust forward.

Within seconds, he was there, the heat of his come spilling over his hand, and he bit his bottom lip.

"Fucking hell! You have an iron grip pulsing around me. I can't..."

Jason felt Harry's rhythm stutter, then the man buried himself deep, leaning over Jason's back and breathing hot air onto his already sweat-slicked skin. Harry inhaled and rose from his position, Jason wincing when he withdrew.

"Are you okay?"

Jason still had a firm grip on the covers, and his body was drawn tight like a bow because he knew he'd collapse in a heap if he let go.

Harry nudged him. "Are you still alive?" He pushed against Jason's hip, sending him rolling to his side out of the wet patch.

"I'm fine," Jason said. "I think it's time to sleep now, isn't it?"

Harry snorted. Jason could hear him moving around, but he didn't have any spare energy to move. It was all he could do to keep breathing. As lost in his hazy thoughts as he was, he jumped when Harry wiped him clean with a warm flannel.

"We need to change the sheets."

"It's on top of the cover. It can wait until tomorrow." Jason wasn't entirely sure his words came out as words, but Harry must have understood something because Jason felt the covers being moved, and Harry rolled him to his other side before spreading the duvet over his body. Jason drifted until the bed dipped, and he rolled towards Harry, nuzzling into his side and pressing a kiss to his chest.

He had to remember to return the favour after he'd had a little nap.

"Do you want your usual, Jason?" the owner said when she sidled up to the table.

The woman was in her fifties, but she was the sweetest woman he'd ever met. If he'd been straight, he would've snapped her up in no time. All he could offer her were his smiles, his wit and his business.

"Yes, please, Doreen." He grinned at her.

"Be still my heart. That smile wakes me up every time." She winked and fanned herself. "And what can I get you, handsome?"

"Hey, hands off," Jason said. "He's mine."

Doreen smirked. "I wondered whether that would provoke a reaction from him," she told Harry.

Harry's cheeks darkened, and he dropped his gaze, rubbing at his eye. He was cute when he was flustered. "Um, pancakes, please? With syrup?"

"Of course, sweetheart. What about drinks?"

"Coffee," they both said in unison.

Jason laughed. Harry had kept his word about making the second time last the previous night. He'd kept Jason on the edge for about an hour before Jason begged for release. They'd fallen asleep again afterwards, and the sun had woken them this morning. Jason had forgotten to close his curtains because Harry had been interested in seeing the moonlight shining on Jason's skin. It had been a good job he'd not brought his camera because Jason doubted they would've slept enough if he had. Before heading to the Duck & Waffle, they'd dropped by Harry's flat to get him a change of clothes since he hadn't brought any with him. Something he wouldn't do again now that Jason had put his foot down.

Jason reached for Harry's hand across the table. "Do you know where we're heading this morning?"

Harry nodded. "I thought we could visit Anglesey Abbey in Lode. They've got some wonderful, picturesque areas. If that fails, then maybe take a drive through the area and see what we can find. Do you have to be back at any particular time?"

"Nope. I'm all yours, assuming you want me."

Harry's mouth curled at the corners, and he ducked his head, though he flipped over his hand and gripped Jason's.

For someone who hadn't thought he'd be able to have a relationship, he was doing a damn fine job of being in one.

He couldn't help the voice in the back of his head from telling him that time would show he wasn't worth it, but he tried to squash it down.

After eating their fill of pancakes—or rather, Jason eating all his and half of the stack of Harry's the man hadn't been able to eat—they left with a wave for Doreen. Jason had persuaded Harry to let him drive, arguing that Harry could concentrate on the scenery and take pictures if he didn't have to concentrate on the road. He couldn't argue with the logic and had reluctantly agreed. Reluctant because Harry pouted all the way to the café.

Once they climbed into the car, Jason aimed east and told Harry to choose some music if he wanted to.

"Are you okay without any?"

Jason snorted. "There are other choices to pop music, you know."

"I know, but there always seems to be some thrown in there no matter which station you choose."

"What about classical?"

Harry was silent, and Jason glanced over at him before returning to the road ahead. The expression on Harry's face told Jason what he thought of that idea.

The drive to the National Trust property took them around fifteen minutes, and there wasn't a lot to see on the way. Jason hoped the historic house and gardens could provide Harry with the landscape photographs he wanted. They paid for entry to the gardens, and Jason threaded his fingers through Harry's before setting off, a barely concealed smile on his face. This was something he had never done with any of the people he'd seen in his past, spending time together because they could.

They followed the path past the house and headed for the entrance to the surrounding area.

"I received a call from Amanda Bagworth yesterday," Harry said, tightening his grip on Jason's hand. "Did things go okay with her?"

Jason didn't reply for a moment, trying to gather his thoughts enough to explain how it went.

"You don't have to tell me anything. I wanted to be sure you liked her, but if you gave her my number, I assume you did. It doesn't matter."

Harry's word-vomit ended, and Jason's mouth twitched. "I'm happy to tell you everything. I was trying to figure out how I felt about it. It's weird to tell a stranger about my life, my inner thoughts and my feelings. It's almost like I shouldn't be doing it, but Amanda put me at ease, and I found her to be a comforting presence, which helped me to open up a bit. At least until the alarm went off, anyway."

Harry's eyes widened. "Oh, no! Typical. How much time did you get to speak with her?"

"Around half an hour, which was good for a first session. It eases me into it. I have booked another appointment for Monday. I'll be able to do the full hour because I'm not working."

Harry nodded absently, staring around. Jason removed his hands from Harry's, causing the man to frown at him. "What's wrong?"

"You have your 'I see something I like' look on your face."

Harry raised his eyebrows. "Does that mean I have that look on my face every time I see you?"

Jason snorted. "I don't know. I'll have to check now." He nodded down the path. "Lead the way. You get the photos you need, and I'll follow behind. It's no hardship." He winked.

Harry backhanded his shoulder and set off. "You can still talk even if I'm taking photos."

"We spoke mainly about work and how I felt being the crew commander, what happened at the fire the other day, a little about you." Harry glanced back at him at that, then stopped and crouched, lifting the camera to his face.

"Good things, I hope."

"Is there anything else I could say?" Jason watched Harry adjust the lens, and he held his breath when the man's finger depressed the button to take a photo. He was as beautiful as a well-planned bonfire that consumed everything that was thrown on it without causing problems.

"You could've told her all the issues I have."

Harry's words brought him back to the present. "That's what you're supposed to do, not me."

Harry frowned and came to stand in front of him, cupping his jaw. "Don't censor yourself because of me. If there's something you need to tell Amanda, tell her. I won't be offended."

Jason's eyes widened, and he ducked his head. "I don't want to upset you."

Harry smiled. "You won't. I want you to heal the same way I want myself to heal. To do that, we need to open up about things the other person might not want to be known. But that's the good thing about Amanda; she keeps things between her and us." He paused, staring off into the distance. "I remember when I visited the first psychologist when I was eight. He was a nice man, but he said something that always stuck with me. *You are stronger than your mind makes you believe.* I don't know why that struck me as significant, but it seems to be true. My mind tells me I'm not strong, but when something happens, I find the strength I didn't realise I had."

"You are strong. You're stronger than I am."

Harry raised his chin. "We're both stronger than we think we are, and I think these sessions will be good for us."

They began walking again. "I still want to talk to you, though. In addition to Amanda, I mean. I don't want any secrets from you."

Harry pulled him to a stop again, and Jason saw tears brimming. "I don't want secrets from you either." He wiped his face, the tears overflowing. "Sorry."

Jason cupped his face and swiped the tears away with his thumbs. "Don't be sorry. I don't know how to make relationships work, Harry. I'm the last person anyone would come to for advice, but I want to try with you, which is more than I've wanted to in the past. You mean more to me than anyone else ever has."

More tears flowed, and Harry tried to duck his head, but Jason wouldn't let him. Instead, he lifted Harry's face for a soft kiss. A click sounded, and Jason pulled back, turning his head. Harry held his arm outstretched and had taken a photo of them.

"I want a copy of that."

"If it's any good." Harry grinned and sniffed, wiping his eyes of the remaining tears. "Would you like to come to dinner at Mum's house tomorrow? She'd love to meet you."

Jason swallowed hard and stared at Harry, eyes wide. "Um, okay?"

"Why does that sound like a question?"

"Because it was. I have never met anyone's parents before, but let's do it. That reminds me, though. Paul is holding a pre-Christmas get-together on 21 December. It's an all afternoon and evening thing because he wanted to make sure everyone from the station could attend, and some of them will work either day shift or night shift. You can bring your friends as well if you want."

"Sounds good. I'll ask, although Al probably won't come."

Harry stopped to take some photos of an arch of trees, and Jason frowned. "Why not?"

Harry stood and sighed, crossing his arms over his chest. He didn't meet Jason's gaze, and he knew he wasn't going to like what Harry was going to say. "He has a thing for me, I'm told. I never realised."

"Why does that matter?"

Harry faced Jason. "He and I..." He waved his hands back and forth.

Jason clenched his jaw against the jealousy flowing through him and took several seconds to get his breathing and heart under control. "It still shouldn't matter. If he's your friend, he should be ecstatic for you, even if it means you aren't with him."

"You'd think, wouldn't you?" Harry pressed his lips together. "It doesn't help that I'm not making things easy for us to talk. I want to pretend it never happened and ignore it, but he wants to talk something through. I keep putting him off."

"It would be easier to get it over and done with." Jason made himself say the words, though he'd prefer it if Harry wasn't within two hundred yards of the man who might persuade Harry to change his mind about them.

"Yeah, I suppose."

"Ring him. Meet up with him tonight, and I'll be there when you're done."

Harry stepped closer and wrapped his arms around his neck. "You, Jason Townsend, are a wonderful man."

Jason snorted. "You wouldn't think that if you were in my mind right now. What I want to do to the guy would have me in prison for years."

"Which is why you're wonderful because, despite those thoughts, you still want to help me salvage my friendship."

"Hmm."

"Come on. Let's get some more photos."

"Hold on. Message Al first."

Harry blew out his cheeks but complied, typing something on his phone before sliding it back into his pocket. "Done."

"Good." Jason held out his hand. "Let's see what this garden has to offer. You never know what nook and crannies it might have."

Harry gasped. "We are not doing anything like that in public!"

Jason's mouth opened in mock shock. "You wound me with your words. I meant nooks and crannies that few people see and might be good for unique photos." Jason huffed. "You have no faith." He lifted his nose into the air and strode away, the corners of his mouth twitching.

Harry's laughter followed him through the trees. Bringing laughter to their lives was something Jason could always promise. He loved making people laugh, even if it was at his own expense. But Harry's laughter was the medicine he needed to mend the broken pieces of his soul. He hadn't realised it until then.

Chapter 20

Harry

It was like Harry had seen another side of Jason he'd not known existed. Though Harry got plenty of photos, only a quarter of them would be helpful for his contract; he'd been interested in taking photos of Jason and catching him unawares several times through the hours. Jason insisted on taking some pictures of Harry, too, and Harry tried to get some of the two of them. As far as days went, this was one to remember for many years to come.

Harry pushed Jason back against the car when they were ready to leave and grabbed the back of his head, pulling him down for a kiss. When there was nothing in their way, Harry could see a future spread out before them, but it wasn't always possible to see it. At that moment, he could see them growing old together. It terrified him. He'd always expected to be alone. He'd resigned himself to the fact and had become comfortable in the knowledge, enjoying the company of those he wanted to spend time with and not worrying about going home to an empty house.

Now, though, there was Jason, and Harry was petrified. Many things became more important, more visible, riskier when he had someone else to think about. It wasn't his life he had to contend with; it was Jason's, too.

Today had shown him what he was missing. He was scared to keep Jason in his life, and he was scared that Jason would leave. How was that for a conundrum? He brushed aside his worries, choosing to bring the thought to Amanda on his first session, needing to find a balance between what he could live with and what he couldn't live without.

He ran his tongue along the seam of Jason's lip and gained access, deepening the kiss but keeping it steady and slow. Jason grew hard against his stomach, and he pressed closer, putting pressure on his groin, and received a moan into his mouth.

"Don't start something we can't finish," Jason said, pulling back.

Harry lifted his chin. "Who said we can't finish?"

Jason chuckled. "I did." He pushed against Harry, who stepped back. Jason clicked the button to unlock the car and opened the driver's door. "Where to now?"

Harry narrowed his eyes but checked his watch. "Let's find somewhere to have lunch, then if you're okay, we can drive around for a bit and see what we find."

"Providing it includes food, then yes, I'm happy."

Harry snorted when Jason climbed into the car after blowing him a kiss. He rounded the car, and his phone beeped. The message was from Al.

AL: I can be there for seven?

HARRY: *Perfect, thanks.*

"Did Al reply?" Jason asked when he started the engine.

"Yes. He's coming around at seven tonight." Harry knew the conversation had to happen, but he wasn't looking forward to it, unsure if he would end up losing a friend at the end of the night.

Jason's hand came to rest on his leg. "You'll be fine. If it makes you feel better, I can wait in the car outside, then you know I'm close by."

Harry gave a lopsided grin. "No, you don't need to do that. I'll call you when it's done and let you know what happened. You can come over after that if you like?"

"Let's see how things go. You might stay friends and want to hang out."

He said the words, but his hand tightened on Harry's thigh. "Even if we hang out, you can come over. I'll call Joey and Clemency and see if they're free, and you can meet everyone. I'm sure everything will be fine." Harry squeezed Jason's hand, then messaged Joey.

HARRY: *I'm going to speak with Al tonight about the situation. Regardless of how it goes, do you want to come over and you can meet Jason afterwards? I'm going to invite Clemency, too.*

He rested his head back and rolled it towards the side window, watching the scenery rush past. The situation with Al wasn't ideal, and he had a feeling his friend wouldn't take his disappointment lightly. Harry hoped he could mitigate the damage he was about to inflict on their friendship.

Harry and Jason spent the rest of the afternoon driving through villages and the countryside to see what they could find. Jason had persuaded Harry to listen to some pop music, and although it wasn't horrible, it wasn't Harry's idea of fun, either. Harry had needed little persuasion for Jason to pose for some provocative pictures when they found somewhere deserted. It hadn't been more than removing his shirt and undoing his jeans, but it was all Harry could do to stay behind the camera and not join him for some afternoon fun in the sun.

As the sun sank towards the horizon, Jason drove them back towards his apartment so Harry could drop him off before heading home.

"I've had a great day. Thank you for coming with me."

Jason copied what Harry had done earlier that day and pressed him against the car, trapping him there. Not that Harry was in a rush to go anywhere.

"It was fun. Make sure I get to see those photos you took of me. I might have a career in modelling if the firefighter gig doesn't work out."

The corners of Harry's eyes crinkled. "As if you'd ever give that up." He slid his arms around Jason's neck.

Jason tightened his hold and stared at him. "I would if you asked me to." Harry's eyes widened, but Jason's did, too. "Holy fuck," Jason murmured. "I never thought I'd ever say that, but fuck if it's not true."

Harry's heart raced, and he couldn't find anything to say straight away. After several long seconds, he coughed. "Well, rest assured, I will never ask that of you."

Jason huffed. "I never expected to find someone who meant more to me than my job did." He lowered his head, brushing his lips against Harry's mouth. "Let me know once you've finished talking with Al. I'll bring some beer."

"Deal." The subject of Al was uncomfortable but less so than Jason's words. Harry kissed him with meaning, leaving them both breathless, then climbed into the driver's seat and waved, pulling away from the kerb.

He had a couple of hours before Al arrived, and he wanted to look at some of the photos they'd taken. When he settled at his desk with a coffee, he loaded the pictures and brightened when the first one he'd taken opened. It was of Jason when he'd bent down to tie his shoelaces. Harry hadn't been able to resist the sight of that ass in tight denim. He snorted. Who was he kidding? There was nothing about Jason he didn't like.

He arranged the photos into two folders. One for personal photos for him and Jason to look through later, and the other for work photos. While he sorted through them, he checked and was pleased to realise several of them might work for the Addams brief he'd received.

Shutting down the computer, he darted under the shower spray and washed off before dressing and making coffee. He had a feeling the night was going to be a long one.

Al knocked at the door right on time, and when Harry opened the door, he raised his eyebrows at the messy hair and dark circles under his friend's eyes.

"Come on in."

Al wandered through to the living room and dropped onto the sofa without a word. Harry blew out a breath and closed the door, following in the wake of the unhappy man.

"Do you want a coffee?" he asked from the doorway.

Al shook his head, and Harry settled into the armchair, surprised Al hadn't taken that spot like he usually did. "What did you want to talk to me about?" Harry asked, tucking his legs beneath him.

Al closed his eyes and rubbed his hands over his face. Harry jumped when he shifted forward on the seat and faced him. "I want you to choose me, Harry. Me. Not some...worthless joker. Me." Al exhaled. "After everything we've been through together, I thought you would choose me. I've been there every step of the way. Choose me, Harry, not him."

Harry rubbed his eye, the twitch never more evident than now, and exhaled, knowing he was going to upset Al. "I appreciate everything you've done for me, Al, but it was never more than comfort. I thought it was the same for you. If I'd realised you had feelings for me, I would've put a stop to it long ago."

"That's why I didn't say anything. I thought you'd grow to love me." Al's voice sounded broken, torn.

"Al, I'm sorry."

Al rose and paced behind the sofa, holding the back of his neck. "Are you not even willing to try?"

Harry's shoulders slumped. "I can't, Al. Even for you, I can't pretend to feel something I don't. I'm sorry."

"We could go back to the way things were before?" Al said.

"No, we can't. I'm with Jason now. Even if we don't last long, I'm with him now. I won't cheat on him."

"I know you won't cheat. I wasn't saying that. Get rid of him. He's a troublemaker."

Harry clenched his teeth and stood. "No, he isn't, and I'd like for you to stop the name-calling. Jason has problems, the same as you and I. He's dealing with shit; we're dealing with shit. Just because you don't understand it doesn't mean it's not happening." Harry inhaled. "I've invited everyone over tonight for a beer or two. If you can't be civil, I'm going to ask you to leave, but I'd like it if you got to know him."

Al said nothing but sank back onto the sofa. He rubbed his hands together. "Why him?"

Harry snorted. "I have no fucking clue." He stared out of the window, watching the darkness spread across the city. "He wormed his way into my life before I even realised it."

They were silent for several minutes, then Al said, "I'll meet him, but I can't stay and watch you together. Not yet."

Harry faced him, leaned back against the windowsill and nodded. "That's fair enough. I think you'll get along well once you get to know him."

Al's mouth curled at the corners, a small semblance of a smile. "Maybe, but not yet."

"Understood." He pulled his phone out and messaged Jason, Joey and Clemency.

HARRY: *We've finished talking. You're welcome whenever.*
JASON: *On my way.*

A knock sounded, and Harry frowned. "Who's that?"

He strode for the door and opened it to find Joey and Clemency smiling at him.

"What—?" He shook his head. "Never mind." He left the door open and returned to Al. "Guess they're eager for drinks."

"Always, my dear. Always," Clemency said, affecting a posh tone. "I have to get in my alcohol allowance before I go to sleep. Paris awaits."

Harry hugged her. "Are they sending you again?"

She nodded. "Yes," she said, returning to her usual voice, and settled into the bean bag. "I'm leaving on Tuesday and staying for two weeks." Her smile widened. "Two weeks in Paris! Can you believe it! Your photos did the trick!"

"Will you be working the whole time?" Harry called as he exited the living room, heading for the kitchen and ignoring her words.

"No. They want me there for fittings, the show rehearsals and the show itself, but the rest of the time is mine alone."

Joey snorted. "Does your bank balance know you are going to Paris?"

Harry caught the tail end of the throw she'd aimed at him, the cushion smacking him in the face. He held out bottles to everyone.

"Are you two back to being BFFs again?" Clemency asked, then downed her drink.

Al shifted on the sofa and faked a smile. "We're good. I need to head out in a bit, but I said I'd meet Jason first."

Joey glanced at Harry with his eyebrows raised, and Harry shrugged, so Joey changed the subject. He couldn't believe Joey had been right about the whole thing, and he hoped Al would forgive him eventually.

Harry rose again when there was a knock. Jason stood there, uncertainty on his face, and Harry felt a weight lifted from him. "Come in."

"Is everything okay?" Jason asked in a low voice.

"Yeah. Al understands though he's upset for obvious reasons. He wants to meet you, but he won't be staying. Said it would be too hard for him right now, which I get."

Jason cupped the back of Harry's neck. "And you?"

"I'm all right. Sad, but I'm good." He lifted his head for a kiss, then tugged Jason forward. "Let's get it out of the way."

Jason lifted his other hand. "I bring gifts."

Harry grinned at the beer cans. "Are you trying to get me drunk, Mr Townsend?"

"Will it get me into your bed easier?"

"No." Jason frowned, and Harry sniggered. "You're already going to be in my bed."

"Damn it! I could've saved that money."

Harry backhanded his chest, laughing. "Hey. This is Jason. Jason, I think you know Joey."

"Yes, fault of the job," Jason said with a grin.

"This is Clemency."

"And you're the firefighter." Clemency winked. "Fellow model here. We'll have to swap stories."

"Clemency, behave." Harry inhaled. "And this is Al." He wasn't sure what Al would do.

"Nice to meet you, Jason. I've heard a lot about you."

"Same goes to you. Harry is always telling me funny anecdotes you get up to."

Harry gasped. "I do not!" Jason grinned. "Sit your butt down before you get me into trouble."

Jason winked and dropped to the floor beside the armchair, resting the beer on the coffee table.

"I have to go, but it was nice meeting you. See you soon, guys and gals." Al strode away, and Harry followed.

"Hey, are you all right?"

Al screwed up his face. "I will be. Give me time. I won't always run when he's here, but I need time."

"Okay. If you need anything, let me know."

"I will." Al hugged him, and Harry could feel the man's reluctance to let go, though let go he did. "I'll see you soon."

"Take it easy."

Al waved and closed the door, and Harry stared at it for several seconds. Would Al come back? Or was this goodbye? He turned when he heard someone step into the hallway.

"Is he okay?" Joey asked.

Harry gritted his teeth. "I don't know."

Joey squeezed his shoulder. "It's not your fault, Harry. You never promised him anyway, but maybe being intimate wasn't a good idea."

"I know that now." Harry rolled his eyes. "Come on. I need a beer." He brushed past Joey but stopped when Joey caught his arm.

"I'll keep reaching out to him and check he's okay. It'll put our minds at ease."

"Thanks."

Harry sank into the armchair, running his hand across Jason's head. Jason hooked his elbow over Harry's leg and nestled closer while still talking to Clemency about Paris. He felt Al's absence, but there wasn't much more he could do to help the man heal. Harry should've seen it coming and should've stopped things from going as far as they had. He hoped Al would forgive him because he didn't want their friends to become middlemen, so to speak.

"You're meeting his mother!"

Clemency's words dragged Harry from his thoughts, and he snorted at her tone. "Stop trying to worry him. He'll be fine." He leaned down and dropped a kiss on Jason's head. "You'll be fine."

"We'll be there as well," Joey said. "This I have to see."

"For god's sake. It's not like she's Cruella."

"True, but you are her son," Joey said. He glanced at Jason. "Might want to bring protective equipment." He smirked.

"Joey, stop it!" Harry threw the nearest cushion at him.

"What! I'm yanking his tail! It's what friends do."

"Yeah, but he'll change his mind, and then I'll have to change it back again. Stop being an asshole and choose the film."

Joey's eyes twinkled, but he grabbed the remote. "Any recommendations?"

"Have you ever seen *The Thirteenth Floor*?" Jason asked.

"Is it a horror?" Clemency screwed her face up.

"No, it's a sci-fi thriller type of film. It's from the late 90s, but it's pretty good."

Joey clicked through the options, a small crease between his eyes. "Here it is. Shall we?"

"Go for it," Harry said, and Clemency nodded.

They settled in to watch, but Joey caught their attention. "Why don't you two swap seats with me? Jason will end up with a numb ass if he stays on the floor for long."

They played musical chairs while the credits were on, then Harry sat back, and Jason laid on his side with his head on Harry's lap. He linked their fingers together. While the film played, Harry kept glancing at Jason, the lights from the TV playing across his face. He couldn't believe they were here. At this stage in a relationship. If a psychic had predicted this, he would've never believed it until he saw it for himself. His mother would be beside herself tomorrow after believing Harry would never let anyone in.

He had a reason for that though, and it was something he needed to talk through with Amanda because if he couldn't get over it, he and Jason didn't stand a chance. If that was the case, he needed to end their relationship before it went any further. It wasn't fair on Jason if Harry couldn't give it his all. And he wanted to. He truly wanted to. That he would have to give Jason up was like a knife being forced through his body. He shivered.

Jason peered up at him. "You okay?" he whispered.

Harry nodded. He would be okay. He needed to be okay.

Chapter 21

Jason

J ason brushed his hands down the front of his shirt, staring at his reflection in the mirror. He rubbed his jaw, wondering if he should've left a little stubble to make him look older or more put together. Harry had told him his mother would love him, but Jason wasn't sure. He looked the part, dressed up as he was, but wasn't it what was inside that counted to most people? Would she see past his outer shell and find him unworthy of being with her son?

"Where the hell are you going dressed like that?" Dillon asked with a smirk. "Who are you pretending to be? It's not Halloween, you know?"

Jason paused with his hands on the doorknob. "I have a date."

Dillon sniggered. "Who the fuck would ever take a chance on you? You're not worth the air they breathe." He strode over to Jason, who stood straighter, refusing to cower.

He clenched his jaw. "I'm taking them to a restaurant."

Dillon narrowed his eyes. "Where did you get the money to afford that?"

Jason swallowed hard. "I've been working with Mrs Jameson."

"That old bat? What's she got you doing?" Dillon howled with laughter. "Oh, don't tell me. She's teaching you how to please the ladies? Oh, I forgot, you don't swing that way."

"I do the gardening for her."

Dillon grinned. "I bet that's not all you do."

"Jesus, Dillon! She's sixty-eight." Jason opened the front door, and Dillon slammed his hand against it, shutting it again.

"Why are you putting yourself through this, Jason? You know it won't work out. They never do. How many times have you been out on a date this past year?" Jason said nothing. "Exactly. They figure out how much trouble you cause and run for the hills. Why not make your life easier and forget about it, eh?"

Jason wanted nothing more than to punch his brother in the face, but he couldn't mess up the chance Paul had given him. He inhaled. "It doesn't matter how many times I try; I'll try again."

He pulled hard on the door and slipped out before Dillon could say anything further. Jason had to keep reminding himself that Dillon was upset with him; that was all. The moment he could be a decent member of society, Jason could pay him back and make him proud of him. He turned eighteen in three months, and he would show Dillon what he'd made of himself.

Jason came back to the present and inhaled through his nose, not wanting to remember his eighteenth birthday.

He grinned at his reflection, trying to infuse his body with confidence, then entered the living room. Whistles met him, and he grinned, spinning in a circle.

"Look at you all spiffed up," Ford said.

"They're bound to let you off with a pardon looking like that," Ulrich deadpanned.

Jason picked up a cushion and threw it at him. "Asshole!"

Ford hooted. "You ready to meet the parent?"

"Ready as ever."

"What are you taking with you?" Ulrich asked.

"I bought a bottle of red wine. I was told it went well with a roast dinner."

Ford nodded. "Excellent choice. What time do you have to be there?"

"Harry's picking me up in a few minutes."

"Ooh, a proper date. Nice."

Jason stuck up his middle finger. "What are you two's plans for today?"

Ford glanced at Ulrich, then glanced down. Ulrich said, "Not got anything planned. We'll see where the day takes me."

Jason wished Ulrich would see what was right in front of him: Ford. He shook his head and pulled his phone out of his pocket when it vibrated. "Right, well, I'm off. Wish me luck."

"Break a leg," Ulrich said.

Ford backhanded him. "That's for a play, you idiot." He rolled his eyes. "You'll do great, Jason. Have fun."

Jason picked up his coat and shrugged into it, hiding his nervousness through movement. He wandered down the hallway towards the lift, scraping his fingers through his hair and linking them at his nape. He bounced his shoulders and shook his hands out, then aimed for the stairs instead of the lift. He jogged down to the ground floor, hoping to get rid of his excess energy, and exited into the foyer. Harry had got a parking space right outside, and Jason opened the door and got blasted by a gust of wind and what felt like a bucket of water. He raced for the car, holding his coat over his head, and climbed in.

"Did you not check outside the door before you opened it?" Harry said with a laugh.

Jason mock-frowned at him. "Your beauty distracted me. It's your fault."

Harry leaned over and pecked him on the lips, then put the car into gear, but Jason could see his cheeks turning red. The compliments made Harry uncomfortable, but Jason wouldn't stop saying them because they were true. There was nothing he would change about Harry. Of course, he would've liked Harry to be free of his nightmares and guilt, but that was because he didn't want Harry to suffer, not because it would change who he was.

"Mum said it was roast beef today. I hope that's okay."

Jason's stomach growled. "I think my stomach says yes."

Harry joked, "I'm glad your stomach approves." He glanced to the side, then refocused on the road. "You look good."

"Thanks." He smoothed a hand down his front again, shifting on the seat. "Um, when did you say you were seeing Amanda?"

"I'm meeting with her on Wednesday."

Jason's leg bounced while he watched the scenery, trying not to think about his brother's thoughts on his dating abilities. A hand rested on his knee, and he stopped bouncing. He peered at Harry, who wore a small smile.

"Don't be nervous. Mum's great. She'll love you, and you'll love her."

Jason nodded and rested his hand on top of Harry's. He stared ahead of him and inhaled, pushing all thoughts of Dillon aside. He could pretend to have it together in the same way he had for many years. This was nothing different.

Harry pulled the car into his mother's driveway and killed the engine. "Let's do this."

Jason forced a smile at Harry, bringing his confident persona to the forefront. "Let's."

Harry grabbed his hand, and they headed for the door.

"Mum! We're here!"

Jason braced himself for the disappointed look he'd received all his life and pasted a small smile onto his face. When Harry's mother emerged from what Jason assumed was the kitchen, he liked her. She was the same height as Harry, with the same black hair and green eyes, but her hair was long and curly, kept back with a clip. She had lines around her eyes and mouth, which showed the laughter she'd had in her life. Her clothes, however, were not what he'd been expecting. She wore pink leggings and a flower print, knee-length dress. It gave her an exotic air.

She wiped her hands on her apron and grabbed Harry's face, bringing him towards her for a kiss. Jason rolled his lips inwards to stop himself from laughing at the sight. Harry kissed his mother, then wrapped her in a hug, whispering in her ear.

Her gaze flicked to him, and Jason swallowed, discreetly wiping his hands on his jeans. "I'm glad you could be here." She pulled back. "Aren't you going to introduce us, Harry?"

Harry smirked. "Mum, this is Jason. Jason, my mum, Esme."

"Nice to meet you."

Esme stood and put her hands on her hips, narrowing her eyes at him. He cleared his throat and shifted on his feet. When she still said nothing, he glanced at Harry, who had a hand over his mouth, as if that would hide his smirk.

"Hmm. Are you sure you want to keep him, Harry?" Jason's heart dropped, and his gaze hit the floor. "I could do with someone as fit and healthy as him helping around the house."

Jason snapped his focus to her again, seeing a grin on her face. His heart jumped, and he exhaled, shaking his head. "Shit," he muttered with a smile. "All right. You got me."

Harry laughed, holding his sides, while Esme stepped closer, cupping Jason's jaw. "Anyone who my son believes is worth his time is worth *my* time. You're welcome here. Anytime at all. Whether or not Harry is here."

A lump formed in his throat, and he couldn't speak. Tears brimmed, and he blinked to get rid of them. Esme pressed a kiss to his cheek and turned away.

"Dinner is in half an hour. You two are on table setting duty."

"Where's Naomi?" Harry asked when they followed.

"She's on her way with Adam." Esme disappeared into the kitchen. "Joey and Clemency were leaving when I last spoke to them."

Jason chuckled at Harry's grimace and received a shove in response. "You wait. I've done nothing to deserve the painful conversation that is coming our way."

Harry pouted and led the way to the dining room. It reminded him of the one from his childhood home, but he chose to remember it full of life with his parents instead of stark and foreboding with his brother. The room had a fireplace in the centre of the outside wall, two dressers on either side of it, and a large ten-person table that appeared too large for the room.

"I know. Mum enjoys having people around, and she's hoping there will be plenty of family to have around soon."

Harry's cheeks darkened, and he busied himself opening the drawers in the dresser and bringing out cutlery.

"Are the cups or glasses in here as well?" Jason asked. "Oh, crap. I've just remembered!" He held up the bottle of wine he'd been holding.

Harry snorted. "Go give it to her then." He pointed towards the kitchen. "Turn left outside the door and follow it to the back of the house."

"Are you not coming with me?"

Harry raised his eyebrows. "Do you need me to hold your hand?"

Jason pursed his lips and narrowed his eyes. "No," he said, although he agreed in his head. He was a big boy. He could deal with one woman.

The scent of food increased the closer he got to the kitchen area, but he got derailed by the photos hanging in the hallway. He saw many pictures of Esme, Harry and a woman, who he assumed was Naomi. There were several older pictures higher up the wall of Esme with a man and then the complete family with a small child. Jason assumed this was Harry's brother, John. He couldn't begin to understand how it felt to lose a brother, but he knew how it felt to lose a parent. He exhaled and hoped these therapy sessions would be beneficial to them both.

Jason continued and reminded himself several times not to hold the bottle too tight; otherwise, it would end up broken. He smoothed a hand down his shirt and bit his lip when he entered the hub of Esme's house. The radio played, and Esme hummed along while she dealt with pans and plates.

He cleared his throat, not wanting to make her jump. She lit up as she glanced over her shoulder. "I brought this for you. I forgot to give it to you earlier."

Esme bustled over and took the bottle from his hands. "Ooh, lovely. This will go well with the beef. We can have it with lunch." She placed the bottle on the side and faced him again. "Jason, time for the inquisition."

"Already? Don't I get a reprieve until everyone is here?" he joked.

Esme smirked. "Do you want me to ask all these questions when everyone is here?" She cocked her head.

Jason grimaced. "Probably not."

"Good boy. Tell me, who do you have around you?"

Jason frowned. "Sorry?"

Esme waved her hand and turned back to the oven. "Friends, family, acquaintances, lovers, whatever. Who do you have in your life?"

Jason sniffed, unsure why she needed this information but willing to go with the flow. "Harry, obviously. The only lover I need. I have friends from work, other firefighters, and I'm good friends with the station commander, Paul and his husband, and their friends Ave and George Oxford. My best friend, Jasmine, is a wedding planner's assistant."

"I know Ave and George. Lovely couple. Harry told me your parents died. I'm sorry."

Jason shrugged, leaning his hip against the counter and crossing his arms. "Thanks."

"Can you tell me about them?"

Jason licked his lips and grazed his bottom lip with his teeth. "They died in a train accident on the way back from visiting a friend."

Esme came to stand beside him. "I'm sorry to hear that, but I meant, can you tell me about what they were like before they died. What was your life like?"

Jason frowned. "Why?"

Esme's mouth curved, and she patted his arm. "You can tell a lot about a person from the memories they talk about and the ones they don't." She returned to the cooker. "I can remember many things about our life before the fire, but there are some that are painful, even for me. Most of those are moments between my husband and me because the memories of my children are the best memories to have, regardless of how painful they are."

"I'm sorry for your loss."

Esme smiled at him. "Thank you."

They were silent while Esme pottered around, and Jason thought about her question. "They would always say 'I love you' whenever they were leaving each other or us. It didn't matter where we were or what we were doing; they would always say it. I never understood why, and as a thirteen-year-old, it was embarrassing to have your parents say it at the school gates."

"I can imagine, but it's a beautiful memory."

Jason nodded. "We used to have picnics in the living room on the weekend." Jason grinned. "We'd put on a film, make some popcorn, grab some sweets and drinks and pretend we were at the cinema. I don't know how many times we had to clean that carpet from spilt drinks." Jason hugged himself.

"The bane of parenthood. Spills and stains are a staple for us." Esme handed him a bottle opener. "Could you air the wine because I'm about to dish up the food? Naomi better arrive soon, or she'll have to reheat it."

Jason focused on the wine bottle, removing the cork with no trouble. He grabbed seven glasses from the cupboard Esme pointed him towards, then hooked them all in his fingers and hooked the bottle in the crook of his elbow, heading back towards Harry.

"Thank you for telling me, Jason," Esme said. He glanced over his shoulder and smiled, then carried on to his boyfriend.

"How was it?" Harry asked. He looked like he'd been running his hands through his hair and pacing the floor.

"You left me to deal with her," Jason said in a forlorn voice.

"Oh, god. What did she do? I told her to be kind." Harry came over and removed the glasses from Jason's hand.

Jason snorted. "She was lovely. She asked me about my parents."

Harry winced. "I'm sorry. I told her they'd died, but I didn't think she would ask you about them."

"It was okay. She asked me about what they were like when they were alive. It made me remember a couple of things I'd forgotten." Jason placed the bottle on the table. "She would be a good psychologist."

Harry sniggered. "Yes, she'd get everyone to spill their secrets within seconds, guaranteed."

"I'm here! I'm here! Sorry!"

Jason watched a tall, slender woman rush past the dining room doorway and, he assumed, through to the kitchen.

"Now, there's a surprise," Harry said. At Jason's raised eyebrows, he continued, "She's alone. Maybe I don't have to deal with pop music conversations today after all."

Jason grinned. "I think I have the perfect conversation starter."

Harry pressed a finger into Jason's chest. "Don't even think about it."

"How are you going to stop me?"

Harry slid his hands around Jason's neck and pulled him closer. "I can think of many ways to change the topic, especially if it means you'll be sleeping in a cold bed tonight."

"That's mean."

Harry tilted his head. "Is it? Hmm, maybe I need to think of something else instead then." His finger followed a pattern across Jason's shirt, but Jason's gaze was caught on the lip Harry had between his teeth. He tugged on Jason's shirt, kissing him, then pressing kisses along his jaw. "Maybe I need to invite my friends over for a drink tonight. We can all watch a film until the early hours of the morning."

Jason's eyes closed at the seductive purr of Harry's words, but they flew open again when the words registered. He pulled back. "Fine. No pop music."

Harry quirked the side of his mouth. "I thought you'd see things my way." He stepped back, but Jason dragged him close again.

"Remember, payback is a bitch." He nipped Harry's earlobe and moved away. He adjusted the glasses and wine bottle while Harry greeted his sister.

"Jason, this is Naomi."

"Nice to meet you, Naomi." Jason shook hands with her, noticing she looked more like their father than their mother from what Jason had seen in the photographs.

"You, too. Do you have any single friends? Any that aren't losers like most of the men I meet?" Sadness clouded her features.

"Hey! I resent that!" Joey stepped into the dining room with Clemency following behind. "I'm not a loser!"

Naomi snorted. "I'm not talking about you. Anyway, you bat for the other team. You don't count."

Jason flicked through his mental list of crew members and found a potential target. "Maybe. I need to check if he's single first, though."

Naomi beamed. "Thanks. I'm giving up on musicians. They're all after groupies instead of something more long-lasting." She dropped into a chair. "Maybe a firefighter is what the doctor ordered."

Jason chuckled, and Harry said, "Naomi! Stop talking about them like they're pieces of meat!"

"What? I bet you have loads of women and men lusting after you when you're all dressed up in uniform, don't you?" She aimed the question at Jason.

He glanced at Harry and grinned. "More often than is comfortable."

Harry palmed his head and groaned. Joey, Clemency and Naomi hooted.

"Dinner's ready. Come and get your plates!" Esme called. "And I heard that, Naomi. I think we're needing another discussion about being on your best behaviour."

"Mu-um! I'm thirty-two years old!" Naomi whined when they entered the kitchen.

"Hmm." Esme pursed her lips at her daughter. "Jason is not a pimp, you know. You can easily meet decent men if you stop choosing the ones who talk to *you* like a piece of meat." She narrowed her eyes. "I heard that part, too."

Jason bantered with them. "It's absolutely fine. I'm used to it."

"Really?" Naomi said. "Tell me more."

Jason grinned. "I have plenty of stories to tell."

"It's all lies, I tell you! Lies!" Joey called.

Harry groaned. "Please, stop them, Mum. This can only end in disaster."

Chapter 22

Harry

Harry had made the appointment with Amanda for nine o'clock in the morning to give him the rest of the day for his studio clients. He had expected to go to her office at the hospital, but she had offered to visit him at home instead, which made his life easier. It was because it would make him feel more comfortable, especially since it was his first session. He fluffed the bean bag chairs again and brushed a few crumbs off the coffee table into his hand, depositing them in the small bin beside the TV. His stomach churned, and he was glad he had only eaten one slice of toast for breakfast. He tucked a few papers away in his desk and surveyed the room. It appeared tidy enough.

Shuffling through to the kitchen, he boiled the kettle and set out two mugs on the counter, almost dropping one on the floor in his haste. He didn't know if Amanda drank tea or coffee and decided to wait until she arrived before making anything.

The knock sounded when he pulled the milk from the fridge, and he dropped the carton to the floor. Thankfully, it didn't burst open. He placed it on the counter, wiped his hands on his jeans and strode to the front door.

"Good morning," Amanda said with a smile.

"Morning. Come in." Harry stepped back, allowing her room to enter, rubbing his hand over his face. He closed the door, asking, "Would you like a drink?"

"I'd love a cup of tea if you have any, please."

"Sure." He showed her to the living room, then backtracked, swiping a hand over his forehead. He blew out his cheeks in an exhale and fixed their drinks. He could've done with coffee, but he thought the extra caffeine might not be the best idea when potentially talking about his past.

When he entered the living room, he saw Amanda had taken a corner of the sofa, and inwardly, he relaxed at being able to sit in his armchair. Hopefully, being surrounded by his usual seat would help him relax and not flee the building. Now that he was here, he wasn't sure this was the best course of action for him. There was a reason he hadn't sought any therapy since he was a child. Then, he remembered Jason, and the reason he was doing this cleared his mind.

"Thank you," Amanda said, accepting the cup. "Just what I need on this bitter day."

"I've not been outside yet. Is it as cold as they predicted?"

Amanda nodded. "Definitely. The weather reports said it wouldn't snow, but it feels cold enough to."

The typical British subject for when the population is nervous. Harry almost snorted his tea instead of sipping it. He tucked his legs underneath him and got as comfortable as he could, given the situation. His nose tickled, and he rubbed it.

"Okay. What would you like to get from these sessions?"

Harry raised his eyebrows. "Um, I..." He blew out a breath and sniffed. "I want to get past what happened when I was younger. I want to build a relationship with Jason that is about us and not what happened to my family. I don't know if that makes sense, but I want the best start for our relationship that we can get."

The corners of her mouth curled up. "That sounds like a wonderful reason." She leaned towards the coffee table and placed her mug on it, then removed her coat. "Sorry, it's nice and warm in here." She folded the coat and placed it on the sofa beside her.

Harry's nose twitched again, and he frowned, glancing around. He'd turned all the plugs and electrics off, even the kettle, before he'd come into the room.

"Everything okay?"

His gaze snapped to Amanda's. "Yes, sorry. My mind wandered."

"It's fine. Do you have any concerns about your relationship with Jason at the moment?"

Harry winced. He had concerns, but he hated bringing them up.

Amanda crossed her legs and cradled her cup again. "What we discuss stays between us here. I won't say anything to Jason if that's what you're worried about."

"No, I'm not worried about that. In fact, I'm comfortable with you discussing what I say with him." He exhaled. "My concern is to do with his job. I always swore I wouldn't be with someone who put his life in danger. I've lost enough without potentially losing someone else." He shook his head, and his mouth twitched. "Then Jason happened."

Amanda chuckled. "He is a force of nature, isn't he?"

Harry laughed. "That's one way to put it." He sniffed and glanced around again. He thought he'd scented smoke, but there was no way. He must be coming down with a cold.

"How do you feel about Jason's job?"

"Honestly? I would prefer it if he didn't do it, but it's part of who he is. I would never ask him to stop doing what he loved." He sniffed again, uncurled his legs and put his cup down.

"Is everything okay? You seem a little distracted."

"Sorry. I need to..." He went about checking the plugs and electrics in the living room but couldn't find the source of the smell. It was the same scent he had become accustomed to when Jason was around, but he wasn't around then. He didn't know why he could smell it. The only thing he could think of was that something was on fire that he couldn't see. His heart raced, and his chest hurt. His gaze ran around the room several times. "We need to get out."

Amanda stood. "Why?"

"Something's on fire. I can smell it, but I can't find it. We need to get out of the building." Nausea churned in him, and his hands trembled.

"I can't smell anything."

He paced around the room, trying to find the source. He waved his hand across his face. "It's in my nose. It's like what

I smell when Jason is near, and although I've got used to that when he's here, he's not here now. Why can I smell it? Something must be on fire." He grabbed Amanda's hand and headed for the doorway.

"Harry, wait! I think it's me." He faced her, frowning. "I smoke. It could be on my clothes, although I try not to smoke before seeing clients. I've been told my clothes have a lingering smoky scent."

"It...It..." He tried to understand what she was saying, but his breathing increased, making his head fuzzy.

"Harry, I need you to calm down. Breathe for me. Concentrate on my voice and come back to where we are. We're in your living room. We're safe. We're safe."

He didn't know how long it took for him to figure out he was sitting on the floor with his back against the wall. His head was between his knees, and Amanda knelt in front of him.

"How are you feeling, Harry?"

He took stock of his body and emotions. "Tired. Worn out."

"Understandably. I apologise for not realising this was a trigger for you. If I had, I would've been more careful."

Harry waved her away. "It's fine." He glanced around the room. "Are you sure there's no fire?"

"Yes, I'm sure. Does the scent of smoke trigger you itself or the unexpectedness of it?"

Harry tilted his head. "It must be not expecting it because I can handle the scent of it around Jason because he comes home smelling like a bonfire most days."

"Okay. Let's try something. Smell my coat and see if that's the scent you noticed."

She held out her coat, and Harry sniffed at it and nodded. "Yeah. As I said, it's like what Jason smells like, but slightly different. I'm used to it around him and his friends, but nowhere else." His jaw went slack. "I'm getting used to the panic, though."

"You don't have to get used to it. We can work on it. Find better ways for you to deal with panic attacks when they happen." She stood, holding out a hand to help him up. "Let's finish our tea, and we can book another session."

"I'm okay. We can continue—"

Amanda held up her hand. "I know, but you'll feel better after a nap. Even if it's an hour. Get some rest before going out into the world."

Harry cocked his head. "You're not like any therapist I've known before."

Amanda's mouth curved into a smile. "I work differently to many other psychologists. I found my clients appreciate the way I change their therapy to be unique to them. There's no hard and fast rule about how your sessions should go because everyone is different. They need different things. What you need will differ from what Jason needs."

Harry dropped into his armchair. "That makes sense."

They spoke for a few minutes longer and made a second appointment for the following week. After she left, Harry sent a message to Jason because he knew he would be concerned about him.

HARRY: *Session finished early. I had a panic attack, but I'm fine. Don't worry about me. I'm going for a nap, then will go to the studio later. See you later.*

He climbed into bed, exhaustion flowing over him. Dragging Jason's pillow closer to him, he breathed in the smoky, earthy scent, not at all upset by it now. It comforted him. How strange that one scent in various scenarios could have a different effect on him. He didn't understand the psychology behind it, but hopefully, Amanda could help him.

"Jason mentioned that he'd told you about the cause of the fire when you were younger. What do you think of that information?"

Harry pulled the blanket tighter around his legs while he thought about Amanda's question. After three weeks, he was getting used to the way she tried to get him to open up. Truth was, he'd not given Jason's words extensive thought, and he told Amanda as such.

"I pushed it aside and ignored it. It was easier than dealing with it."

"In what way?"

Harry exhaled. "If I ignored it, I wouldn't have to think about it. I wouldn't have to dig around my memories and remember what happened. I could continue to pretend it had happened to someone else."

"Do you think it would be better to work through it with someone you trust? They could be there when you read the report or when someone talks to you about their findings?"

Harry's chest felt like a weight was pressing on him, and he was going to throw up, but he breathed through it, counting in his head. He threw her a smile. "I don't think that will help. Would you like another drink?" He pushed the blanket aside.

"I don't need another drink, thank you. Harry, what's going through your head now?" Amanda leaned forward, resting her elbows on her knees.

Harry dropped his head. He knew this was her way of asking him to be honest with her. "I don't want other people seeing how weak I am, and I know if there is someone else there, they'll witness my breakdown."

"What if it was Jason or me? Or one of your friends? Would you feel the same way?"

He threaded his fingers together, clenched them, then released them several times. His face twisted, knowing he would have to go through this, anyway. "It would be better with Jason, Joey or you. Clemency is away, and Al...well, I've not seen a lot of him lately."

"Why not? You mentioned before that you were best friends."

Harry nodded. "We are...were. I don't know what we are anymore. Al and I had a...friends with benefits agreement over the years. Not often, just when the memories were excessive. He saw more into our relationship than I realised until Joey brought it to my attention that he was in love with me." Harry huffed a laugh. "I hadn't seen it, and it fractured our friendship."

"I'm sorry to hear that."

She said nothing for a minute, but Harry waited her out. He knew she was pausing to see if Harry said anything else, but there wasn't much more to say about the situation with Al. Harry had sent several messages, inviting Al to come over, and received some in return, but none that agreed to meet up.

"How about Joey? He wouldn't be too close to the situation like Jason would and unlikely to psychoanalyze your every word." She grinned at him, and he smirked. "He could go through the file with you and answer some questions you have. If he doesn't know the answer, I'm sure he'd know who to ask."

Harry swallowed hard. "Okay."

Amanda sat upright, dragging her diary closer. "Right. Although it's nearly Christmas, I would suggest arranging the visit with Joey between now and New Year. You can get it out of the way and start a fresh year with fresh eyes. How does that sound?"

"I'll ask him."

"Brilliant. Let me know what the date will be once you've arranged it, and I will make a note in my diary in case you need to talk to me that day. How does that sound?"

"Terrifying." He snorted.

"I understand that. Trust me, though, you will do better knowing the facts of the accident rather than hurting from what you believe is the truth."

Harry blew out a breath, staring at the ceiling. "I know."

"We're all here for you, Harry. We'll all help with what we can."

"Thank you."

He felt like he'd been put through a wringer when she'd left. It was late in the day, and he didn't have any appointments, which was fantastic. Jason wasn't due to arrive until dinner, so Harry ran a bath and sank until his head was the only thing above the water. The heat seeped into his muscles and relaxed the last of his tension. He allowed his thoughts to come and go as they pleased, not focusing on anything in particular.

When the water cooled enough to make him shiver, he climbed out and wrapped the large fluffy towel around him. It had been on the radiator and was warm enough to ward off the chill of the flat. He rushed to the bedroom and climbed into bed, towel and all, and pulled the covers over his shoulders. He knew it would warm up soon enough and waited it out. Once he stopped feeling like an icicle, he thrust his hand out and grabbed his phone.

There was a message from Jason.

JASON: *I hope everything went well. I'm awake, but I won't come over until dinner as we agreed. I know you like to have a nap after speaking with her. I'm bringing food with me. Don't order anything.*

Harry beamed at Jason's need to always look after him. If he was honest, Harry loved it, and he loved returning the favour, though usually, his care of Jason was of the sexual kind. He typed out his reply.

HARRY: *As always, thank you for bringing food. You are right that I need a nap. I've had a lovely soak in the bath, although it would've been one hundred times better if you had been in there with me. I'll see you in a couple of hours. I love you.*

It was only after he sent it he realised what he'd written. There, in black and white, were the three words he hadn't expected to say to anyone except his family. For once, he didn't succumb to the panic wanting to shield him; he breathed through it and nodded. He *did* love Jason, and however fast it had happened, he refused to hide from it any longer. He grinned to himself, wondering what Jason's reaction would be.

Chapter 23

Jason

I *love you.*

The words were seared onto Jason's retinas while he cooked the lasagne. He almost burnt it because he couldn't believe Harry had written them, and more that he deserved them, but he was working on that with Amanda. His brother's voice was less prevalent in his mind, even after only a few sessions. Either that, or he was getting better at ignoring it.

He rested the oven dish on the counter to cool and raced to his bedroom. The need to see Harry pushed everything else aside, and he jumped into the shower before dressing again. He wanted to talk to him, tell him how *he* felt. Although he'd known he'd felt something for Harry from the start, the deeper emotions had snuck up on him. He snorted. At least it felt that way, but he was sure Paul and his crew would deny that. They had bets going on when he and Harry were going to get married. Jason wasn't ready for that yet, but he wasn't opposed to it, either, whereas before, he would've run into a burning building to get away from it. Not because he didn't want it, but because he thought he'd bring unnecessary trouble to his partner's door.

He attached a lid to the oven dish and wrapped a tea towel around it. Luckily, he didn't have far to go to his car. When he parked near Harry's building, his heart pounded as fast as his breaths were coming, and his entire body tingled. His hands clenched around the steering wheel, and he tried to control the shaking of his hands. The fluttering in his stomach had him frowning. He couldn't figure out why he seemed nervous.

Then, his hands dropped to his lap, and he stared through the windscreen, not seeing anything when he realised what he was feeling was *hope*. He had never let himself hope for anything before. Too frightened that it would be taken away. Even his crew members becoming friends and his position at the station had not been something he had hoped for, just something that had happened.

He rubbed at his chest, not feeling the knot of tension that usually resided there. He could make this work. *They* could make this work. He knew it. With those words, a weight lifted from his shoulders, and he grinned.

Climbing out of the car with the lasagne, he jogged across the road and into Harry's building. He didn't even wait for the lift. He ran up the stairs as fast as he could, grateful for his training, though he was out of breath when he knocked on Harry's door.

Harry opened the door, his bottom lip caught between his teeth. "Hi."

Jason was overwhelmed. He stepped inside and past Harry, ducking into the kitchen to put the oven dish down, then back to where Harry waited with a frown. Jason didn't want that expression on Harry's face, so he cupped his jaw and kissed him with everything he had in him. In the end, he was lightheaded enough that he needed to pull back for air, but he herded Harry towards his bedroom, needing to feel him.

"What about dinner?"

Jason shook his head, a lump stuck in his throat. He couldn't say the words yet. He needed to *show* Harry how he felt first. For once, Jason was the one in charge.

He stared into Harry's eyes while his hands smoothed down his sides and gripped the hem of his T-shirt. At the first touch of his fingers against Harry's stomach, the man inhaled and trembled beneath his skin. He ran his hands higher, the T-shirt bunching up and up until he yanked it over his head. All the while, Jason guided Harry backwards, careful of any obstacles in their way. Jason lowered his head, nipping Harry's bottom lip, his fingers sliding along the waistband. He slipped a finger between the fabric and Harry's skin, the heat evidence at once. Jason kept Harry's mouth busy while he flipped open the button and unzipped the jeans. The moment he had room to manoeuvre, Jason slipped his hand down and took hold of the erection and groaned into Harry's mouth. He stroked from root to tip, the uncut skin sliding along the hard shaft.

Harry moaned, his head dropping backwards and his eyelids fluttering closed. Jason took the opportunity to kiss down his lover's neck while he pushed the jeans down with one hand. He wanted Harry naked. He wanted to worship every inch of him. Jason flicked his tongue over the straining nipples in turn, then continued lower, dropping to his knees. The jeans and boxers were easy to pull down but difficult to remove when Harry was trying to keep his balance.

By the time Harry was as naked as the day he was born, Jason had fastened his mouth to the head of Harry's cock. He could feel it twitch and lengthen with every lick and suck, which encouraged him all the more. Talking about his feelings was difficult but *showing* how he felt was easier. He would give Harry the words but later.

"Jesus Christ, Jason. Your mouth feels amazing."

Harry's fingers threaded through Jason's hair, and his eyes closed. Concentrating on making Harry tremble with need, he worked the man's dick, giving him everything Jason had learnt over the years. The trembling in Harry's body increased until he warned Jason of his impending release, but Jason refused, pulling off and grinning at Harry's growl.

He stood, guiding Harry to the bed, laying him on his back. Harry tucked his hands behind his head with a smirk. "I'm all yours."

Jason took in the display of skin, cataloguing every inch while he divested himself of his clothing, then he grabbed the lube and condom from the bedside table before crawling up Harry's body. He couldn't wait to get his cock inside of him, and he wasted no time in slicking

Harry's shaft. Having prepared himself in the shower before he'd driven over, Jason didn't need any prep. He straddled Harry's hips and held the dick to his entrance.

Locking gazes with Harry, he sank in one go. They groaned in unison, and Harry's hands came down to rest on Jason's hips. Jason brushed them aside, and Harry transferred his grip to the covers beneath him. Keeping Harry deep inside, Jason circled his hips, feeling the fullness move within him and glancing off his prostate on every pass. He bit his lip and stared at Harry, whose eyes had half-closed while his mouth had opened.

Jason rested his hands on Harry's chest, making sure to rest one finger on each of his nipples, then lifted himself off a short distance. He dropped down again, and Harry gasped. Jason repeated the action, never coming off fully, but with each movement, his fingers grazed Harry's nipples, which Jason knew were as sensitive as his own.

After several lifts, he stayed down and circled his hips once, then rose again. While his body screamed at him to go faster and harder, he refused. He wanted this to last. He wanted Harry writhing beneath him until neither could last any longer. It didn't matter how long it took, but he needed to show Harry everything.

His cock wept, spreading precome along Harry's abs, the sight sending sparks along his nerve endings. Without even touching his dick, he was close. Could he come hands-free this way? The thought flew out of his head when Harry lifted his hips in time with Jason's movements. The man hit his prostate directly, and Jason saw stars.

"Fuck! Jason, I want you to come because I'm fucking close."

The hoarse, strained tone was music to Jason's ears because it confirmed Harry's words. He increased his speed, and their skin slapped together with sweat dripping down his spine and forehead. Jason felt Harry's stomach tighten beneath his hands, and Harry groaned, his head arching backwards when he came. Jason slammed his hips down again, and Harry's cock hit his prostate dead on. His orgasm barrelled through him, and he could do nothing but close his eyes and feel while his entire body clenched in release.

When he could open his eyes, he saw Harry smiling at him in the lazy perusal he liked to give. According to Harry, seeing Jason sweaty and flushed from climax was one of his favourite things.

Jason lowered his hands to the bed, allowing him to get closer to Harry, though kept his cock deep inside him. He licked his lips and set his heart free with the first words he'd spoken since arriving at Harry's flat. "Those three words seem too small to hold everything I feel for you, but never doubt that I love you."

Tears leaked from Harry's eyes, and Jason lowered his head to meet him in a soft kiss filled with meaning.

"I hope you're not hogging those beers all to yourself," Matias said with a grin.

"Of course I am. If I set them free, they'll be gone within seconds, and then what would I drink?" Jason said.

"There's plenty to drink."

Jason smirked. "Then why do I need to give these up?"

Matias rolled his eyes. "How are things with you?"

He knew what Matias was asking. "I'm better now that I'm talking to Amanda. She's bloody amazing at making me see what's right in front of my eyes."

"And that's not the man you're talking about." Matias sniggered.

"Nope. Although he's amazing, too." Jason glanced at Matias, seeing a frown on his face. "What's wrong?"

Sadness crossed Matias's face. "I want that. I'm not made to be alone, but I don't want to settle either. I tried that, and it didn't work. Now I have to attend my brother's wedding alone."

"Ouch. Nothing worse than going stag to something like that. Do you not have a friend you could take?" Jason felt for the guy. Although he didn't have a family of his own, he'd heard many stories from his friends that told him being alone at a wedding would bring nothing but interference from family members.

Matias shook his head. "I've left it too late. My friends are busy that weekend. It won't be bad I suppose, because we're staying in the Whittaker Hotel." He shook his head. "I know, I know. Staying at a hotel in the same city you live in is ridiculous, but Isabella wanted to treat us all. I can't argue with her."

Jason chuckled. "Little sisters are the worst, I'm told." He frowned. "Is your sister marrying a man with the surname Mitchell?"

Matias glanced at him. "Yeah. How did you know that?"

Jason grinned. "My friend, Jasmine." He pointed to where she was talking with Harry. "She's the wedding planner's assistant. She'll be there."

"Ah, I've met Eli, but not Jasmine. Well, at least I know who I can go to if I need to escape."

Jason snorted. "I'll introduce you again later, but to warn you, if you ask for her help, expect her to set you to work."

"I'd prefer to work if it meant I wasn't alone all night."

"Don't say that within hearing range of her."

"Of who?"

Jason smiled at Dean. "Jasmine. She's not afraid to cross boundaries and make people do her bidding."

"That's a good thing, isn't it?" Dean asked, sitting on the porch steps.

"Unless it's you that has to do it."

They laughed. Jason watched the men and women mingling in the back garden at Paul's home. Paul and Quinn had insisted on opening their house for an early Christmas celebration for the entire station. Paul had invited that many people they had split into the back garden despite the air being wintry. Everyone who had braved the cold was wrapped up in coats, hats and scarves, even Jason, who loved the colder weather. From his vantage point on the decking, he could see Harry's red nose and knew the man would warm it in Jason's neck later. He usually tried to steal Jason's heat.

"What are your plans for Christmas, Dean?" Matias asked, bringing Jason back to the conversation.

Dean brightened. "Dad and Sally are coming up for a visit and staying with us for a few days. We're hoping to get in to see the pantomime this year, though we've left booking the tickets late." He snorted. "Dad couldn't decide what date they were coming. I can't book it until he decides. We may end up going in January instead."

"What are they performing this year?" Jason asked.

"Jack and the Beanstalk."

"Should be good. I went to see The Snowman last year. It was fantastic," Matias said.

"Maybe we should make it a station outing," Jason said. "It's a shame we can't all be there at the same time."

"It's something to think about for next year, maybe," Dean said. "What are you doing for Christmas?" he asked Jason.

"Harry is spending Christmas Day with his mum and sister because I'm working, but on Christmas Eve, a friend has invited us to join in the celebration at Crush."

"Don't they throw a party every year?"

Jason nodded. "Yeah. The owner, Tom, closes the bar to the public. The party is only for family and friends, and those who others invited. I went last year, and it was great."

"Who do you know to get an invitation?" Matias grinned and nudged his shoulder.

Jason gave a lopsided grin. "I know lots of people, but Charlie invited Harry and me. If either of you is interested, let me know, and I'll speak with Charlie."

Dean shook his head. "Thanks, but we'll be with Dad."

"Matias?"

"I might take you up on that. My family will drive me crazy by mid-afternoon, I'm sure."

"All right. I'll let you know." Jason pulled out his phone and messaged Charlie. "He's usually good at replying unless he's slammed at work."

"Come on, you lot!" Paul shouted. "It's time for volleyball."

Jason screwed up his face. "Volleyball? Since when do we play volleyball?" He didn't argue and instead stood and followed the others to the grassy area. More people spilt out of the house.

"Right, we have enough people for four teams. Each team will play the others, then we will have a semi-final and a final after that. It should keep us nice and warm before our main meal." Paul grinned and clapped his hands together.

Quinn rolled his eyes. "Good luck, everyone. I'm going to make said meal. Have fun!"

Jason slipped through the crowd to stand next to Harry. "Hey, handsome. Want to be on my team?"

Harry squinted at him. "We're not allowed."

Jason frowned. "Who said?"

"Paul." He nodded in his boss's direction. "Partners have to split up."

"But we work well together." Jason knew he was pouting, but he wanted to be on Harry's team.

"Button it, hose guy. You're on my team," Nash said.

Sighing, Jason dropped a kiss on Harry's lips and followed Nash.

"Red Team against Blue Team first," Paul said. "No, your station crew colour is not the same as your volleyball team."

"We're up." Nash smacked the back of his hand against Jason's chest.

"Which colour are we?"

"Blue."

"It would've been easier if we had our station colours," Jason grumbled but followed Nash onto the makeshift court. Clay from White Watch and Ian joined them. "Hey, how come some people aren't joining in?"

Paul glared at him. "Some people have a choice. You don't." He quirked his mouth and returned his focus to setting up the net.

Jason huffed and removed his gloves, shoving them deep into his pockets. Nash was team captain, so he and Valerie, Red Team's captain, tossed for the ball. Valerie won. The match started, and within seconds, there were points on either team. Volleyball had never been Jason's favourite sport, but he would admit that it was easier to play it on grass than sand. There was plenty of shoving and knocking into each other, and by the end of the fifteen-minute match, the opposing team had won.

He shook hands with the Red Team, then grabbed a drink, loosening his scarf, and drank it in one go.

Hands slid around his waist, and he glanced over his shoulder to see Harry resting his chin.

"When are you playing?" Jason asked.

"I'll be in the next game."

Jason pivoted in Harry's arms and wrapped his arms around Harry's neck. "Are you enjoying yourself?"

"Everyone is great. It's weird seeing some of the guys in clothes, but..." Harry leered.

He trailed off, and Jason tilted his head. "You don't want to see them without their clothes. Only I get to do that for you."

"You do, and any time you want to."

Jason nudged their noses together, and the coldness of Harry's was a stark contrast to his own. He kissed him, a simple press of their lips, but he found he didn't want to pull away. So, he didn't. Instead, he opened his mouth and licked along the seam of Harry's mouth, waiting until the man gasped to slide his tongue inside. Jason breathed through his nose, deepening the kiss, wanting to taste his lover every time he licked his lips after they parted.

Harry pulled back with a gasp and hid his face in Jason's neck. It was only then that he heard the whistling and cheering from the garden. He focused on the occupants, who were grinning and clapping for them. Jason held up his middle finger and buried his head in Harry's shoulders.

"Sorry."

"'S'okay."

"Harry! Your turn!"

Jason stepped out of Harry's grip and tilted his chin up. "Go get 'em."

"I'm rubbish at volleyball."

"Doesn't matter. Try to have fun. The score doesn't matter." Jason kissed him one last time, then Harry strode to his team. "Love you!"

Harry whirled around, mouth open, and silence descended on the garden. Jason hadn't intended to say that as loud as it came out, but he refused to take it back. He loved Harry, and he didn't care who knew it.

Jason winked at Harry, whose cheeks had turned a delicious rosy red, then perched on a chair on the decking. Things were looking up, and he was happier than he had been for a long time. He tethered his bottom lip between his teeth to keep his smile from becoming crazy-looking and inhaled, taking everything in to remember it for years to come. He glanced around the area and found Harry's camera on the table. Jason was no photographer, but he could hold his own. He removed the cap and lifted it to his eye, moving the dial Harry had shown him to focus it, then aimed it at the match. He clicked the button and checked on the small screen. It looked okay, but he wasn't good at this. He didn't care, though, and continued taking photos here and there until the match ended. Yellow Team won that one, and Harry came bounding back with a smile.

"I said you'd be all right," Jason said.

"Did you get some photos?"

Jason shrugged. "Yeah. Not sure how good they are, though."

"Doesn't matter. All that matters is that you took them."

"I'll let you be the judge of that when you get them onto the computer at home."

Home. The word that related to either Jason's or Harry's place. Either one held a piece of Jason's heart now. Like the man in front of him.

Chapter 24

Matias

Matias watched Jason and Harry together and rubbed at his chest. He wanted that what they had. When he'd first found out Harry was seeing Jason, it had hurt Matias. After all the talk about Harry not dating a firefighter, and then he starts a relationship with Jason. It stung. He wouldn't deny it. At first, he was angry because he'd thought Harry had lied to him, but when he'd eavesdropped and asked questions, he'd found out it hadn't been their choice.

Those words had reminded him of what his mother had always told him about how she'd met his father. At first, they had hated each other, but the more they saw each other, the more feelings grew until they had no choice but to accept the other as the love of their life.

Matias had moped for a few days, then picked himself back up again. It wasn't meant to be. That was what he needed to remind him—repeatedly if need be. When he found the person he was supposed to spend the rest of his life with, he would know. He wished they would hurry and enter his life. He was lonely.

"Hey." Someone nudged his shoulder, knocking him from his thoughts.

"What?" he said to Nash.

"What's got you all melancholy?" Nash sipped his beer, appearing glassy-eyed.

"Nothing."

"It sure doesn't seem like nothing."

Matias shook his head. "Ever the nosey-parker."

"What! I'm interested."

"I know. I'm pulling your leg, Nash." Matias scowled. "I'm having to go to my sister's wedding without a plus one, and I won't enjoy the family's reaction to it."

"Ah. Not good." Nash cocked his head. "I could always go with you if you want?"

"That would've been great, but I've had to take time off for it. You'll be working."

"Damn. What about one of the other guys?" Nash gestured around them.

It was an idea, but he didn't want to put them through the million questions his family would throw their way by thinking they were a couple. "I couldn't do that to them. I'll be fine on my own. It's better that way, anyway. I wouldn't want to sic my family on someone who wasn't interested in me. They'd run for the hills." Matias snorted.

"Talking of interested..." Nash trailed off when Jason and his friend, Jasmine, wandered their way.

Matias side-eyed Nash, saw his gaze fixated on Jasmine, and bit his lip to stop his laughter.

"Matias, Nash, this is Jasmine."

Jasmine held out her hand. "I'm his better half." She smirked.

"Hey! That's not strictly true. Harry is my better half. You're my best friend, meaning you're my better other half."

Jasmine grimaced. "I'm not sure that's a thing, but I'm going to assume that was a compliment."

Matias chuckled. "Nice to meet you, Jasmine. Jason tells me you're part of my sister's wedding."

"I am. I am Eli's assistant. I run around and fetch whatever he needs. I try to predict what that will sometimes be, but it doesn't always work out. One day, I'll have my own company, I hope, but until then, Eli is a blast to work for. He's bloody amazing at what he does."

"I'm glad to hear it."

"Matias has a bit of a problem," Jason said.

Jasmine frowned, glancing between them. "Okay...?"

Matias sighed. "It's fine, Jason. Don't worry."

"No, it's not fine." He turned to Jasmine. "He's going stag to the wedding, and he knows his family will be all over him about it. Can you keep an eye out for him and help him out where he needs it?"

Jasmine brightened. "Of course! I know what it's like. I have a big family who wants everyone to be blissful and married with kids, but I'm content being single. That doesn't mean I don't hate it when I have to attend parties alone, but I've found it's better than taking someone and getting their hopes up."

Matias hadn't thought of it that way. "That seals it. I'm going alone. Even if it kills me. I could always hide away somewhere."

"I know the exact place you can hide, too," Jasmine said. "There is a room at the hotel that is for Eli's people. If you need a breather, let me know, and I'll get you in there. No one will know where you are."

Matias grinned. "Thank you, Jasmine. That would be fantastic."

"No problem at all."

Now, he had to get through his final suit adjustment appointment, and he'd be good. It was a shame those appointments had family members attending, too. He would've preferred dealing with it himself, but his mother had insisted.

At least he had a hideaway. That should help him a bit.

He hoped Eli didn't mind.

Chapter 25

Harry

The party the previous day had gone on late into the night. People had come and gone throughout the day, and Paul and Quinn were never far away from the festivities. After Harry and Jason had left around midnight, they arrived back at Harry's flat and crashed into bed, getting undressed before their heads hit the pillows. It'd been great fun, even though socialising was not Harry's forte.

Now, though, Harry had to contend with the visit from Joey he had put off as long as he could. It hadn't been something he wanted to do this close to Christmas, but if there was something he needed to know about the fire, he wanted to find out before he faced his mother. Stalling the visit hadn't helped him to deal with the knowledge he had to get through it, and he'd finally called Joey and set a time.

Harry was so tense, he'd thought he'd break into tiny pieces if the wind blew at him. He wasn't sure the cereal he'd eaten that morning had been the best idea because it felt like lead now.

He was startled when the front door opened, and Joey strode in. His expression was neutral, which didn't help Harry's nerves.

"Morning," he said, trying to breathe through his nose to ease the tightening in his chest.

"Good morning." Joey came to stand before him and squeezed his shoulder. "Are you sure you're ready for this?"

"No. Not even a little, but I need to know."

"Are you sure you don't want Jason here with you? Or someone else?"

Harry shook his head. "It's better if I work through it myself first. Jason is coming over after lunch."

"Good." Joey squinted at him. "I'll make you a cup of tea. You sit down. I'll be there in a minute."

Harry, too distracted to argue, curled himself into the armchair and pulled a blanket over his legs. The room wasn't cold, but there was a chill in his bones he wasn't sure he could get rid of until he'd finished talking with Joey. He was certain it had been his fault, but Jason had told him it wasn't. It didn't seem right, though. How could it have been a faulty wire? Harry had knocked into the oven that night. That must have been how it started. His mind went around and around until Joey came into the room. Harry cupped his hands around the too-hot cup, distracting himself from the memories.

Joey sank into the seat closest to him and sipped his drink before placing it on the table. He rested his elbows on his knees and cocked his head at Harry. "Are you sure?"

Harry nodded. "Amanda said I need to know the facts before I can begin to understand my thoughts and feelings. She's right. I've never spoken to anyone about the fire, except my original therapist, and he didn't say anything different from what I told him."

Joey's eyebrows drew together. "He should've explained what had happened to the house. That's on him. You wouldn't have been dealing with this guilt for all these years if he'd told you how the fire started. If I had known, I would've said something. I'm sorry."

"It's not your fault, Joey. After all these years, you would've thought I'd known. There was no reason to think otherwise. I'm still not certain it wasn't my fault."

"That's what we're here to find out."

Joey pulled a file from a bag he'd draped over his shoulder that Harry hadn't seen. He set the bag to one side, but Harry's focus was on the brown-coloured folder.

"How do you want to do this? Do you want me to read the documents to you, or do you want to read them and ask questions?" Joey asked.

"Can you read it, please?"

Joey nodded and sat back, crossing his ankle over his knee and resting the file on his legs. "If at any point you need me to stop or want to ask a question, do it."

Harry nodded, staring at the steam rising from his cup while Joey read through the first details about the property address and date. His throat closed, and he shivered.

Joey cleared his throat. "Fire detail." Harry shut his eyes. "Fire Origin: Portable heater in the guest bedroom. Igniting object: Paper. Material first ignited: Paper beneath the socket. Possible cause: A portable heater in the guest bedroom was plugged into a socket. Description..." Joey inhaled. "After investigating the property, we found that the portable heater had a faulty wire. It was being used in the guest bedroom. We conclude that the faulty wiring in the heater had sent sparks onto the pile of paper beneath the socket, causing the fire to smoulder initially before igniting more flammable objects. Injuries: None." Joey paused. "Fatalities: Two."

Harry took deep breaths, trying not to lose his composure while memories of that night bombarded him. He knew Joey was talking to him, but all Harry could hear was a muffled ringing in his ears. He dropped his cup and crumpled, lost in the tears of remembrance. Pictures and voices swirled around his head, too quick for him to catch more than a glimpse. Heat. Yellow. Crying. Orange. Smoke. Yelling. Round and round.

A strong, sure voice arrowed through his mind, and he latched onto the presence, focusing on it and following where it went. Harry blinked open his eyes, feeling heavy and tired, and found a man cradling him, talking to him, though Harry couldn't discern the words. He closed his eyes again, breathing in and taking the scent that somehow comforted him.

With effort, Harry opened his eyes again, inhaling and exhaling to wake himself up. His eyes rolled with the need for more sleep, but he fought against it. There was something he needed to do.

"He's coming around."

A tightening started on his bicep, and he grimaced, trying to lift a hand to push it away.

"A little longer, Harry. That's it."

The pressure released, and he exhaled. Something squeezed his hand, and he dragged his eyes open, not realising he'd closed them again. Jason's face swam before him.

"What happened?"

At least that was what he tried to say, but his mouth tasted of cotton wool, and he couldn't swallow easily. Something pressed against his lips, and he automatically opened his mouth, closing it around the tube. Cool liquid filled his mouth. It was taken away before he was ready, and he frowned.

"You can have some more in a little while," a voice said. It wasn't Jason because his lips hadn't moved.

Harry rolled his head to the side, taking in more details the more aware he became of his surroundings. He laid on the sofa, a cushion beneath his head, with several people in the room with him. He recognised Jason and Joey, but the other man and woman, he didn't know.

He coughed. "What happened?" He tried to sit upright, but hands pushed him back down.

"Not yet. A little more rest first."

Jason squeezed his hand. "You had an anxiety attack, I think. You passed out."

"What?" The last thing he remembered was talking to Joey...and with that, everything came flooding back. The report. The memories. The pain. His breathing increased again.

"Harry, I need you to listen to me, okay?" The man he didn't recognise leaned in front of him, resting a mask over his nose and mouth. "Breathe for me. In and out. Slower. That's it. Good. Keep it going."

He followed the man's instructions until the spots in front of his eyes disappeared. He relaxed back into the cushions and closed his eyes. The report had said the fire wasn't his fault. It was the heater they used to warm the guest bedroom because it hadn't had a radiator in there. Whenever someone came to visit, they'd heat the room with that portable heater and leave it going through the night. How many times had they done the same thing?

"Harry?" Jason's voice caught his attention. "How are you feeling?"

"Rough," he said.

Jason nodded. "Understandable."

"We're going to try getting you to sit up, Harry. Keep the mask on for me, and let us take your weight, okay? If you feel queasy or lightheaded, let us know."

Harry focused on the unknown man, and finally, the uniform came into focus. The man was a paramedic. Had they called an ambulance for him?

"Harry?"

He refocused on the man's face and nodded.

"On three. One, two, three."

The paramedic and Jason took most of Harry's weight as they moved him into an upright position. His head swam, but he closed his eyes and breathed through his nose to settle the nausea. When he felt like he wouldn't puke, he glanced around him again.

His flat didn't appear any different, but something was. He couldn't figure out what.

"Any dizziness?" Harry shook his head. "Nausea?" He nodded. "Pain anywhere?" He shook his head. "Good. Let's take the mask off now and see how you do."

The paramedic removed the oxygen mask and set it aside. Harry bounced a little when Jason settled beside him, and Harry sent a smile in his direction.

"You gave us a scare there, Harry," Jason said, and when Harry studied his face, he saw deep lines and a pale complexion.

"I'm good," he said. "Tired, though."

"That's to be expected," the paramedic said with a smile. "In case you didn't catch it when I arrived, my name is Casey, and this is Chloe. I'm going to take a few more observations on you before I deem you fit enough, okay?"

Harry nodded. "Was it a panic attack?"

"It seems so. Your friend said you started having difficulty breathing, then passed out. He called us because he couldn't bring you around. When we arrived, you'd started waking up."

"How long have I been out of it?" He glanced at Jason with a frown.

Joey answered. "You were unconscious for around three minutes before I called the ambulance. It's been fifteen minutes since they arrived."

Casey continued, "You weren't unconscious when we arrived because you were moving around, but you didn't want to wake up." He smirked. "Lazybones that you are."

Harry snorted. "First time this has ever happened."

"And hopefully, the last," Jason said.

The others made small talk while Harry rested his head back against the sofa. He was exhausted. A hand rested against his head. Harry rolled his head towards Jason.

"I'm okay."

"All right. I think you're fine now. I'd like you to have someone with you for the next twenty-four hours, in case, but I think you'll feel better after a long nap," Casey said.

"I will, thanks."

"No problem."

Harry watched from his position on the sofa while Casey and Chloe packed up their equipment and said goodbye, Joey seeing them out. He rolled his head to look at Jason again.

"Sorry for scaring you."

Jason huffed a laugh. "You're a menace. Come on. Let's get you to bed."

"I'll be fine here for a while," Harry argued.

"No. Doctor's orders. Sleep."

Harry's eyelids drooped, but he let Jason pull him to standing with Harry holding his hands in a tight grip because his legs felt like jelly. Jason leaned down and lifted Harry into his arms.

"I can walk, you know!" Harry said after grabbing Jason around the neck.

"I know, but I'd prefer to carry you."

Harry couldn't argue with that and dropped his head onto Jason's shoulder. He must've worried the man a lot for him to be this careful with him. What was different between this panic attack and the ones before? Why did he faint with this one? It didn't matter anymore. He'd get some sleep and discuss it with Joey and Jason when he woke.

Jason laid him on the bed, pulling the covers from beneath him. "Do you want your jeans on or off?"

"Off, please," Harry mumbled, already feeling comfortable on the soft mattress.

Jason removed his jeans and covered him with the duvet. "Get some sleep. I won't leave the flat. Shout me if you need something."

"Hmm," was the best he could do.

Harry woke, wrapped in a cocoon, overheated and sweaty. Not the good kind of sweaty. The room was dark, and when Harry tried to push the covers away, arms tightened around him. His mouth twitched. He needed the bathroom, though, and he pushed at the weights until they loosened enough for him to slip out of bed.

He padded across the hallway, closing the door behind him before switching on the light, not wanting to disturb Jason. He did his business and washed his hands, staring at his reflection. A pale face, black eyes and dry lips peered back at him. He yawned. He must've slept the entire day away, and he could still manage some more.

Not bothering to fight the inevitable, he strode back to the bedroom and snuggled under the covers in Jason's arms.

The next time he woke, there was a weak strip of light peeking into the room. Relaxed enough to not want to move, he gazed at the dust particles floating in the sunbeam. With it being close to Christmas, a bright beam of sun told of late morning. He couldn't be bothered to turn his head to check the time. He had nowhere to be that day.

Jason rubbed at his nose and opened his eyes, a smile spreading across his face when he glanced at Harry. "Morning."

Harry's gaze took in everything about Jason's sleep-ruffled face, from the creases in his cheek from where it had been laying on the pillow to the bleariness in his eyes to the shadow on his jaw. "I love you," he murmured, sliding his hand along the whiskers that had appeared overnight.

Jason's eyes brightened. "And I love you."

"How did we get here?" Harry's mouth curled. "And I don't mean physically."

Jason grinned, then sobered. "I don't know, but I'm glad about it. Whatever we have to go through to come out the other side is worth it if I have you with me. Waiting for me. Helping me."

Harry couldn't see Jason any longer, tears filling his eyes. "Waiting for *each other*. Helping *each other*," he amended.

"Together."

Harry leaned in and brushed his mouth over Jason's. Jason opened to Harry's tongue, and he slipped inside, wishing they could stay in their cocoon forever. He kept the kiss slow, not needing anything more than that. The comfort of knowing he had someone by his side when trouble came knocking gave him more peace than anything else.

They spent long minutes tasting each other, not pushing for more, until they rested their foreheads together and breathed.

"I wish I could spend Christmas with you," Jason said, pulling Harry over to rest on his chest.

"It's just a day. We can celebrate Christmas whenever we want to. Besides, you'll be home after dinner, so there's still Christmas night and the following day. It's fine." Jason hummed. "It's not a problem, Jason. Stop worrying. I'll be spending the day with Mum and Naomi, and the evening with you. What more could I ask?"

What Jason didn't realise was that he would drop by the station on Christmas day at some point. He wouldn't be able to spend the entire day without visiting, and he'd promised Paul some cookies. Harry ducked his head and beamed into Jason's chest. Despite what had happened the previous day, he felt lighter, though the memories still lingered, in a way, he hoped they would. The memory of what he'd lost would remind him how brief life was. No one ever knew how much time they had. He needed to live each day to its fullest and celebrate what he'd achieved—what they'd achieved. It was the best thing he could do to memorialise his dad and brother.

"I love you," he whispered, then squeaked when Jason rolled them over to brace himself over Harry.

Jason lowered to his forearms, his hands bracketing Harry's face. "I love you with everything I was, everything I am, and everything I will be." Jason frowned. "Fuck! I need paper!"

Harry bit his lip when Jason scrambled to the bedside table. "Why?"

"I have to write that down. It'd be perfect for my wedding vows."

Harry's breath hitched. "Wedding?"

Jason smirked. "Not yet, sweetheart, but someday." He refocused on the paper. "Now, what did I say?" he murmured, scribbling away.

Harry stared at him and grinned. He had a boyfriend, a job, friends, family—a future. Something to look forward to. He couldn't be happier.

Chapter 26

Jason

Jason was itching for his shift to end. The Christmas day hours had seemed longer than any other. It had been busy, which was usual for a day where there was plenty of cooking and celebrations. Even then, the hours seemed to crawl. He'd had a pleasant surprise when Harry had dropped by with a box of cookies for them, but he didn't stay long. Enough for a long, deep kiss to the cheers of the station.

When six o'clock finally came, and he handed over to Matias, who was the crew commander for Blue Watch, he couldn't wait to get out of there. No offence to anyone because he wasn't the only one rushing to leave.

He climbed into his car and headed straight for home. He wanted to make sure he was as smoke-free as he could get before he went over to Harry's flat because, with the gift he'd bought Harry, he didn't want anything else that might trigger a panic attack. He hoped he'd done the right thing. Harry's mother had cried when he'd told her what he was planning, but Esme had helped get the things together he needed.

In the shower, he washed three times with different shampoos and shower gels until he was satisfied, then he dressed as fast as he could. He paused in the living room to make sure he had everything he needed, then, with a grin, he grabbed it all and got in the car again. He didn't need to be back at work until six o'clock the next evening, which gave him under twenty-four hours with Harry.

By the time he parked and grabbed everything from the car, he vibrated with excitement. He couldn't remember the last time he'd been excited about Christmas. Last year, he had spent the afternoon with Paul and Quinn and their two kids, and come to think about it, he had done the same for the past few years, too, if he'd not been working. This year, he had no plans to visit anyone except Harry. They would meet up with others over the next few days instead.

He stopped outside Harry's door and inhaled. He would've loved to propose to Harry this year, but neither of them was ready for that. Soon, though.

The door opened before he'd even had the chance to knock, and he grinned at his boyfriend's eagerness.

"Ho, ho, ho! Merry Christmas," Jason said.

Harry snickered. "Merry Christmas to you. To what do I owe the pleasure of your company?"

Jason narrowed his eyes. "I told you I was coming over."

Harry grabbed his coat and yanked him inside the flat. "Get in here, you doofus. I was trying to be funny."

"Leave the jokes to me, darling." Harry backhanded his chest and strode to the living room. "What? Don't I get a kiss?"

"Not if you're being an idiot."

Harry's voice carried from the other room, and Jason grinned. He removed his shoes, balancing the bags and boxes he'd brought with him. When he entered the living room, he smiled at the twinkling lights they'd put up two days before. After Harry's incident and then sleeping for around twenty hours, he'd had plenty of energy, and they'd decided to decorate his flat. They had to ransack supermarkets and shops to get some things, and even Esme had sent some things over for them, but eventually, they had the place looking festive.

"I could always take these to someone else?" he said, shrugging.

Harry chuckled and stepped closer, holding two bottles of beer. "Come on. Sit down and rest up. I've heard you've been busy today."

Jason placed the boxes and bags on the sofa and accepted the bottle from Harry, using his other arm to drag him close for a kiss. When Harry's cherry flavour burst over his tongue, he groaned, holding him tighter.

"God, I needed that."

Harry pushed him onto the armchair and straddled his thighs. "I've missed you."

"You, too." Jason exhaled through his nose and closed his eyes, enjoying the sensation of having Harry close to him.

Harry pet his chest. "Are you okay?"

"Yeah, I'm worn out, to be honest. It was a long day after a long night." There had been too many fires to count, but all were superficial and easy to put out, except one. There had been no one inside the office building, but something had caused the fire that had blackened the sky for several hours before the crew had it under control. Only time would tell what the cause had been. As for the previous evening, they'd shown up at the Crush Christmas party and spent many long hours enjoying the company of their friends, old and new.

"I have something that might cheer you up a bit," Harry said.

"You mean seeing you and drinking beer is not all?"

Harry bit his lip and slid off his lap to the floor, right next to the tree. "Here." He held out a palm-sized box.

Jason beamed and accepted the gift. Checking the label, he saw it was from Harry. He unwrapped the paper, lifted the lid and removed the tissue paper, then he stared. Nestled in with more tissue paper was a small keyring. He held it up to the light to see it better. It took him a minute to understand the etched pattern, but then it came into focus. On the clear plastic square was a hand-drawn etching of the photograph Harry had taken of them when they'd kissed at Anglesey Abbey. It didn't have the colours of the photograph, but the feeling it brought up in him was incredible.

"Do you like it?"

Harry's voice was quiet, and Jason glanced at him. "I love it. I can have it with me all the time now." Harry's cheeks darkened, and he fidgeted. "I have something for you. Well, more than one thing, but I'd like you to open this one first." He reached for the bag closest to him and pulled out a wrapped square gift, handing it to Harry. "Come sit with me," he said, wanting Harry close.

Harry climbed onto his lap and ripped open the paper. A plastic packet fell out, and Harry grinned at the cherry-flavoured sweets. Below it sat a burgundy-coloured photo album, and Jason's heart raced at what Harry would think because it wasn't empty.

"It's gorgeous." His hands caressed the suede cover.

"Look inside."

Harry glanced at him, opened the cover and stilled. On the first page sat the photograph of his parents and their three children before the fire had changed their lives. Jason felt Harry's breath hitch, and he tightened his hold.

"There's more, but if it's overwhelming for you, we can do it another time. This is yours. You have time to look at it. It doesn't have to be now."

Harry ran his finger over the faces of each of the people in the photo, then turned the page. The second page showed their house, including the front garden with the double swing set. Harry swiped at his eyes but couldn't help but smile.

"I have many stories about what happened in that garden."

"I'd love to hear them."

He turned the page and blew out a breath when his parents came into view, holding John as a newborn.

Tears streamed down his face, and he flipped through each page. Photos of his childhood—before and after the incident—held his focus, bringing tears of joy and sadness. When he reached the end, he closed it and put it on the table, curling himself into Jason.

"Thank you."

"You're welcome, sweetheart."

They sat there, listening to the Christmas music playing on the radio, and held each other. Jason's memories were as close to the surface as no doubt Harry's were, but he pushed them back, not wanting them to intrude on the peacefulness he'd found.

Jason's stomach interrupted the silence by growling, and they both laughed.

"I better feed you before you eat me instead," Harry said, rising from his position.

"I'd happily eat you." Jason winked.

"Later." Harry grinned. "We don't have a roast dinner today."

Jason's heart sank a little. "Why?"

"I didn't think you'd want one after eating at the station. I do have something else for you."

Jason cocked his head. "What?"

"Pancakes."

He brightened. "Pancakes! You are the awesomest, bestest, wonderfullest person in the entire universe."

Harry beamed. "I don't think they're words."

"Doesn't matter. You understand my meaning."

Harry licked his lips. "Yes, I do, and the same goes for you."

He wrapped his hands around Jason's waist and lifted his chin, sealing their mouths in a chaste but heartfelt kiss.

"This is the best day ever!" Jason said, his stomach growling in agreement.

"I'm glad you think so because if I have to think about my mother and the gift you bought her, I might hide in a cupboard somewhere."

Jason withheld his chuckle, though the corners of his mouth twitched. "Whatever do you mean? Did she not like her calendar?"

"Oh, she liked it, but the idea of my mother perving over a sexy firefighter calendar—one of whom is my boyfriend—is not something I intend to think about often. Ever, in fact."

Jason held his stomach and wiped his eyes. "I thought she might like something to brighten up her kitchen."

"Well, it does that," Harry said, entering the kitchen.

Jason slid his arms around Harry's waist again, trapping him between the counter and his body. "Are you jealous?"

Harry snorted. "No."

Jason frowned and pulled back. "You're not?"

Harry pivoted in place, facing Jason and linking his fingers behind his neck. "I have the real thing, not a photo."

Jason rewarded him with another kiss, but his stomach interrupted them again, and his cheeks heated. "Sorry."

"Let me get you fed." Harry waved him away and set to work.

"Did you give the photos to the rest of the station crews?" he asked.

"I put them in individual envelopes and decorated them with Christmas stickers, then asked Paul to hand them out for me. Hopefully, they'll like them."

"They'll love them," Jason said. "It's not that often we get candid photos of us when we're messing around with each other. They'll appreciate them more than they'll let you know."

"What do you mean?"

Jason sighed. "Many of the firefighters at the station have been transferred or requested to be transferred there for less than stellar reasons. It makes them withdrawn and harder to befriend. There aren't many that have relationships or families, and to have something that shows them in what they might have considered before to be a weakened state, they will hopefully see what we see and know they have friends and family. You might receive nothing more than a thank you, but I know it will be more heartfelt than anything."

"I hate it that people are still against the LGBTQ+ community."

"It takes generations to change the mindset of humanity," Jason mumbled, remembering hearing that from a documentary he watched about the subject.

"True." Harry plated the food, and the scent wafted across to him, making his mouth water. "Sit down. I'll bring it to you."

Jason traipsed to the table and sat in his usual seat, glancing out of the window. "It would be nice if it would snow tonight. I can't remember the last time we had snow on Christmas Day."

Harry set a plate of steaming pancakes in front of him and sat beside him with his own plate. "It would be nice, but I bet White Watch will curse you if it does."

"That's true." He looked at the ceiling. "I take it back! Don't snow! Please, don't snow!" Harry hooted, and Jason cleared his throat. "Have you heard from Al?"

Harry crossed his arms and leaned on the table. "Only a message to say Happy Christmas. I can't believe I messed up so badly with him. I was in my own head. I didn't see he had problems, too."

"It's not your fault, Harry. You can't help how you feel or don't feel." He rested his hands on Harry's arm. "He's keeping in contact. That's a good thing. At least he's not ignoring you. He might need time."

"Joey said he was keeping an eye on him. They've got together a few times. Al has that, I suppose. I would hate for him to lose all of his friends because of what happened."

"I'm sure he'll come around."

Harry gave a small smile. "I hope he does."

They finished their pancakes while Harry filled him in on what happened at his mother's house that day. They would visit Esme the next day for a couple of hours because Esme refused to send Jason's gifts home with him. She insisted on seeing him, which was nice of her. Once the kitchen was clean, they grabbed a tub of chocolates and settled in front of the TV, watching A *Nightmare Before Christmas*.

Snuggled up under a blanket with Harry with the lights off and the TV glowing brightly, Jason never wanted to move.

This was home.

Did you enjoy this book? What happens when the wedding planner ends up as a fake date for a guest? Read Breathing Fire to read Matias and Eli's story.

Sign up to my newsletter to get a free stories, exclusive content and early access: https://elouiseeast.com/newsletter

About Elouise East

I am Elouise East but feel free to call me Elli. I write sweet and steamy connections in gay romance. I also touch on taboo stories under the name Elouise R East.

Books that tell the stories where friendship and family are the focal point - be it blood family or chosen - is very important to me. That's why I include a variety of personalities, talents, ages, situations and abilities as I believe a story needs, or a character needs. I want my characters to be real, to be relatable, to be free to have whatever views they tell me they have. And trust me, most of the time, I do not have *any* say in the matter!

My characters come to life on the page for me as well as my readers. Their stories unfold in front of me, and I have very little input into how they want to be shown. Just like real life, the lives of my characters change with every choice, every interaction and every conversation. And I wouldn't have it any other way.

I write books that are emotionally realistic, even if liberties are taken with other aspects of my stories. I don't know any other way to write. It comes from deep inside.

Who am I? A single parent to two children who make life worth living. An avid reader who still devours every book she can get her hands on. A student of learning about any subject that takes her fancy. An author of books she would read herself. And a romantic at heart who loves anything cheesy.

Who's in?

Stalk me here... ;-)
Website : https://elouiseeast.com
Newsletter : https://elouiseeast.com/newsletter
All links : https://elouiseeast.com/links

Books by Elouise ast

Love in Flames
Fight Fire with Fire
Out of the Frying Pan
Smokescreen
Breathing Fire

Club Royal
Rogue Royal
Secretive Royal
Grieving Royal
Disowned Royal
Trained Royal
Awakened Royal
Commanding Royal

Crush
Love Conquers
Instant Desire

Too Many Secrets
Collide
When Fantasies Collide
When Dreams Collide
When Pleasures Collide
When Cravings Collide